You'll also enjoy this Reuben Frost Mystery

MURDER FOR LUNCH

"The characters are portrayed with wickedly informed satire.... Murphy has exhibited more than enough potential to do for the legal world what the tongue-in-cheek Emma Lathen mysteries have done to demystify investment banking."

Time

"Emma Lathen fans, and others who search for the American mystery of manners, will undoubtedly find *Murder for Lunch* highly enjoyable and will be eager to meet again the team of Frost and Luis Bautista."

Wilson Library Bulletin

"A first mystery worth a prolonged stay in an armchair."

The Washington Post Book World

"Reuben Frost is an intelligent, no-nonsense lawyer, good at his profession and good at finding murderers.... Murphy promises Frost will solve more murders. He's given himself a hard act to follow."

United Press International

Also by Haughton Murphy
Published by Fawcett Crest Books:

MURDER FOR LUNCH

MURDER TAKES A PARTNER

Haughton Murphy

FAWCETT CREST • NEW YORK

For Phyllis and Mary

REHEARSAL

1

REUBEN FROST WALKED BRISKLY DOWN FIFTH AVENUE, between Fifty-fourth and Fifty-third streets. He was quite content, having just finished a companionable lunch of Welsh rarebit at his club, the Gotham. Recently retired as a senior partner of Chase & Ward, the downtown Wall Street law firm where he had worked all his professional life, Frost had made a midday visit to the Gotham a part of his daily routine.

It was a beautiful day, and as he walked, Frost savored the bright April sunshine. It made Fifth Avenue look splendid, he thought. His only regret was seeing the ever-increasing number of Senegalese peddlers along the Avenue hawking their Vuitton and Gucci rip-offs; they made stylish Fifth Avenue resemble the main thoroughfare of a Third World capital. An old friend of the Mayor's, he had complained in the past about these peddlers, but had been told that the City's law enforcement resources had to be allocated to the suppression of murder and dope-dealing rather than to an aesthetic cleanup of Fifth Avenue.

Frost understood, though he did not share, the Mayor's priorities. But in the long view, these priorities were probably correct. After all, the peddlers still could not ruin Fifth Avenue. The distinguished-looking men of affairs and smartly dressed women who crowded its sidewalks this early afternoon—coupled with the open-faced, clean-cut out-of-town tourists who stared in wonderment at it all—made the Avenue vital and attractive. The tourists, especially, were a good sign; New York, after its great fiscal crisis of the 1970s, had regained its élan and was once again a magnet for visitors. The City, like Frost himself, was in good health.

At the corner of Fifty-third Street, Frost's sense of well-being was momentarily interrupted as he lost his footing in one of those sloping indentations in the curb installed for people in wheelchairs. He recovered his balance without falling, but not before thinking, however briefly, that at seventy-five he was subject to the vulnerabilities of old age after all.

As he regained his balance, Frost was aware of a strong, steadying hand on his forearm. He turned to find Hailey Coles, one of the most promising young dancers from the National Ballet Company, at his side. An absolute slip of a girl, weighing at most ninety pounds, she nonetheless held the old lawyer in a firm grip.

"Are you all right, Mr. Frost?" she asked, a look of concern in her large green eyes.

"Hailey! How are you? Yes, I'm fine," Frost said. "These damned ruts in the curb. I know they're for the handicapped, but my guess is they *create* more cripples than they help."

The young woman smiled, reversed her dance bag of rehearsal gear from left shoulder to right, and put her arm in Frost's.

"You're not heading to the theatre, are you?" she asked.

"Well, yes I am. We've got a directors' meeting today and we're also supposed to see a rehearsal of *Chávez Concerto*."

"Oh, yes, I forgot that was today," the girl said.

"You're not in it?" Frost asked.

"No, thank God," Coles said, realizing too late that she was being indiscreet, especially to the Chairman of the Board of NatBallet (as it had been called for short ever since its founding in 1970).

"Why do you say that?"

"Well, Mr. Frost, I shouldn't be telling tales out of school, but I don't think rehearsals are going too well. The music's awfully difficult, and Clifton's playing cat-and-mouse with Veronica and Laura."

The young dancer was referring to Veronica Maywood, the reigning star of NatBallet since its founding, and her recent and formidable rival, Laura Russell. And to Clifton Holt, the Company's Artistic Director and principal choreographer.

"I'm sorry to hear that," Frost said.

"But don't worry. We artists are very temperamental, but we always get the show on stage." Hailey Coles squeezed Frost's arm as she spoke. Frost looked approvingly at his eighteen-year-old companion as they approached the Zacklin Theatre.

"I've got to run, Mr. Frost. I'm late for rehearsal. I hope you enjoy the new ballet."

"Thank you, Hailey," Frost replied. "And thank you for keeping me upright on Fifth Avenue."

The girl laughed, dashed off toward the stage door, and waved back at Frost. He entered the theatre, now even more content than he had been walking down Fifth Avenue in the spring sunshine.

Reuben Frost groped his way down the darkened aisle of the Zacklin Theatre and took his seat in row

L. From long experience he knew that this row was far enough back to permit him to see both the choreographic patterns formed on stage and the dancers' feet—exquisite or clumsy—as they performed.

Frost had warm feelings about both the Zacklin and NatBallet. His wife, Cynthia, a distinguished star of American Ballet Theatre in the 1940s and '50s, had been one of the founders of the Company. Her title had been simply "ballet mistress," but she had been more than that—one of the subversives who had encouraged others to leave American Ballet Theatre, the New York City Ballet and other companies to join the slate-clean, brand-new NatBallet; one of the group who had defined the Company's shape and purpose; and, together with her husband, one of the money-grubbers who had amassed the considerable funding needed to start NatBallet from absolute scratch.

Frost had always been supportive of his wife's artistic efforts, onstage and off. He had met her on a double date in 1940 when he was a hardworking young Chase & Ward associate and she a young ballerina starting to attract the critical acclaim that was to increase steadily until her retirement from dancing, in 1956. Married at the end of World War II, after as stable a courtship as the War had permitted, the Frosts had, over forty years, become (if possible) steadily more devoted one to the other, notwithstanding the enormous statistical increase in divorce in the very circles in New York City in which they traveled.

Frost had been drawn into the orbit of NatBallet affairs gradually. He had come to love the ballet through his wife's determined efforts. With Cynthia beside him in the audience or before him on stage, his eyes had been opened to the beauties, the technical secrets and—yes—the tricks of the dance. As his own interest grew and became more sophisticated, he had been gratified to see the public's interest in dance expand as well. Never a sports fan, he took considerable satisfaction from the fact that the total American audience for professional dance events now exceeded the combined live audience for all professional sports, notwithstanding the Refrigerator, Dr. J. and the rest of the country's overpaid athletes.

Frost's interest in NatBallet had grown avuncular as Cynthia introduced him to more and more of the members of the Company. The older ones, who had taken a considerable professional risk in leaving established companies to join the new, untested (and precariously funded) NatBallet, were known as the "domestic defectors," a title the press derived from the Western flights of Nureyev and other Russian dancers and teachers fleeing the artistic treadmills of the Kirov and the Bolshoi.

Finally Reuben Frost's attachment to NatBallet had become downright paternal as Cynthia drew him into even closer contact with the Company and its affairs. (Not that putting the bite on his friends and colleagues in the corporate and legal communities had been exactly passive. Anything but. Frost had called in intangible chits, twisted arms and in general performed the gentle extortion that passes in polite New York society under the name "fund-raising.")

It was largely through Frost's efforts, and those of an old investment-banking client and colleague, William Burbank, that NatBallet now had its own theatrical home. Three years or more had been needed to marry together the elements required to erect the Zacklin Theatre: straight-out commercial greed (Everett Zacklin's desire to erect an enormous office and cooperative-apartment complex on West Fifty-third

Street), artistic *Lebensraum* (the desire of the management of NatBallet for a larger stage, more seats and expanded space for rehearsals), civic do-goodism (the desire of the City Planning Commission, when selling its soul to the Great God Bulk, to command a price for it), and the amiable pragmatism of the City's Mayor (eager to be both friend of the City's real estate lobby and patron of the arts, a straddling act he was able to perform by encouraging the Zacklin colossus).

A complex package of tax abatements, tax-exempt bonds, zoning variances, landmark waivers, Federal and state development grants, and sweetheart mortgages from the City's leading banks had all been necessary to launch the Zacklin project. Not to mention the enthusiasm of one of the burgeoning investment-banking firms—enthusiasm enhanced after a lunch of the senior partners with the Mayor—for occupying most of Zacklin's commercial floor space, and the seemingly insatiable desire of the possessors of flight capital or hit-record royalties for the deluxe duplex—or triplex or quadruplex—apartments that Zacklin had to offer atop his multi-use edifice.

As far as Frost was concerned, the important rabbit that emerged from the builder's capacious hat was the theatre, the construction of which was a condition to the zoning variances Zacklin needed. Zacklin had originally resisted the grandiose plans Clifton Holt had devised, aided and abetted by both Cynthia and (as his enthusiasm grew) Reuben Frost. Then Reuben, shrewdly sensing the solution after a dinner with Zacklin and his wife, Rhoda, suggested naming the theatre the Zacklin. (Frost had in fact been revolted by the idea, but Mrs. Zacklin had thought it just fine and persuaded her husband to accede to the physical, acoustic, artistic and aesthetic wishes of Clifton Holt in designing the new theatre—the new *Zacklin* Theatre. Frost had suppressed his reservations and maintained a longer perspective on the whole matter. It was clear to him that Holt's reputation would continue to grow. He had already received the Handel Medallion, the City's highest award for cultural achievement, and it seemed only a question of time before he became one of the "honorees" (hateful word) at the Kennedy Center in Washington. Coupled with the four Oscars that the choreographer had already won for motion-picture direction, it seemed obvious to Frost that this heap of honors would fuel a movement to rename the Zacklin Theatre after Holt—possibly at a very public ceremony at which Rhoda Zacklin would preside over the change.)

All the tenants in both the commercial and residential space professed to be pleased with Everett Zacklin's development. There had been some minor rumblings from the apartment owners, whose chandelier-lined entryway stood beside the alley leading to the stage door. This minority felt that the ragtag assemblage of dancers in rehearsal clothes often seen emerging from the theatre was undignified; but other apartment owners thought just the opposite, and liked the idea of their proximity to NatBallet's glamour and artistic prestige.

Those at NatBallet were pleased, too. Dreams of clean, well-lighted studios, air-conditioned dressing rooms, storage space for scenery, a stage floor that all dancers who used it pronounced the best in America, and wing space that permitted dignified—and safe—stage exits were all realized. (No more need for stage-hands to grab a male dancer in mid-flight as he leaped into a *grand jeté* from the stage into nonexistent landing space in the wings; no more forty-minute intermissions while the simplest scenic drops were trundled back and forth from temporary quarters across the street.)

Reuben Frost's part in the Zacklin negotiations had been the culmination of his legal career, and had helped allay his reservations about retiring. Under the inexorable rules at Chase & Ward, he had been required to retire as the firm's Executive Partner in 1978 and to retire altogether as a partner in 1982. He was, of course, still "of counsel" to the firm—a quite luxurious title, in actuality; while it did not permit him to share in the firm's considerable profits, it did allow him to have an office, to carry on legal work for those who still called for his personal services, to keep a secretary, and to get assistance when necessary from the firm's pool of bright young associate lawyers.

The Zacklin negotiations had enabled Frost to remain active, giving him the supportive feeling that he was still capable of performing well as a lawyer. They involved just what he liked: complex financial arrangements, the chance to draft difficult legal documents in clear and straightforward language, the opportunity to use to the fullest the negotiating skills developed over almost a half-century of practice.

The directors of NatBallet, in part in recognition of his work in procuring the Zacklin Theatre and in part knowing a good and available commodity when they saw it, had prevailed upon Reuben to become Chairman of the Board. It was another welcome affirmation of his usefulness, and his wife, aware of his occasional sadness at being retired and growing old, urged him to take the job.

Normally the Theatre and the rehearsal studios were dark on Monday—the Company performed on a Tuesday-through-Sunday week—but Holt, ever the demanding taskmaster, had insisted on extra rehearsals for his new work, set to the music of César Chávez' *Piano Concerto*. Frost had reluctantly agreed to Holt's request, though knowing painfully well the damage this would do to the Company's budget (and perhaps to the rehearsals necessary to sustain other ballets already in the repertory); but Holt, as NatBallet's Artistic Director, had final say in such matters, subject only to restraint from the Board if his proposed actions threatened the Company with insolvency. The stage rehearsal of the second movement of *Chávez Concerto* had been scheduled as a prelude to the Board meeting—or perhaps as a peace offering for the strain rehearsing the work had placed on the Company's budget.

While he waited, Frost looked around the semidarkened theatre, still feeling a slight sense of wonder that it had ever been built. The interior was not entirely to his liking; the red velvet plush was, he thought, reminiscent of faded and tacky movie palaces of the '20s; but then, so was the principal auditorium of the Kennedy Center in Washington. Everything else about the theatre was fine—excellent acoustics, clear sightlines from any location and a 3,500-seat capacity that accommodated NatBallet's growing audience.

Frost's reverie was broken by the arrival of Andrea Turnbull, one of his fellow directors and a perpetual trial to him. Turnbull, a wealthy widow from Syracuse, had moved to New York City two years earlier, apparently with the intention of making a name for herself within the City's artistic establishment. Her bountiful donations—two large annual contributions that the Company hoped would become a habit and the generous underwriting of two new productions (*Chávez Concerto* being one of them)—had easily won her a place on NatBallet's Board.

But while her neat, large checks were attractive, Andrea Turnbull was not. Frost, if the truth were known, found her just this side of repulsive. She was overweight, with straggly brown hair and clothes that looked as if they had been purchased in a thrift shop. While other wealthy women of her age—Frost guessed her to be roughly fifty-five—were often obsessed with face-lifts and the latest treatment designed to smooth out wrinkles, Andrea Turnbull could not even be bothered to have the simple electrolysis that would have removed the slight but noticeable mustache above her upper lip.

Not much was known about Mrs. Turnbull except that her husband had left her a substantial fortune, earned in a profitable farm-equipment and automobile dealership in Syracuse, augmented by shrewd plunges in the stock market. As far as was known, she had no friends, or at least any who would publicly acknowledge their friendship. The result was a fanatical devotion to NatBallet and a seemingly endless amount of time to meddle in its affairs. Unlike the other directors, who deferred almost without question to Clifton Holt's artistic judgments, she was constantly giving Holt advice on all subjects—what ballets to have in the repertory, what dancers to feature and promote, even what the design of the Company's program should look like.

Holt was not a notably patient man, and he had more than once caused Mrs. Turnbull to threaten to snap her checkbook shut. But each time Frost, as a reluctant but effective peacemaker, had resolved the conflict. He had grown battle-weary in the process and now groaned inwardly as the woman approached; he knew from the expression on her face that a new storm was brewing.

"Reuben, thank God I've caught you here alone. I must talk to you," she said as she pushed in front of Frost, making clear that she wanted to sit next to him.

"Fine, Andrea. What is it this time?" Frost asked, trying to keep a tone of resignation out of his voice.

"Did you see *Paganini Variations* Friday night?"

"No, we weren't here on Friday."

"Disgraceful! Clifton let that Cassidy boy dance the lead. He's not ready for a part like that. He should be learning basics in the corps, not attempting lead roles for which he is not suited."

Paganini Variations, one of Clifton Holt's earliest works, had become the "signature" ballet of the Company. Universally praised by NatBallet's followers—and grudgingly admired even by those who were normally critical of the Company and Holt as a choreographer— its performances were often used by Holt to signal to the public which dancers were then in favor. Veronica Maywood had begun dancing the major female role when she had been promoted to principal dancer twelve years before. She was considered the authoritative interpreter of the part, though she had had a number of partners in the ballet, most recently Aaron Cassidy, a strikingly handsome twenty-year-old who was steadily advancing to the top ranks of the Company— advancement that was well deserved in the opinion of most, though apparently not in Andrea Turnbull's.

"The role calls for a noble prince, Reuben," Turnbull went on, pressing her case. "Cassidy is a colt and dances like a colt. He's clumsy and awkward, and I—"

"Andrea, dear, you are of course entitled to your views, but most people think Cassidy is very good— just the sort of bravura young blood the Company needs," Frost said. "Certainly Clifton thinks that."

"I know Clifton thinks that. And Clifton is wrong.

That boy is *not* promising, and neither you nor Clifton can convince me otherwise. I think Clifton and he must have something going, if you ask me."

Frost was able to ignore Turnbull's sexual innuendo by turning—eagerly—to greet Adelaide Simms, who had come up beside him. Mrs. Simms, who had married into a major perfume fortune, was a cheerful lady of goodwill who had been a friend of the Frosts for many years. Reuben got to his feet and kissed her on both cheeks (or, more precisely, made a vaguely kissing sound as he rubbed against each of her cheeks).

"How are you, Adelaide?" Frost asked.

"Wonderful, Reuben. Couldn't be better. Are we in for a treat this afternoon?"

"We shall see," Reuben answered. "But you know Clifton can always produce surprises."

"He certainly can," Andrea Turnbull chimed in. "I was just telling Reuben what stupid judgment Clifton is showing by pushing that Cassidy boy."

Neither Frost nor Simms had a chance to reply, as other members of the Board began arriving. Frost took the occasion to leave his seat and greet the newcomers, leaving Adelaide Simms to listen to Mrs. Turnbull's latest grievance.

As the assembled group talked, a dozen members of the Company filed onto the dimly lit stage. As always at a ballet rehearsal, they appeared in various types of motley, carefully and thoughtfully selected to suggest insouciance: a Rolling Stones sweat shirt here, flaming pink leg warmers there; a torn and dirty T-shirt on one boy, an exotic turban on another girl. Only Veronica Maywood and Laura Russell, who would rehearse the lead part, wore any semblance of a costume. Both wore identical green chiffon shifts designed for the performance. Aaron Cassidy and Roy Irwin, their male counterparts, were by contrast wearing sweat shirts and warm-up pants.

Kirk Drinan, one of the Company's pianists, nervously picked out difficult passages from the piano transcription of Chávez' dissonant work. Frost could not help hearing them as he returned to his seat. He had more than a little apprehension about Clifton Holt's latest undertaking. He was unfamiliar with the music, but Cynthia had heard a record of it and had pronounced it undanceable. Part of the interest in Holt's ballets was watching the resolution of difficult problems the choreographer created for himself; if Cynthia was right—and the excerpts Frost was now hearing indicated that she was—Holt this time had set himself the ultimately impossible task of making a ballet to ferociously difficult music.

Frost had another feeling of foreboding as well, after his brief encounter with Hailey Coles. Ever since the premiere of *Paganini Variations,* Veronica Maywood had been Holt's favorite ballerina (and, for a period in the late 1970s, his mistress). In virtually all Holt's works since, and certainly the major ones, the leading female parts had been made on her. But now, for the first time, Holt was rehearsing two dancers—Maywood and Laura Russell—and had not indicated which of them would dance the premiere. There was no question that Russell was outstanding, dancing at nineteen with a maturity that one expected only in a more seasoned performer. But Maywood had always been the favorite and was thought by many to be dancing exceptionally well during the current season.

Frost knew that Maywood was both strong-willed and temperamental. He hoped, as he took his seat beside Andrea Turnbull, that Holt's decision would not create fireworks; he knew from long experience that fireworks within the Company had a way of throwing off sparks and burning others, creating unwanted morale problems in the process.

"I see he has Cassidy in this one too," Turnbull grumbled. "I'm not sure that I paid the money for this ballet as a vehicle for that pretty-boy."

"Andrea, we'll have to talk about this later. Right now I think Clifton is about to begin."

Holt had come on stage. Although he had long since given up dancing, he maintained a slim, wiry profile. Never a *danseur noble*, never a handsome prince, he nonetheless had an immediately recognizable air of authority—one, Frost reflected, that would have been as effective in a corporate boardroom as on the stage of the Zacklin. Something about his manner and his brisk, choppy and decisive movements said Don't cross me, don't tread on me.

After talking briefly to Maywood and Russell, Holt came down the steps leading from the stage into the orchestra. He seemed oblivious of the Board members seated behind him. He had apparently told Veronica Maywood and Roy Irwin to dance the rehearsal, as Laura Russell and Aaron Cassidy moved to the side of the stage.

All the dancers, except Russell and Cassidy at the side, left the stage, and Holt signaled Kirk Drinan to begin playing. The music that emerged could best be described as prickly. It was reminiscent of Stravinsky's *Rite of Spring,* but without Stravinsky's undeniable inventiveness and with a decided Latin overlay. Twelve corps dancers—six girls, six boys—entered from the wings, forming rapidly dissolving patterns to the complex music. Then Maywood and Irwin came out and started a *pas de deux*. They had scarcely begun when Holt stopped them. He went forward to the edge of the orchestra pit and spoke to them in a voice inaudible to those in the auditorium. Maywood dramatically shrugged her shoulders, but did not speak.

The *pas de deux* resumed. This time Holt allowed it to continue only slightly longer than before. Again Holt talked to the dancers. This time Maywood could be heard saying from the stage that she was "uncomfortable doing the steps that way. It's simply too awkward."

"You mean too hard?" Holt said, this time in a mocking voice that could be heard.

"No, Clifton, not too hard. Just too damned clumsy and awkward. I don't feel right doing it."

Holt did not respond but only beckoned to the pianist to begin the passage again. This time the duet of the dancers continued for five minutes. Maywood had said the steps were not hard; to the spectator they nonetheless seemed extraordinarily complex—sharp, jagged, syncopated movements executed in unorthodox positions—and both dancers were sweating hard when Holt again stopped the music.

This time the choreographer went back up the steps to the stage, took the dancers aside, and talked to them quietly, his arms and legs outlining the movements as he wanted them executed. Russell and Cassidy came closer to hear the conversation, anxious to avoid similar problems when they rehearsed.

From the auditorium, the talk did not seem agitated, though what was actually being said could not be heard. The clustered group on the stage appeared to be a quintet of professionals discussing a technical problem. Then the atmosphere changed. Veronica Maywood stepped back away from Holt and her partner and began shouting.

"Clifton, this music is impossible, and you know it.

I refuse to go on with it. I feel like a goddamn Mexican jumping bean, doing the goddamn Mexican hat dance! These steps are just plain clumsy and designed to make us—or at least me—look weird and ungraceful. Let Laura do it if she wants to. You're being perverse, Clifton, and I'm not going to be a part of it!"

Maywood grabbed her towel from the side of the stage and walked off. The corps members, peeking out from the wings to see the excitement, looked stunned, as did Roy Irwin, watching his partner disappear. Only Laura Russell seemed serene, as she stood staring at her slippered feet.

Clifton Holt was furious. What would he do? Go on with Laura Russell? No, he turned to the small group seated in the audience. "Ladies and gentlemen, I apologize. We do not seem as far along as I had hoped with our ballet. I think we should cut our losses and call this rehearsal off. Thank you for coming, and better luck next time."

"See what I mean, Reuben?" Andrea Turnbull said to Frost in great excitement. "The man is a monster. Trying to do the impossible and torturing his dancers. We've got to do something."

"This is neither the time nor the place, Andrea," Frost answered. "Let's get upstairs to the Board meeting. I have a feeling it's going to be interesting."

BOARD MEETING

2

THE UNKNOWING MIGHT THINK THAT NATBALLET'S BOARD of Directors, as the governing body of one of America's leading cultural institutions, would meet in comfortable, rarefied and beautifully furnished surroundings. The reality was quite different. The Board met in a cramped, oblong room in the Zacklin Theatre, two floors above the stage and on the same level as the principal rehearsal studio.

Today there were twenty-six members of the Board (out of a total of thirty-five) present for the spring meeting. As they filed into the room after Clifton Holt's disastrous rehearsal, they seated themselves on wooden funeral-parlor chairs arranged around four portable metal tables, pushed together in a long rectangle. Although new, the room was narrow and windowless; there was no aura of corporate grandeur, no echoes of J. P. Morgan or John D. Rockefeller, let alone Otto Kahn or Mrs. Belmont.

The room and its arrangements—the hard wooden chairs, the bare gray tables, the legal pads and pencils and the collection of duplicated materials distributed at each place—made a statement. The statement said:

Yes, we will provide you with a seat, a sharpened pencil and a pad (one each), and a certain amount of information about NatBallet (the duplicated material). But don't expect food or drink, or comfort that would make you want to linger. In other words, we welcome you, but don't stay too long (and don't get too deeply involved in our affairs). The ambience was closer to that of a criminal-court jury room than to that of the Cabinet Room at the White House.

The unknowing might also think that the purpose of this Board of Directors was to give patrician, thoughtful artistic advice to Clifton Holt and his colleagues. Such was not the case. The Board did, as it would today, go through the motions of ratifying decisions made by Holt about promotions in the Company. And if anything happened to Holt, the Board would appoint a new Director. But as long as Holt was in place, the artistic operations of the Company—the aspects of the Company's existence that were seen by the public—were almost entirely his responsibility.

Although never spoken too loudly, the central purpose of the Board was to raise money, to find the wherewithal to pay dancers and musicians and stagehands and wardrobe mistresses a living wage, to provide money for scenery and costumes, and to buy roughly thirty thousand pairs of ballet slippers each season (at $25 a pair). And all without raising ticket prices to a level that would make admission to Nat-Ballet performances affordable only by arbitrageurs and rock promoters.

Other companies over the years had made the mistake of allowing Board members to make artistic decisions; with the rarest exceptions, these attempts had been disastrous. The directors could, and did, express their opinions—often in very strong terms—to Holt.

And the financial reins held by the Board imposed practical limits on what he could do. But Holt, shrewd enough to recognize the budgetary limits—which were lenient as such things went—had never had a serious dispute over money with the Board. Its members, in turn, had never overruled his artistic policies and judgments.

Some cynics might have said that the Board was deliberately inflated in size to reduce its decision-making efficiency. Other cynics (and they were right) realized that the larger the Board, the greater the contributions that could be exacted from its members. The unspoken rule was that each director was responsible for donating or personally raising at least $25,000 a year. Of course appropriate exceptions were made. Monsignor Joseph Carroll, the president of a local Catholic university, was excused. So was Bartlett Empson, a gentleman, a snob, an encyclopedic source of information about ballet history and an astute critic—and an aging bachelor of modest means. But most of the others had large bank balances, or their spouses did, or their fathers did, or the foundations they headed did. Or failing direct access to wealth themselves, they were sufficiently well connected with the rich to make them effective fund-raisers.

The fact that most Board members were rich or regularly associated with the rich did not necessarily make them genteel and couth. Mrs. Turnbull was not. Nor was Hugh Warner, whose real estate enterprises were under the protection of the bankruptcy court much of the time (though this did not seem to affect his personal generosity toward NatBallet). Nor was Kenneth Franklin, a wealthy Wall Street commodities broker whose political contributions had enabled him to serve as an American ambassador in Europe, whence he had returned as (forevermore) Ambassador Franklin, though diplomatic he was not.

Privately, Reuben Frost was particularly contemptuous of Franklin. He regarded him as a vulgarian, a man single-mindedly devoted to making money and one whose pretensions as "the Ambassador" in no way masked his avarice and lack of taste and intellectual polish. Frost conceded that taste and intellect were probably not necessary in the commodities business, but thought they would have been useful to Franklin in his pose as a devoted patron of the arts. Pushed by his second wife, a former stewardess with pretensions even grander than her husband's, Franklin had feigned sufficient interest in the dance to be named to the NatBallet Board. (His feigned interest, needless to say, being bolstered by frequent and generous contributions.)

Franklin was at Reuben's side when he entered the meeting room. "That Maywood is quite a spitfire, isn't she?" Franklin said to Frost. "What did she say to old Cliff—'Mexican-jumping-bean music'?"

"Something like that," Frost coolly replied.

Franklin seemed quite amused at the piece of living theatre he had just seen downstairs in the Zacklin auditorium. None of his colleagues shared his amusement, appalled as they were by Maywood's behavior (if they were especially fond of Holt) or Holt's (if their loyalties were with the ballerina) or the behavior of both (if they were objective about the matter and concerned above all about the Company).

In general, the assembling group was a subdued one. Monsignor Carroll, more used, as a former pastor, to scenes of grief and disaster than most, tried to cheer up Adelaide Simms and David Weiss, the elegant designer of equally elegant women's clothes, by an insistent conversation about the City's erratic spring weather.

Others were glum and silent, including Jack Navikoff, a blond, deeply tanned overgrown beachboy of fifty-odd. Navikoff had been the producer of Holt's last three movies and in the process had become Holt's close friend and confidant (and, more than likely, his lover). Holt by choice did not serve on the NatBallet Board—not out of any sense of artistic purity, but because its proceedings quite frankly bored him. Instead Navikoff had been named as a director at Holt's insistence.

Those within Navikoff's hearing did not overtly criticize Holt for his part in the set-to with the Company's leading ballerina. For they had learned from experience that Navikoff was not only Holt's mouthpiece, but his eyes and ears as well. Only Andrea Turnbull, extending the tirade she had started with Frost downstairs in the orchestra of the theatre, continued to broadcast her negative views of the Company's Artistic Director.

"I think Clifton is around the bend," she said to Hugh Warner. "Veronica Maywood was absolutely right. He is trying to do the impossible with that crazy Chávez music. And I am paying for it!" she said loudly, leaning into Warner's face.

"Well, I agree with you that it all seems terribly messy," Warner replied in his oleaginous baritone. "But she said herself the steps weren't difficult. I think she feels threatened by Clifton's interest in Laura."

"Perhaps, though I don't think Veronica is like that," Turnbull replied, with some petulance. "But if his stupid ballet—*my* ballet—ever sees the light of day, it will be very good for Roy. He is twice the dancer that Aaron is."

"To each his own, Andrea," Warner answered. "Time will tell."

Frost, overhearing the conversation, marveled at Warner's highly perceptive judgment, so aptly expressed in cliché. But it was time for business, and Frost took his customary seat at the head of the table. On his left was Jeanine Saperstein, a culture maven whose aggressive energy had battered down the doors of several artistic institutions in the City—doors that in many cases would probably have been closed to one of such acutely deficient intellect, but for her brassiness and shamelessness. (There were *some* limits to what money could buy, and Ms. Saperstein, possessor of the proceeds of a large and messy divorce settlement that had permitted Mr. Saperstein to marry a pretty, young, intelligent—and quiet—museum assistant, came perilously close to them.)

The woman was the nominal secretary of the Board and, at each meeting, read the minutes in dramatic tones more suggestive of a bad tragedienne than of an efficient secretary. Next to her was Jocelyn Taylor, a bright young Smith graduate, passionate balletomane, and all-purpose Girl Friday on NatBallet's staff, who actually kept the minutes and wrote them up after each meeting. (This was a task quite beyond Ms. Saperstein's capabilities. As Cynthia Frost had once observed to Reuben, Jeanine had clearly been told by her mother before she started school that she *must* participate in each of her classes—that is, make herself heard even if she had nothing to say. This habit from school had continued into later life and was evident at the numerous board and committee meetings she now attended; she still raised her hand and talked whether or not her contributions were pertinent. Framing her words—one could not really say framing her thoughts—

and seeking attention from the "Chair," as she trendily called Reuben, would have left little time for taking minutes.)

At Frost's right was David Weiss, Vice Chairman of the Board. A multimillionaire from his successful career as a high-fashion couturier—and perfume seller, jeans maker and (most recently) men's designer—Weiss was a handsome, asexual (as far as anyone knew or could speculate) and utterly charming man. He was particularly useful in beguiling the latest Texas millionaire who had discovered the "bal-*lay*," or the Upstate Assemblyman responsible for NatBallet's New York State Council on the Arts' appropriation—or more particularly, in beguiling their wives who (in the case of Mrs. Texas) wore his dresses or (in the case of Mrs. Assemblyman) had seen pictures of them.

Next to Weiss was Peter Howard, a young man of thirty-two, pleasant enough to be with once one recognized that he had a very low energy level. He purported to do some sort of teaching at the New School—closer investigation would have revealed that it was a rather basic night-school course in "the contemporary novel"—and otherwise appeared to devote his time to NatBallet. He served on the Board at his mother's request, his mother being a wealthy grain heiress so generous in her many benefactions that she herself could not with any efficiency serve on the boards of all the charities to which she bountifully contributed. Peter's amiability and reasonable intelligence had been spotted early. He had been offered the presidency of NatBallet three years earlier and had accepted, on condition that his duties would be only part-time. Within this constraint, he was good value for the Company. Well liked by the dancers, he acted as an ombudsman between the dancers and Holt, and also between the dancers and the business side of the operation. He held "open door" office hours twice a week, and listened patiently to the real or imagined grievances of the dancers, musicians and other personnel who stopped by to see him. He appeared to enjoy his job as President and, were he willing to spend a trifle more time and a bit more energy in carrying out his duties, would have been a truly effective figure not only in terms of the Company but also in the world of the arts generally.

"The meeting will please come to order," Frost called out as the group sat down. "Jeanine, will you read the minutes from the January meeting?"

The January meeting had been most routine, but Ms. Saperstein, reading Jocelyn Taylor's crisp minutes, managed to raise and lower her voice dramatically and endow the description of the proceedings with false suspense, a little like Joan Sutherland singing "Three Blind Mice."

A motion to approve the minutes was carried, and Frost called on Ambassador Franklin to give the treasurer's report. The Company was on budget, he reported, taking the group through the duplicated financial materials that had been distributed. Everyone knew that the extra rehearsal costs for *Chávez Concerto,* not yet reflected in the books, would probably change that; but box-office receipts were ahead of last year's, as were donations. So a spirit of modest well-being pervaded the room as the meeting proceeded.

Frost took advantage of this mood to move quickly to the next item on the agenda, which he knew would be controversial: the question of promoting three of the Company's dancers. He called on Navikoff to make a report. (Since suggestions for promotions by tradition originated only with Holt—the Board was involved really only because of the increased salary commitments the promotions made necessary—it had seemed appropriate to name Navikoff the chairman of the promotions committee, since he was most privy to Holt's thinking on such matters.)

"Yes, Reuben, I'm happy to report," Navikoff said. Frost, who considered himself quite expert on the subject, was sure that Navikoff normally wore contact lenses; to him the man's not-quite-right turning of the head and slight hesitation in focusing were giveaways. Now, however, Navikoff was wearing outsize shell-rimmed glasses. Did the glasses contain real prescription lenses, Frost wondered, or were they simply a prop to enhance Navikoff's "serious" (that is, non-pretty-boy) side? Frost did not know the answer, but he had a strong suspicion that the glasses were fake.

"As you all know," Navikoff began, "it is customary to make promotions from the corps to soloist at this time of year and to make promotions to principal as well. I've talked with Clifton about this, and to Arne Petersen, the Assistant Artistic Director. Grace Russell, who's on my committee, and Bartlett Empson, who is too, have also talked to them. And on this basis, we are prepared to recommend making Hailey Coles and Nancy Baker soloists and Aaron Cassidy a principal.

"Just to talk about them for a minute," Navikoff continued. "Hailey is a charmer, as I think everyone here will agree. She's only eighteen, but she's been in the Company for two years now and she's danced wonderfully everything that's come her way, including the Sugar-Plum in *Nutcracker*. I understand she's also rehearsing the lead role in *Paganini Variations*. Everyone thinks she's great—long-legged, pretty and capable of both a seamless adagio and incredible speed. Don't you agree, Bartlett?"

"Absolutely," Empson answered. "She's got a way to go, of course, at her young age. But she reminds me of the young Patty McBride. Able to do just about anything, and with real spirit. She's going to go far. So is Nancy Baker, for that matter," said Empson, pre-empting Navikoff's report. "She's extraordinary in Clifton's *Cinderella* and that Chopin piano ballet. I don't like that one very much, but she's been able to make something of the young girl's part for the first time ever. You remember even Veronica never looked very good in it."

"Thank you, Bartlett," Navikoff went on. "I guess that brings us to Aaron Cassidy. We now have sixteen principal dancers, though if you leave out Roberta and Sam, who are all but retired, it's only fourteen who are active. That's a low number—we had eighteen, remember, two years ago. Clifton feels very strongly that Aaron is ready. He's tall, and he's a wonderful partner, and he's just what the Company needs. The ballerinas can only look good if they have good partners—and Aaron can make them look good."

"Does anyone have any comments?" Frost asked the group. Andrea Turnbull put up her hand at once and Frost called on her.

"I don't have any quarrel with the girls," she said. "They seem all right to me. But I've said over and over again to anyone who would listen that Aaron Cassidy is simply not a first-class dancer. Handsome he is—very handsome. And that goes a long way with some," she continued, pointedly. "But technically he is not up to being a principal dancer—or at least, that's my judgment. Doesn't anyone agree?" She looked around the table plaintively.

"Andrea, there is no question that Aaron is not the finest dancer we have," Empson said. "But I'm sure he's going to get better. Don't forget he didn't go to our school, and he has a lot of little mannerisms that he has to unlearn. He's got to learn to hold his shoulders correctly, for one thing. But that's easy, and I certainly have no objection to promoting him now."

"Anyone else?" Frost asked.

"If Clifton wants him, let him have him," said Kenneth Franklin.

"I agree," said Jeanine Saperstein. "When one's time has come, one's time has come. We have to recognize it."

Frost ignored the secretary's inanity. "Do I take it, then, that all three appointments should be made? Or should we vote on them separately?"

"I move that we accept all three recommendations," David Weiss said, with Monsignor Carroll offering a quick second.

Frost took a formal vote by a show of hands. It was unanimous, except for Andrea Turnbull, who sat sullenly at her end of the table and refused to vote either aye or nay.

"Very well," Frost said. "Will you let Clifton know, Jack? I assume he'll want to convey the good news right away."

"Yes, indeed," Navikoff replied.

"Mr. Chairman, can I ask a question?" Adelaide Simms called out from the other end of the room.

"What is it, Adelaide?" Frost asked.

"I think the appointments we've just approved are fine," Simms began. "Aaron, Hailey and Nancy will all, I'm sure, do credit to the Company. But I'm troubled by one thing, Mr. Navikoff, and that's the failure to promote Gerald Hazard. He became a soloist what—ten years ago? And I really don't understand why he's not promoted to principal. My own opinion is that he is one of the finest we have—he's elegant, his technique is impeccable and it appears that he can do anything. I remember one night last season when he did the Bournonville variations, Clifton's *Jazz Café* and the *Corsaire pas de deux* all in one evening. So just what is his status?"

"I agree with you, Adelaide," said Beth Allen. Mrs. Allen was a shy, unassuming woman with an intense interest in the ballet and quiet, confident judgment in what she saw. She now overcame her shyness, for Adelaide Simms had struck on an issue about which she too felt strongly. "Gerald is an immensely valuable asset. He's a quick study and can learn a role in no time. That program you mentioned, Adelaide, was a good example. The three boys who could do the first dancer in *Jazz Café* were all injured. Gerald learned it overnight and did a very creditable job—along with carrying the rest of the program. I think he deserves principal status."

"Sometimes I think we'd be better off with the New York City Ballet's old system," Jeanine Saperstein interrupted. "You know, no rankings, no principals or soloists. It would certainly save a lot of trouble."

"That's a subject for another time, I think, Jeanine," Frost snapped, annoyed at Saperstein's irrelevant interruption. "I think you're right to raise the question, Adelaide, and I think we should discuss it." Both Cynthia and Reuben Frost agreed with the woman's assessment. Gerald Hazard was an excellent dancer with only one problem: Clifton Holt did not like him. The question of Hazard's promotion had come up twice before, but nothing had been done because of Holt's opposition. He was sure the same would happen this time, but it seemed worthwhile to convey to Navikoff (and thus to Holt) the wide support Hazard had on the Board.

"I know Gerald pretty well," Peter Howard said. "I know he feels terribly frustrated about being stuck as a soloist; he's talked to me about it several times. And while I know it's not relevant to the issue, Gerald, unlike many of the dancers, does have family responsibilities—his wife and two little boys who are just about school age."

"He's sort of funny-looking, don't you think?" Ambassador Franklin asked.

"He has red hair, Mr. Ambassador, if that's what you mean," said Adelaide Simms, a flaming (and natural) redhead herself, as the group laughed. "I've never found him so. Granted he's not as handsome as young Aaron or Roy Irwin, for that matter. But there's nothing especially unusual-looking about him. And he dances so beautifully that you certainly don't notice any imperfections in his looks when he's on stage."

"I was just asking," said Franklin.

"Does anyone else want to speak?" Frost asked. "Bartlett?"

"I agree with Adelaide and Beth. Gerald is a real asset to us. And I also agree with Peter Howard that he might well leave us if he's not promoted soon. But . . ." Bartlett Empson's voice trailed off. He seemed about to say something, then stopped. He did, however, stare at Jack Navikoff, who now looked increasingly uncomfortable.

"As chairman of the promotions committee, perhaps I should say something," Navikoff said. "I'm impressed with the depth of support for Gerald you are showing, as I have been in the past. All I can say is that I will report this back to Clifton and perhaps we can review the bidding."

So there it was. An artistic issue had been discussed, but the Board had not forced the Artistic Director's hand. And Jack Navikoff, Frost was almost certain, wouldn't now force it either.

Frost was about to ask if there were any other matters to be brought up when Maria Craig, one of the Company ballet mistresses, burst into the room. The look of distress on her face was evident. She looked around, spotted Frost, and went and whispered in his ear.

"Oh, my God!" Frost called out. After some more whispering with Craig, he turned to his colleagues.

"Ladies and gentlemen, I think we'd better adjourn. Clifton Holt has been stabbed outside the stage door downstairs."

CONFUSION

FROST'S ANNOUNCEMENT ELECTRIFIED HIS AUDIENCE. Some of the directors sprang up and started shouting questions at Maria Craig; others slumped back in their chairs in a state of shock. Frost firmly grabbed Ms. Craig by the arm and propelled her toward the door, moving so fast that the other Board members were left behind.

Still gripping the reluctant young woman's arm—she wanted to stand still and elaborate on her dramatic tale—he led her to the bank of two large elevators normally used to take dancers to the stage level and decisively banged the call button. Again his companion tried to talk, but Frost's stern look silenced her. An elevator stopped, its down signal ringing, and Frost pushed the woman into it ahead of him. As the door began to close, David Weiss and Peter Howard were running to catch it. Frost did nothing to keep the doors from closing.

Once the elevator had started down, Frost turned to his companion and looked her straight in the eye. "What happened, Maria?" he asked with intensity.

"I don't know, Mr. Frost. I was standing in the

wings talking to some of the dancers when Hailey Coles came in from the stage door. She was yelling, 'Clifton has been stabbed! Get a doctor!' Jeb Crosby—you know, the stage manager—was standing near us and tried to call for help from the phone at the side of the stage. He was shouting and cursing because the house operator didn't pick up, but then he got through and I heard him asking for the police and an ambulance."

"But for God's sake, what about Clifton?" Frost demanded.

"Everybody was too stunned to do anything for a minute; we were all hypnotized listening to Jeb shout at the operator. Hailey snapped us out of it with her screaming. 'We've got to do something—he's bleeding to death!' she kept shouting. Then Veronica Maywood, who was standing with me, yelled out and asked if he was dead. Hailey screamed again—she was quite hysterical by then—and said 'No.' Veronica and Aaron, who had also been standing there with us, ran outside. Then several people did. And that's when I came up to get you."

The elevator doors opened and Frost found himself in the midst of an unsettling scene—some of the dancers and stagehands calling for a doctor and an ambulance, others shouting for the police. Many started gathering around Frost as he emerged from the elevator, his old-lawyer's dignity in sharp contrast to the dramatic panic around him.

"Jeb!" he cried, spotting the stage manager. "Have you called an ambulance?"

"Yes, Mr. Frost. It's on its way," Crosby answered.

"What about a doctor?"

"We've called Edwards," Crosby replied, referring

to Martin Edwards, the company's orthopedist, whose office was around the corner.

"And the police?"

"Yes, I just got through to nine-one-one," Crosby said.

Satisfied that the necessary had been done, Frost headed for the stage door. It opened onto a long, dimly lit alley that led to Fifty-third Street. He saw the outstretched figure of Holt about halfway down the alley, with Veronica Maywood bent over him. The choreographer was still wearing the clothes he had worn at the earlier disastrous rehearsal, and Maywood had frantically ripped open his shirt. The fiery ballerina was no longer talking about Mexican jumping beans; instead she was desperately trying to staunch the bleeding from what appeared to be a triangle of three knife wounds in Holt's chest.

Maywood moaned softly as she held her scarf over Holt's chest. "Oh, Cliff, Cliff, no, no!" she cried. Aaron Cassidy and four or five other dancers stood by, watching helplessly.

"Is he still alive?" Frost barked at the nursing ballerina. One could not tell from looking at Holt's ravaged, blood-soaked figure or gaunt, alabaster-colored face.

"Yes! But his pulse is getting fainter. Where is the ambulance?" Maywood shouted.

As she spoke, a cacophony of distant sirens grew louder and, within seconds, the blinking red lights of not one but three police squad cars became visible. Four uniformed police officers—three men and a woman—came running down the stage-door alley, their hands on undrawn service revolvers. Two more officers followed them by seconds.

"Okay, get back, everybody," the first patrolman to

reach Holt's lifeless figure called out. He and a colleague pushed Maywood away.

"Stabbing," the first one said.

"Yeah," said his companion.

Before they could do anything for Holt, an ambulance, its siren screaming, pulled into the narrow alleyway, upending a garbage can in the process. In what seemed a matter of seconds the medics had jumped out of the ambulance and put Holt on a stretcher.

"Tyler Emergency?" the police sergeant who had taken charge asked.

"Right," one of the medics answered.

"Collins, you go with the ambulance," the sergeant said, pointing to one of the other officers.

The ambulance was gone as quickly as it had arrived. The sergeant then asked the crowd to move back into the theatre. Cowed and scared, they did so, observing as they went the other police officers securing the bloody area where Holt's body had rested moments before.

Once inside the Zacklin, the sergeant started asking questions. The group automatically deferred to Frost, who now stood next to the police officer.

"All right, who's in charge here?" the sergeant asked the stunned group.

"I suppose I am," Frost replied. He introduced himself to the officer, one Sergeant Peter Madden.

Before he could ask the next question, Madden was interrupted by cries of "Sergeant! Sergeant!" from the alleyway. Two of the other officers burst through the door. "They caught the guy!" one of them said. "He walked right into the arms of two patrolmen around the corner."

"Good going. How did they get him?" Madden asked.

"This gentleman here"—the officer who was speaking pointed to a visibly winded middle-aged civilian behind him—"was chasing the guy down the street, shouting that he was a murderer. The two patrolmen came around the corner just as the perpetrator was approaching."

"Sure they got the right guy?" the sergeant asked.

"Yes, indeed, officer," the civilian witness said, speaking with some effort. "I was coming out of the apartment house next door—I live there—and as I came along Fifty-third Street, I heard a strange sound from the stage-door alley—not a scream, but more like a painful groan. Next thing I knew, this young black kid came into the street with a knife in his hand. I could see a man lying in the alleyway, so I started screaming and chased the kid. He threw the knife in the gutter and then started running.

"He wasn't all that fast," the man continued. "So I kept up with him to the corner, when the cops grabbed him."

"How about the knife?" the sergeant asked.

"Found," said the woman officer. "Right in the gutter where he'd thrown it. Covered with blood and I'm sure some nice sticky fingerprints. We bagged it and sent it off to the Eighteenth Precinct with the officers who arrested the perp."

"You say this was a black kid?" the sergeant asked quietly.

"Yeah. Black. Twenty years old maybe. Twenty-two at most. And I'd say a junkie by the way he was acting. Higher than a kite," the woman said.

"Okay, let me get back to asking some more questions here," Sergeant Madden said, scanning the mute and fascinated group before him. "Who was the victim? You knew him?" he asked, turning to Frost.

"Yes. Clifton Holt, Artistic Director of the National Ballet Company."

"Anybody see who did it?"

"I . . . I don't know," Frost answered.

"Who found him?" the sergeant asked.

After a pause Vivian Felton, one of the Company's smallest dancers (with one of the smallest voices) said that she had. A delicate wisp in the best of circumstances, she seemed, in her grief and nervousness, even smaller and more vulnerable than usual.

"How did you find him?"

"How? Like, what shape was he in?" Felton asked.

"No, how, like how did you happen to be where the body was?"

"I—I—I was going home after rehearsal. I walked out the stage door, and . . ." She was unable to finish and burst into a flood of tears.

"Okay, miss, just tell me what you saw. Take your time, and don't be nervous. We just want to know what happened."

Felton continued to sob; further questioning would have to wait until she regained her self-control. While he waited, Madden turned toward Frost and spoke to him out of the hearing of the others.

"Excuse me, Mr. . . . um . . . Frost," he said. "You said the victim was the director of this theatre?"

"Yes, officer," Frost answered coolly. "He was one of the greatest choreographers in America—probably in the world."

"Oh, boy. And stabbed by a street-punk junkie."

"Officer, is there anything more I can do for you right now?" Frost asked, anxious to get away and make some telephone calls.

"You didn't see anything yourself?"

"No, I did not."

"Then I guess not. We'll want to question the people here, though, who might have seen something."

"Fine. Shall I ask people not to leave?"

"If you would."

Frost got the crowd's attention—no easy task, given the emotionally charged conversations going on through the backstage area—and conveyed the policeman's request.

"Reuben, surely that doesn't mean us!" barked Ambassador Franklin, who, with the other directors, had long since joined the backstage group and been briefed in whispers as to what had happened.

"I suspect it probably does, Kenneth," Frost replied.

"But we didn't see anything! We were upstairs in the Board meeting!" Franklin pleaded.

"Kenneth, I'm sure all you have to do is tell the police that when they ask you. The crime was committed by a twenty-year-old black junkie who I am sure you do not resemble in any way. Besides, he's been arrested, so put your conscience at rest."

"What are you trying to say, Reuben?" the angered commodities dealer/Ambassador shouted.

"Nothing, Kenneth, nothing. Now please excuse me. I have some things to do." Frost pushed past Franklin, only to run head-on into Andrea Turnbull.

"What is going on, Reuben?" she demanded. "No one will tell me anything!" Jack Navikoff, who was at her side, was visibly shaking and, Frost thought, was pale, in spite of his assiduously cultivated year-round suntan. He said nothing as Turnbull pressed her question.

"Andrea, you know as much as I do. Clifton Holt was stabbed outside the theatre by a young black."

"Did he kill him?" Turnbull asked.

Frost thought he detected just a bit too much

bloodlust in Turnbull's question, but let the matter pass.

"That's what I mean to find out right now," Frost said, moving past Turnbull and the silent Navikoff toward the fire stairs. He quickly went through the fire-resistant door and took the stairs to the basement, where the Company's offices were located. He found Holt's office unlocked and went in and shut the door. He sat down in Holt's beaten-up desk chair—Holt seldom used the office and cared not at all that it looked decrepit and was uncomfortable—and tried to organize his thoughts. He had to call the hospital; no question. And he probably should call Teresa Holt, Clifton's much-put-upon wife. But first he would call Luis Bautista, the City homicide detective who had become his friend several months earlier when they had worked together in solving the murder of his late partner at Chase & Ward, Graham Donovan. Frost was reluctant to admit that the events of the past few minutes had left him tired and a little confused. Bautista could help him out, whether Holt was dead or not—and Frost's quick look at Holt's bloody form had not made him optimistic.

Frost looked through his wallet for Bautista's private number, which the detective had given him during the Donovan investigation. He retrieved it and dialed the number. His luck was good; Bautista himself answered on the first ring. Frost explained the circumstances and Bautista said he would meet Frost at Tyler Hospital.

Frost next dialed Information (as he resolutely called it, despite the telephone company's equally stubborn insistence that what it was providing was "Directory Assistance"), got the hospital number and dialed it. After what seemed an unconscionable amount of switching, he talked to the receptionist in the emergency room, who was set to stonewall him.

"Mr. Frost, you are not a relative of the patient and therefore I can't tell you anything," she announced.

"That is true, madam," Frost replied, speaking slowly and deliberately, his voice signaling that the obstructionist to whom he was talking had better pay attention. "I am, however, the Chairman of the Board of the National Ballet Company, where Mr. Holt is the Artistic Director, and I—"

"That doesn't matter, Mr. Frost—"

"And I am also a friend of Avery Jonas, who I believe is the chairman of *your* board of directors. If I have to call him I will, if you would be good enough to tell me your name."

The icy authority in Frost's voice, and perhaps the substance of his threat as well, changed the woman's attitude. She asked Frost to hold while she got a report. After three minutes, he thought she had put him into telephone limbo forever, but she came back on the line and reported that Holt was still alive, and that the doctors were working on him in the operating room. She did not have anything additional to tell him.

Frost put down the telephone and dialed Information again, to get Teresa Holt's home number. It was, as he feared, unlisted. Frost argued with the operator about the necessity of putting a call through; but again resistance was the order of the day. He hung up on the Directory Assistance operator and, as he did so, spotted Holt's Rolodex on the desk. Thumbing through to "H," he found, under "Holt," an entry for "Teresa" and a number. He dialed it, but reached an answering service that informed him that Mrs. Holt was out of town and would not be back until Friday. At this point he did not feel up to penetrating a third security barrier, so he thanked the answering-service operator and hung up. Besides, the most important thing now seemed to him to be to keep a vigil at the hospital and to see Bautista.

Frost turned out the overhead light in the office and went out. He hurried toward the fire stairs and then hesitated—did he really want to confront Mrs. Turnbull, Ambassador Franklin and the other members of the Board? The answer was no, so he stopped, got his bearings and figured out how to leave the theatre through the orchestra. Not entirely sure of himself, he worked his way through dark backstage warrens to the rehearsal stairs connecting the stage with the orchestra. With the grotesque stabbing of Holt fresh in his mind, the dark and unfamiliar territory seemed both sinister and menacing to him. He was glad when he had reached the exit doors on Fifty-fourth Street, and relieved to find that they opened from the inside.

Sergeant Madden had said no one should leave; but he already felt under the special protection of his friend Detective Bautista. He walked into the street and hailed a cab. Whether Clifton Holt was dead or alive seemed at the moment much more important than answering the routine questions of the police in what was patently an open-and-shut case.

VIGIL

4

REUBEN FROST'S CAB PULLED UP IN THE CIRCULAR DRIVE-way at the emergency entrance of Tyler Hospital. Stepping out, he was momentarily disoriented by the bright neon lights shining against the somber walls of the building. Recovering himself, he walked toward the glass doors marked "EMERGENCY" and pushed one open, his equilibrium being disturbed again by the wails of the sirens of two approaching ambulances.

As he made his way to the receptionist behind a glass partition, two young doctors in white coats, with stethoscopes around their necks, rushed to the door. Frost correctly took them to be interns; both had been summoned by separate emergency calls to meet the ambulances screeching up to the entrance. Before he could get to the reception desk, orderlies wheeled the newly arrived patients in on rolling stretchers—a wizened old white woman looking more dead than alive and a groaning young black man bleeding prodigiously from a head wound.

Three people were in line ahead of Frost at the reception desk: a young girl, in obvious pain and clutching her wrist, laboriously answering what seemed to be an endless number of questions being asked by the plump woman filling out a form on the other side of the partition, and two young men staggering and swaying as they waited their turn.

Frost was impatient. He was, after all, seeking not medical attention but guidance and information. He resented the extensive questioning of the girl at the head of the line—why on earth didn't they take care of her injured arm instead of subjecting her to a cross-examination?—and realized that he would have to wait, however unwillingly, for the young men in front of him to complete the same process.

His young male companions did not share his impatience. Both seemed almost asleep as they swayed back and forth. Frost observed them with both curiosity and distaste and concluded that the one nearer him was petrifyingly drunk—a condition Frost recognized—and the other was strung out on some drug—a condition with which he was much less familiar but one he thought he recognized.

Frost's good nature was soon stretched further by the arrival of a young black woman carrying a screaming baby, who took her place in the line behind him. The mother was approaching hysteria, and as her panic increased, her tiny child screamed louder and louder. Frost could not see anything manifestly wrong with the youngster, but the combined outcries from the baby and its mother indicated that something was very much amiss.

Fortunately, Frost was soon facing the woman at the reception window; the first swaying young man had been given a paper cup of liquid—methadone?—on surrendering a pink card that he carried, and the drunk had been summarily told to take a seat—pending ouster by the hospital security staff.

"Yes?" the fat receptionist officiously said to Frost while, at least in Frost's imagination, looking him over for symptoms that would justify his incursion on her emergency-room turf.

"Good evening, madam. I'm here to see about Clifton Holt. I believe he was brought in here around forty-five minutes ago." He did not make a reference to his intimidating telephone call from the Zacklin.

"What's the name?"

"Holt. H-O-L-T."

"Are you next-of-kin?"

"No, I'm a friend."

"Who brought him?"

"Um, an ambulance. He was stabbed."

The woman gave Frost a "What else is new?" look, but consulted a list on a clipboard at the side of the counter where she sat.

"Clifton Holt?" she asked.

"That's right."

"I haven't much to tell you. He's in surgery now and was in pretty bad shape when he came in."

"I want to wait," Frost said. "What should I do?"

"I don't know what to tell you. You can wait here if you like."

Frost glanced over at the crowded waiting room: crying babies; men and women in obvious pain clutching the distressed parts of their bodies; nervously smoking wives and husbands, fathers and mothers, waiting for some word from the reaches beyond the room's institutional-green walls.

"Do I have a choice?" Frost asked.

"Not really," the receptionist said, in her flat voice. "Mr. Holt, you know, is—"

"Oh, Holt. A dancer or something?"

"Yes, in a manner of speaking."

"There's a reporter here asking about him. And a photographer. You're a friend of his?"

"Yes."

"Just a moment."

The woman picked up the telephone at her side and dialed an internal number.

"Julie?" she asked. "There's a man here about this fellow Holt. What's your name, sir?"

"Reuben Frost."

"Reuben Frost. Says he's a friend."

After a pause, the woman said "Okay" and hung up. "Miss Froelich will be right down, Mr. Frost. She's our public relations officer. Meanwhile, you can wait over there." She pointed to the waiting room Frost had earlier viewed with distaste. But his reluctance to go there was diminished by the screams of the baby in its mother's arms behind him.

Frost did not sit down on the single remaining plastic seat in the waiting area, but instead stood, awkwardly, leaning against the wall beside the entrance. This is a world I never made, he thought, as he observed the pain, misery and anxiety around him. He reflected on his good fortune in never having been in the emergency room of this or any other hospital. His musings were soon interrupted by an attractive young brunette.

"Mr. Frost?" she asked, having singled him out instinctively from the wretched group in the waiting room.

"Yes."

"I'm Julie Froelich. I'm a public relations officer here at the hospital."

"I'm pleased to meet you," Frost replied.

"You know Mr. Holt?"

"Yes. What can you tell me about him?"

"Not much, I'm afraid. He was in critical condition when he arrived and is now being operated on. We won't know anything until Dr. Young or one of the other doctors working on him comes out of the operating room. But he's in good hands, Mr. Frost. She—Dr. Young—is the best."

"She?"

"Yes, Mr. Frost. Abigail Young, our chief surgeon."

Frost felt guilty for having asked his question. It had been entirely innocent, but it seemed clear that Ms. Froelich had interpreted it as a sexist one.

"I see. So what do I do now?"

"Why don't you come with me to my office. The press is here, you know, and I want to ask you some questions about the patient."

"How did the press find out about this?"

"How do they ever find out, Mr. Frost? A policeman, or some tipster, must have called them."

Frost followed the woman out of the emergency waiting area with relief, though the scene on the other side of the door into the hospital proper was scarcely more comforting—a man having his head bandaged, another having an I.V. inserted in his limp arm, other people groaning on stretchers as they awaited attention. Ms. Froelich guided him quickly through the carnage to a large institutional elevator, not unlike the one backstage at the Zacklin.

When they had arrived at the woman's tiny office, she asked Frost to sit down in the metal chair beside her desk. It was soon made evident that she knew Holt was important—the arrival of the reporter and the photographer had confirmed that—but it also became clear that she was not quite sure why. Frost

enlightened her, using for the second time that evening the phrase "one of the finest living choreographers
in America," and Ms. Froelich seemed duly impressed.

"Where is this reporter?" Frost asked.

"Down the hall in one of our reception rooms. He's
from the *Press*."

"Not Arthur Mattison?" Frost asked, thinking with
some distaste of the *Press*'s jack-of-all-trades critic of
all the arts, including dance.

"Stratton. He's a police reporter who's been here
many times before."

"There's no real reason I should see him, do you
think?" Frost said.

"None at all, Mr. Frost. Unless, of course, you want
to."

Ms. Froelich's telephone rang and she picked it up.
After a conversation in monosyllables, she reported
that Holt was still in the operating room, but that the
attending doctors had requested more blood.

"Not a good sign," Frost said.

"No."

"Miss Froelich, could I make some calls? I tried to
reach Mr. Holt's wife earlier but was not successful.
And there are one or two other calls I should make as
well."

"Please feel free. I have a couple of other things to
do, so you can have this office to yourself for the
moment."

"How about long-distance?" Frost asked.

"Just direct-dial on the outside line. The third
button."

"Thank you very much. Oh, and one other thing.
I'm expecting a detective from the Police Department
named Luis Bautista. How will he know where to find
me?"

"I'll call down to Reception and alert them," the woman said. She did so, and then walked out of the room.

Left alone, Frost called the backstage number at the theatre and talked to Moira Burgess, NatBallet's publicity director.

"I'm afraid Clifton is in a very bad way," Frost explained. "He's been in the operating room over an hour now, and they've just asked that more blood be brought in. And there's a reporter here. Some fellow named Stratton from the *Press*. I think you should get over here. And why don't you bring Jeb along for moral support?"

Frost knew that he meant that Burgess should bring Jeb Crosby, the Company stage manager, for *her* moral support; but he wouldn't mind having the cool and unflappable Crosby, devoted as he was to both NatBallet and Clifton Holt, around for reassurance as well. Burgess said she would bring Crosby.

Burgess then asked if Veronica Maywood should come along also.

"I don't know, Moira. She was pretty out-of-control when I saw her at the theatre."

The report Frost now received did not indicate that Maywood's emotions had calmed greatly. But he was sure she could probably not be kept away in any event, so he told Burgess to bring her if that was what the ballerina wanted.

The woman next announced that Jack Navikoff would be coming too.

The more the merrier, Frost thought. But he was really not in a position to restrict the guest list.

Frost then called home to talk to Cynthia.

"Where are you?" she asked.

"In the emergency ward of Tyler Hospital," Frost replied.

"Good God! Are you all right? What's the matter?" Cynthia asked, in a panicky voice.

"Clifton Holt was stabbed outside the Zacklin Theatre. He's now in the operating room," Frost said. "It's horrible—but don't worry about me. But say a prayer for Clifton."

"I don't believe it," Cynthia said. "Who did it? How did it happen?"

"All cut-and-dried, I'm afraid. A young black stabbed Clifton in the stage-door alley and then was caught running down the street."

His wife sighed. "Poor Cliff. What's the prognosis?"

"I don't know, but he's been in surgery for a good long time."

"Should I come over?" Cynthia asked.

"I don't think there's anything you can do, dear," Frost said. "But I've got to stay. I'll be home when we know something."

"Have you talked to Luis?"

"Bautista? Yes, he's on his way here now."

"All right. Well, call me if there's any news. Or anything I can do. And be careful."

"Thanks. Goodbye."

Putting down the telephone, Frost thought again of Teresa Holt. Should he persist and try to reach her? She had not lived with Holt for years. But she was, after all, the wounded man's wife, however much Clifton Holt had made a mockery of his marriage with constant, open and notorious affairs with partners both female and male.

Yes, he would try to assault the fortress of the woman's answering service once again. The operator he reached this time seemed marginally more intelligent than the one he had talked to earlier. She would not give out Teresa's number, nor her whereabouts, but did agree to try to reach her and ask her to call Frost at the hospital extension from which he was speaking.

As he concluded his conversation, Luis Bautista came into the office. The tall, good-looking Puerto Rican, immaculately dressed as usual, shook hands with Frost warmly. The two men, thrown together in the aftermath of the bizarre poisoning of Frost's partner months earlier, had become good friends, as had Cynthia and Bautista's steady girlfriend, the ravishing Francisca Ribiero.

"Reuben! What's happened?" the young detective asked.

"I don't know much more than I told you earlier," Frost replied. He did bring Bautista up to date on Holt's condition as best he could.

"Let me call Manhattan North and see what's going on," Bautista said. He did so, then reported that James Wilson, aged twenty, was being held for robbery and attempted murder. He also confirmed that the police had retrieved Wilson's knife where he had dropped it on Fifty-third Street.

"A nice, straightforward, routine case, Reuben," Bautista said. "Though it was odd, they didn't find a wallet or a watch or anything like that on the kid."

"Could he have thrown them away, like he did the knife?" Frost asked.

"I doubt it. They searched the street pretty carefully."

"It's a terrible thing, Luis. But it looks like no work for you," Frost said, adding quickly, "even if Clifton dies."

"Thank God, Reuben. I've got ten active cases now and don't need another one."

"Well, I appreciate your coming by, Luis. Don't let me keep you."

"Oh, no problem. I'm happy to stay. Some cops 'coop' in their patrol cars in dark alleys; I'm just as happy to do it in beautiful Tyler Hospital." The detective waved his arms about Ms. Froelich's austere little office.

"Coop? What's that?"

"Reuben, where have you been? Don't you remember the big scandal about 'cooping' in the N.Y.P.D. a few years ago? Goofing off. Sleeping when you're supposed to be on patrol—that kind of thing." Bautista was smiling, the small but noticeable nick on one of his bottom teeth showing, as he kidded his older friend with an air of familiarity that would have been emotionally impossible for him to sustain when he had first met Frost at the start of the Donovan investigation—and which Frost, the dignified Wall Street lawyer, would not then have tolerated either.

"Oh, yes, I guess I do remember. Don't get old, Luis: you never remember anything."

"You do pretty well, Reuben—for an old guy."

The two men laughed as Jeb Crosby, Moira Burgess, Veronica Maywood and Jack Navikoff came into the office. The arrivals were startled to see the two men laughing, and the laughing stopped abruptly.

"How is he?" Maywood asked anxiously. "Is he going to die?" She seemed to shrink from such a conclusion.

Again Frost, feeling somewhat like an announcer, recounted what he knew, until interrupted by the ringing of the telephone. Bautista answered it, then handed the instrument over to Frost. It was Teresa Holt.

"Teresa? Where are you?" Frost began.

"In California. Sausalito. Having a glorious time with my old friends the Maxwells. Two months of absolute heaven. But what on earth are you doing at a hospital, Reuben? You're all right, aren't you?"

"Yes, Teresa, I'm all right. It's Clifton."

"Oh?"

"He was stabbed tonight outside the theatre."

"Oh, no," the woman said, barely whispering. "Is he—Reuben, is he dead?"

"No." Frost almost said "Not yet." "He's in the operating room now. We're waiting to hear. And praying."

"Oh, my God, Reuben. Was it—was it anyone we know? Or . . . anyone Clifton might know?"

"I don't think so. Apparently just a junkie out to steal what he could."

"Okay. But then why the stabbing?"

"I don't know, Teresa. I don't think anyone saw what happened. Clifton probably resisted."

Teresa Holt laughed softly. "Oh, Reuben, he was always so stingy. He probably *did* resist. To protect the five dollars in his pocket. He never carried much money. He was always afraid of being robbed. You're sure it was a robbery?"

"Pretty sure."

"It couldn't have been . . . something else?"

"No indication of that, Teresa."

"Well, thank heaven for that, anyway," she said. "I guess I should come back."

"I think so. But that's up to you."

"All right. But could you call my maid—oh, never mind. I can't have you doing my errands. You're obviously doing enough already. Who's there with you?"

"Jeb Crosby and Moira Burgess and . . . a police

detective," Frost said, hoping that Veronica Maywood and Jack Navikoff had not heard the omission of their names.

"Well, all right. I'll get a flight as soon as I can. Probably the day flight first thing in the morning. But call me as soon as you know anything more. And much love, dear Reuben."

Teresa Holt hung up before Frost could get her number. He cursed silently to himself; it would be back to the answering service unless he could locate the Maxwells in Sausalito. Who were they? He did not know.

Ms. Froelich suddenly appeared. She seemed startled by the number of people crowded in and outside her office. But she picked out Reuben and asked him to come with her. He did so, and they walked together down the hall.

"I'm afraid the worst has happened," the woman said quietly. "Mr. Holt died on the operating table. Dr. Young is waiting to talk to you, if you like."

"No, I don't see any point to that. Except perhaps to thank her. But I'd as soon skip that right now."

"As you wish, Mr. Frost. What about the press? There are two reporters and a television crew here now."

"Miss Burgess is the press representative for Nat-Ballet," he said. "She's one of the people back in your office."

"I see. You don't want to talk to them?"

"No. I'll issue a statement on behalf of the Company. Once I pull myself together a bit."

"He was a close friend?"

"He was a *genius,* Miss Froelich. Possibly the greatest living choreographer and the heart and soul of the

National Ballet Company. A friend? Yes, he was. But I am sad for so many more reasons than that."

"I think I understand."

"I'd better tell the others."

Frost turned around and approached the group in Ms. Froelich's office. He told them that Clifton was dead. Jack Navikoff looked as if he had been struck dumb; he said nothing and showed no reaction. Moira Burgess and Jeb Crosby both began crying quietly. Veronica Maywood, temporarily calm before Frost's announcement, now returned to full-range hysteria, alternately sobbing and screaming. She threw her arms around Frost, who did his best to comfort her.

"All right, Veronica," he said quietly, his own eyes getting moist. "Let's be calm. Let's be calm." He patted her gently on the back, and his ministrations at least reduced the volume of her wailing.

"Now," Frost said. "Moira, there are reporters here. I think you and Miss Froelich must see them right away. And the Company has to be told. Jeb, can you do that? You know how to reach everyone."

As the NatBallet stage manager, Jeb Crosby did. Each dancer, from the highest to the lowest, was required to keep Crosby posted as to his or her whereabouts so the stage manager could track down the wayward on those rare occasions when they did not show up at the Zacklin when scheduled for a performance.

"I'd call the principals and soloists first, and let them help you reach the corps members," Frost instructed. "Meanwhile, I'm going home, where I'll try to get Teresa again. And call the Board members too.

"Oh, one thing, Miss Froelich," he continued. "What was the cause of death?"

"A slashed aorta that simply could not be stitched back together," she replied.

"Terrible. Well, I'll be at home if anyone wants or needs me," Frost said.

Bautista, who had been standing quietly in the background, now came forward.

"Come on, Reuben, I'll drive you home."

The two men walked outside Tyler Hospital to Bautista's black unmarked police car, parked in a "no parking" zone outside the emergency-room entrance. Bautista unlocked the door on the passenger side and motioned Frost to the passenger seat. The detective entered on the opposite side and turned on the engine, which immediately started the noisy "fasten-seat-belt" signal.

"Fasten your seat belt, Reuben," Bautista said.

Frost grappled with the strap at the side of the car, but clearly did not know how to manipulate it.

"Cynthia and I never use these things when we go to Long Island," he muttered.

"I'm shocked, Mr. Frost. A good citizen like you, and a lawyer at that, not obeying the laws of the State of New York?" Bautista said, with mock gravity.

Frost thought of two inappropriate responses: (a) he was sufficiently old that preserving his life was perhaps not worth the effort to strap on the infernal Naderesque device now prescribed by the State's authorities and (b) at worst, the fine for noncompliance with the State's latest effort to save its citizens' lives was a mere twenty-five dollars. Neither reason seemed appropriate for the minion of Law and Order sitting beside him.

"All right. I've strapped myself in," Frost said grumpily.

"That's better. That's what I would expect from a

pillar of the legal establishment," Bautista said.

"Um," Frost grunted.

As Bautista coolly drove toward the East Side, Frost recalled that he had only once before ridden in a police car (or its equivalent), when the Mayor had invited him to share a ride downtown from a Gracie Mansion meeting of civic movers and shakers. The Mayor's driver, in traffic, had sounded the siren and flashed the red light in the Mayor's sedan. Frost remembered being childishly pleased at the time, as the Mayor's car moved through congested traffic in a way not available to the ordinary citizen.

The traffic now was not great, and Bautista's deft command of the car quickly brought them to the neighborhood of the Frosts' East Seventieth Street town house. Frost secretly longed for the siren to sound and the red signal light in the rear of the car to flash. Then he thought, What kind of fantasy is this for a seventy-five-year-old man? He was immediately ashamed and hoped against hope that his Walter Mitty dream had not been sensed by Detective Bautista.

As Bautista pulled smartly into Seventieth Street, off Park Avenue, Frost asked him if he would like to come in for a drink or, for that matter, for supper.

"No, sir, I'm afraid not. I've got some things to check on open case number eight tonight."

"Well, okay. Cynthia will be disappointed. But we are going to see you and Francisca next week, I believe. Tuesday, isn't it?"

Reuben and Cynthia, as confirmed devotees of the ballet, were determined to make Bautista and Ms. Ribiero balletomanes as well. With all the zeal and cunning of Jehovah's Witnesses, they conspired ultimately to effect a full-immersion conversion of their new friends; the following Tuesday's NatBallet performance was to be the latest in a series of Scripture lessons.

"Oh, yes, we'll be there. Wouldn't miss it," Bautista said.

"And Luis, thanks for your support tonight. It meant a lot to me," Frost said, as the two men shook hands warmly.

5

FROST LET HIMSELF INTO HIS TOWN HOUSE AND CALLED upstairs to announce his return to Cynthia.

"I just heard it on the TV news, Reuben," she said, as she came to the top of the stairs. "He *is* dead, isn't he?"

"Yes."

"Poor dear, it must have been awful for you at the hospital," she said as she kissed her husband and stroked his forehead.

"The waiting was terrible. He died on the operating table."

"What do you want to do about eating?"

"Can we eat here?"

"Yes. I've got a steak. We can eat anytime."

"I'm afraid I've got to call the directors before I do anything. If I can get Peter Howard—assuming he has enough energy to help—we can divide up the list. It will probably take an hour or so. Is that all right?"

"Fine. Oh, and Arthur Mattison called. He wants a statement from you."

"That must have been an interesting conversation," Frost said. Mattison, the author of a thrice-weekly

column in the *Press* dedicated to cultural subjects, had
recently started a broad-based attack on the Brigham
Foundation's program of grants to the performing arts—
the program of which Cynthia Frost was the visible
and very public head. Acting the outraged populist,
which he did occasionally in print, he had severely
criticized the Brigham program as "elitist" and unre-
sponsive to the needs of minorities and the smaller
arts organizations around the country.

Cynthia had found Mattison's attacks grossly unfair,
given the great efforts she and her staff had made to
identify less obvious organizations for grant assistance.
But trying to explain this to Mattison had been futile;
he had made up his mind and there seemed no way to
change it. The result had been enormous frustration
on Cynthia's part, and confirmed to her and to her
husband something that they had known was true all
along: that they really didn't like Mattison very much.
He was an insufferably vain and self-important man
with views on every aspect of culture, all of which
eventually made their way into the pages of the *Press*.
But his latest volley of attacks had made Cynthia
determined never to speak to him again.

"You're right," Cynthia said. "It was a pretty cool
conversation, though he went on and on about what a
terrible thing Clifton's death was. I was polite, however."

Frost sighed. "I suppose I have to do Mattison's
statement first." He went into the library, worked at
his desk briefly and then went out to see Cynthia,
carrying two sheets of yellow foolscap with him.

"Do you think this is all right?" he asked, reading
from the sheets in his hand:

" 'Clifton Holt's senseless murder has shocked and
saddened everyone in the National Ballet family. Holt

was perhaps the finest choreographer in the world after the generation of George Balanchine and Jerome Robbins. He was the founder of, and the creative genius that sustained, the National Ballet. I will miss him, the Company will miss him and the dance world will miss him.' "

"That's fine," Cynthia said. "But the reference to 'the world' seems a bit strong. Try 'America.' "

" 'Holt was perhaps the finest choreographer in America after the generation,' et cetera. If I do that, can't I take out the 'perhaps'?"

"Yes. Clifton had no competition in this country."

"Would you mind trying to get Moira Burgess to read her this? She was at the hospital, but she should be back at the Zacklin by now. I don't want to talk to Mattison, and Moira can get this to all the papers. Meanwhile I'll use the other line to call the directors."

"Yes, give it to me. I'll call Moira."

Frost went back to the library. He found Peter Howard at home and they agreed to divide the directors, Frost taking the first half of the alphabetical list (thus avoiding both Jeanine Saperstein and Andrea Turnbull).

Frost's calls were perfunctory; he was getting hungry, and this was not a time to hear the Board members' theories about the future direction of NatBallet. He did tell each of those he called that he proposed to place Arne Petersen in acting charge of the Company, and all he talked to concurred. After another call to Howard to make sure he had not found any opposition to Petersen, Frost rang up the Assistant Artistic Director at home to inform him of the decision. The young man seemed to want to talk, so Frost finally asked him to come for dinner. Petersen declined, but said that he would like to come over afterward if that would not be too late. Frost assured him that it would not.

Dinner was ready by the time Reuben had finished his calls, so he and Cynthia took their places in the dining room. It was a large room, its centerpiece an enormous slate-gray marble table. The table seated fourteen easily—one of Reuben's business friends called the setting the "boardroom." But Cynthia and Reuben, as was their custom, sat side by side at one end. They did not eat in the dining room out of any sense of formal propriety; their kitchen was quite small, and eating there was simply not very comfortable.

"Well," Cynthia said, once she had placed the food on the table and sat down. "Just like the old days at Chase & Ward. Work until all hours and then eat and go to bed."

"My dear, your memory really is failing you," Reuben replied. "You might just recall that most of the nights when we ate late and went immediately to bed were due to your performances, not my work. My work schedule was always a model of calm and certitude, as compared with yours."

"Not my recollection, dear; but let's talk about Clifton. Tell me exactly what happened. The news report on television wasn't very clear."

Frost did so, telling her of the alleyway stabbing, the chase of the attacker by a resident of the next-door apartment building, the capture of Jimmy Wilson and the death of Clifton Holt on the Tyler Hospital operating table.

"We're sure this Jimmy Wilson did it?"

"I don't think there's any question about it. Luis Bautista called the precinct house. The kid is twenty, a heroin addict with a record of violence. Just one of those awful, fateful meetings."

"But why Clifton? And why at the stage door? There are robberies around that theatre all the time, but I've never heard of a robbery—let alone a murder—in the stage-door alley. It's a *cul-de-sac*. And Clifton, of all people. He never carried anything valuable. He never even wore a watch, always asking the people around him for the time. It doesn't make sense."

"How was his assailant to know that Holt was a cheapskate?" Frost asked. "Since Clifton wasn't carrying any money, the kid was probably so enraged that he stabbed him."

"Probably so. But what a horrible mess. Though maybe . . ."

"Maybe what, Cynthia?"

"Nothing. It's just that Clifton had become so difficult lately. Look at the ballet he was working on when he died. *Chávez Concerto!* Utterly impossible, yet no one could tell Clifton that. His body of work is marvelous, Reuben, but there hasn't been anything really good since that little Mozart piece three years ago."

"You're right. Though I liked his Aaron Copland ballet last year better than you did," Reuben said.

"Fiddlesticks. But back to Clifton. I'm sure he had not been happy in recent years. He was always a very reserved man—I don't mean just a reserve about women, but a reserve about human beings in general—which meant you never really could be close friends with him. But lately, not only had he been withdrawn, but he had developed some real hatreds—Andrea Turnbull is understandable, but Gerald Hazard and Arne Petersen—why did he dislike them so? Why was he trying to stand in the way of their advancement?"

"I hate to think, Cynthia. Could it be as simple as

the fact that Gerald and Arne are straight and Clifton was not?"

"Perhaps," she replied. "Clifton's sex life was certainly confused and went off in all directions, but I never once thought it interfered with his work. But maybe it did."

"And what about Jack Navikoff? He seemed to be the only person close to Clifton at all in recent months," Reuben said. "He was at the hospital, by the way. Looking and acting, with that suntan of his, like a terra cotta sphinx. No emotion at all. Just *there,* taking everything in but saying nothing."

"I've never figured him out. I've just assumed Clifton and Jack were lovers; I don't have a complete sixth sense about such things, but I'm sure those two were."

"I agree."

"But it was more than that. Clifton and Jack were business partners, after all—and very successful ones, Clifton directing and choreographing those movies that Navikoff produced," Cynthia said. "They got very rich, the two of them. Speaking of which, who gets Clifton's money?"

"Funny you should ask. I am Clifton's executor, if you remember," Reuben said.

"That's why I asked."

"As far as I know, Teresa gets everything, except for the rights to some of the ballets and a specific bequest to Navikoff. I say 'as far as I know' because that's what the will he sent me ten years ago said. He may well have changed it—something I'll have to find out from Melvin Lincoln tomorrow. He never discussed anything personal with me from the time he first asked me to be his executor."

"Why do you think he asked you, anyway?"

"I've never been sure. But he did know us—you longer and better than me—and I think trusted us. And we're older and outside the orbit of his agent, his show-biz lawyers, his publicist and all those other hangers-on—including Navikoff—from his Hollywood days. I think I was meant to be the respectable WASP lawyer who would keep the parasites from dissipating his estate. Do you have a better idea?"

"No," Cynthia said. "I think you're exactly right. It's one thing to leave Navikoff money in the will, but quite another to let him control the estate and Clifton's ballets."

"The one subsequent conversation I ever had with Clifton was about his ballets and who should tend to the licensing of them—a job I really am quite incapable of doing. He said I should do it—consulting with you."

"Good heavens. We'll have to answer all those wonderful letters: 'Dear Mr. Frost, we are a new ballet company in Highland Falls, Montana. While we have only been in existence for three months, we would like very much to perform Mr. Clifton Holt's ballet *Paganini Variations* for our spring concert' . . ."

"No, I don't think so. Clifton's agent, Morris Brooks, will take care of letters like that. The real problem will come when perfectly sound companies want to do works that are not suited for their dancers or their capabilities. But try to tell that to some of the egomaniacs out there," Frost said, motioning in the general direction of the Hudson River.

The doorbell rang as Frost was talking.

"That must be Arne," Frost said, as he went downstairs to open the door. He returned in a moment with Arne Petersen.

Petersen had become a good friend of the Frosts

almost from the time of his arrival from Denmark. A product of the Royal Danish Ballet, he was a dancer of the Bournonville school and had been imported by NatBallet for that reason. Blond and handsome but a trifle on the short side, he had been a very good, but never truly outstanding, dancer. His true forte had turned out to be coaching the small but interesting Bournonville repertory danced by NatBallet. Gradually —no dancer really ever wants to quit outright—he had stopped dancing in favor of coaching, and as his natural skills as a coach developed, he had been appointed Assistant Artistic Director under Clifton Holt.

Petersen sat down at the Frost dinner table and accepted a cup of coffee. Reuben now reminded him of their early meetings when Petersen had first arrived in the United States and, indeed, had stayed with the Frosts.

"Arne, as I told you on the phone, the directors are unanimous in wanting you to take over as the acting head of NatBallet," Frost said.

"Reuben, that's very kind. Very kind indeed. And I should be honored and flattered to do so. On the other hand, I should be realistic. You really don't have any choice, do you?"

Frost was silent for a minute. "You're right, we don't. But I was trying to convey to you, old friend, the confidence the Board has in you."

"Excellent. And how long will it last? Next you'll be appointing a search committee to find a permanent Director—oh, yes, I'll be on the short list as the hometown favorite. But then there will be the *marvelous* director of a ballet school over a Rite-Aid Drugstore in Scranton, Pennsylvania. Never ran a ballet company, mind you, and never lived in New York City.

But he is simply *darling* and *must* receive our attention. I can see it now. . . ."

"That's awfully cynical, Arne," Cynthia said.

". . . Or the wonderful fellow who's the terrific fund-raiser. Doesn't know too much about the ballet—there's even one rumor that he's never seen one—but *is he ever good* with the blue-hairs and the fat cats."

"What on earth makes you think our Board would act that way?" Frost asked indignantly.

"Because I've seen it, Reuben. I've seen these search committees and whom they've picked. And whom they didn't pick—myself included."

"Arne, I had no idea. Have others been looking you over?" Cynthia asked.

"Sure. I'm an obvious target. Moderately successful (though not so successful that I cost too much), nice foreign *and* New York credentials. And growing ever more restless in the shadow of Clifton Holt."

"Arne, we've known you for a very long time," Frost said.

"Going back to when I couldn't even *tale Engelsk*," Petersen added.

"That's right. And I don't think either of us had any idea you were looking around at other companies," Frost said.

"I wasn't looking around. People came to me. Naturally I never said anything about it. Why should I? Whatever competition I was in, the fund-raising smarties or those with artistic pretensions would win. No point in talking about leaving until there's a real alternative."

"But you went to these interviews?"

"Hell, yes. Questions by the hour. Questions by the yard. 'Mr. Petersen, now that you have left Denmark, how do you *really* feel about the Royal Danish Ballet?' 'Do you know Peter Martins?' 'Do you know him well?' Which I always took to be a way of asking whether Peter could help me in getting the rights to perform Balanchine ballets. Or, before he retired as a dancer, whether I could entice him to East Jesus to be the guest artist—for one night—in the Christmas *Nutcracker*."

"And this was all unsolicited?" Frost asked, somewhat incredulously. (He was aware of "headhunters" and high-class employment agencies and, God knows, search committees, but he had not associated such hyper-powered operations with the selection of ballet directors; as Petersen told his tale, he realized that the flesh market operated in this field as in any other.)

"Yes, always. Cynthia, you know what NatBallet means to me. I never would have considered leaving it. Except . . ."

"Except, Arne?" Cynthia prompted.

"Except Clifton had become so difficult. He took charge of everything—casting, programming, coaching, you name it. I didn't have a say in anything. And for over a year at least I've been completely frozen out. Sure, when Clifton went off to Morocco on vacation, I was in charge. Managing the Company for two weeks in the dog days of the season—half the company injured, the other half exhausted. A great chance to put one's stamp on the Company. I don't know why Clifton took a dislike to me. He had been my mentor as a ballet master and as an administrator; then he started to freeze me out—and kept me frozen out."

"I'm sorry," Cynthia said. "I suppose I should have known."

"I was ready for a new search committee—Tucson, Butte, Buffalo, Myrtle Beach—you name it, I was ready."

"But now you have a chance for real development," Frost said.

"Reuben, you've said that. And I'm grateful. All I can hope is that your search committee agrees. But we'll see what we see."

Petersen sprang from the table, kissed both Cynthia and Reuben on the cheek and disappeared. Having once lived in the house, he knew the way out.

Reuben and Cynthia cleared the dishes off the marble dining-room table, then paused for a short while in the living room before going to bed.

"It's been a long day," Reuben said, as he sank down into the living-room sofa and put his feet up on the coffee table (a practice his wife disapproved of, but was resigned to after forty years of marriage).

"And a sad one," Cynthia answered.

"Yes. Very sad. Clifton was an S.O.B., Cynthia, in many, many ways. But a genius nonetheless."

"Absolutely correct," Cynthia replied, then fell silent for a minute or two. Reuben did nothing to break her reverie. Then she spoke again:

"You know, Reuben, if Clifton had to die—had to be killed—it's just as well that it was a street-corner hoodlum who did it. Can you imagine the mess if he had died 'under suspicious circumstances,' as they say in murder mysteries? The number of suspects would be almost as large as the Company's corps de ballet."

"Well, like who, Cynthia?" Frost asked, knowing full well that his wife was right but trying to conceal it.

"Like the young man who just left, Arne Petersen. Willing to consider going to Tucson, for heaven's sake, to get away from Clifton Holt. Or Holt's put-upon wife, betrayed once a night and twice on matinee days. Or your psychotic friend Andrea Turnbull. Or Veronica Maywood, rejected in bed and about to be humiliated by Clifton professionally as well. And I'm sure we've just scratched the surface."

"You're right, as usual," Frost replied, as he drained his glass and got up to head for bed. "But there's no itch, so don't scratch."

"Yes, dear. But all I can say is this Jimmy Wilson prevented an absolute outbreak of the hives."

SEARCHING AROUND

6

REUBEN FROST, DESPITE THE EXERTIONS OF THE PREVIOUS day, was up early Tuesday morning. Over his long legal career he had assumed a variety of roles: director, trustee, arbitrator, even guardian in the case of the minor children of a young colleague who had died suddenly. But as best he could recall, he had never before served as the executor of an estate.

The normal practice, as he had always understood it from his trusts-and-estates partners at Chase & Ward, was to appoint a member of one's family (as Reuben had appointed Cynthia in the case of his own estate) as the executor. Or, failing that, one might name a bank, a close friend or, quite frequently, a member of the law firm that had drawn up the will.

Clifton Holt, with his usual defiance of convention, had not followed the customary course. Given their cold relationship, it was not surprising that he had bypassed his wife, Teresa. But it was odd that he had not named Melvin Lincoln, his personal lawyer at Lincoln & Gold, the entertainment law firm that represented him on a regular basis, especially since Lincoln had prepared the will. Instead he had named

Reuben, which he had announced by sending Frost a copy of his will with a curt handwritten message saying that Frost should note that he was named in it as Holt's executor. Frost had subsequently tried to discuss the matter with Holt, but had never had a truly satisfactory conversation on the subject.

"Reuben, if you're willing to serve, I would be pleased," Holt had said. "I know you'll do whatever's necessary." That was it. No special instructions or requests at all.

Having never heard to the contrary, he assumed that his appointment was still in effect. This he confirmed by calling Melvin Lincoln, whom he arranged to meet later that morning.

After breakfast Frost took a taxi to West Fifty-seventh Street, where the offices of Lincoln & Gold were located. He had never been there before and was startled, as he entered the offices on the forty-fifth floor of a new office building, at the breathtaking view of Central Park from the reception-area windows—and the extraordinary garishness of the interior walls. He guessed that they were painted in "Nancy Reagan red," or something very close to it.

Melvin Lincoln came out to greet his visitor personally. Frost had come to know Lincoln slightly over the years, having encountered him at numerous benefits and cultural events and, more than once, at parties at Holt's duplex apartment. A tall man, he was always immensely cheerful in a gruff, street-smart way.

The two men did, however, have different strategies for confronting advancing age. Frost did it head-on and *au naturel* (helped in this regard by a full head of gray hair)—he used no unguents, sprays or preservatives. Melvin Lincoln, by contrast, seemed determined to use every man-made helper possible to stay the hand of nature—reddish hair dye, the sunlamp and (Frost was pretty sure) the ministrations of a plastic surgeon. The ironic result was to make Lincoln, at sixty-six, appear older than Frost at seventy-five.

Lincoln and Frost shook hands cordially in the lobby and Lincoln guided his guest to a corner suite, where the view encompassed not only Central Park but the Hudson River as well.

"Quite a panorama you have, Melvin," Frost remarked.

"Nice, eh?" Lincoln said. "Have a seat, Reuben."

Frost and Lincoln sat down on opposite sides of a coffee table at one end of the spacious office.

"What an awful thing about Clifton," Lincoln said. "Sometimes I think the crazies have taken over in this town."

"I know. It's true."

"Did the papers have the right story—murdered by a junkie?"

"Yes, that's it. A black named Jimmy Wilson."

"Terrible. Have you talked to Teresa?"

"Yes. She's in California. Sausalito. But I got in touch with her last night. She's flying back today."

"What a goddamn morass."

"How do you mean?" Frost asked.

"I'll explain it to you as we go along," Lincoln said. He picked up a file from the coffee table and pulled out a blue-backed copy of Holt's will. "Here's the will," he said, handing the copy to Frost.

Frost glanced at it quickly; it seemed to be the same as the document Holt had sent to him years earlier. The estate was left entirely to Teresa Holt, except for $5 million to Jack Navikoff and the royalties from several ballets to named individuals at NatBallet. Reuben was appointed the executor, and also the literary executor for granting rights to the ballets Holt had choreographed.

"Yes. This is the same one Clifton sent me long ago," Frost said, after reading it more carefully. "Nothing very unusual about it, except the bequest to Navikoff."

"And except that Clifton had barely spoken to Teresa in recent years."

"True. And how do you account for the Navikoff bequest?"

"There are two possible explanations, I guess. Neither one mutually exclusive," Lincoln said. "Clifton always felt that Jack Navikoff was responsible for his success in Hollywood. He often said that without Jack looking after his business interests his movies would have been failures. But they weren't, as you know. The reality is, Reuben, that Clifton left an estate that is probably worth fifteen million all told—not counting future royalties on his ballets."

"I had no idea it was anything like that. We all knew he was rich, but I at least didn't think he was *that* rich."

"Very few people did; certainly you couldn't tell it from the way he lived. Anyway, I think the bequest to Navikoff was to recognize his help."

"You said there were two reasons."

"Oh, Reuben, you know the other as well as I. Navikoff and Holt were lovers. Clifton never said as much, but they were just too close, too inseparable, not to have been. Don't you agree?"

"I guess I do."

"Now, having examined that will—the signed will—take a look at this," Lincoln said, reaching back into the file. He pulled out another document and handed it to Frost. It was in form a will, but it had not been signed or witnessed. Frost read it carefully and with increasing incredulity. In this version, Holt's entire estate was left to the Clifton Holt Foundation, a charitable foundation with clearly spelled-out purposes: scholarships for young dance students, an emergency revolving loan fund for dancers affiliated with the major companies and an endowment to encourage new choreography. There was no bequest to Navikoff—beyond the forgiveness of an unspecified amount of outstanding debt—and not a penny for the dead man's widow.

"When did you prepare this, Melvin?"

"Last week. I got a note from Clifton about two weeks ago setting forth the new terms he wanted. Then the middle of last week he came in to talk about it some more, and when I found out he was adamant, I went ahead and prepared this. He was supposed to come in tomorrow to sign it."

"But it's crazy, Melvin. He and Teresa *were* still married, weren't they?"

"As far as I know. In fact, Clifton even said so."

"So she could elect against the will and take half the estate?"

"Correct. And I told Clifton that. But if she did elect, look what she would have to do."

"You mean take away funds from the young and the needy?"

"Exactly. Holt wanted to make her look greedy and selfish."

"Shameful. She really wouldn't have had a choice, would she? At least, I assume she has no money of her own?"

"That's what I've always understood. I don't think she has anything other than the apartment where she lives now—Clifton bought that for her three or four years ago—and a monthly allowance of five thousand dollars."

"And what about Navikoff?"

"According to Holt, Navikoff owed him about a hundred thousand. That was to be forgiven. But the five-million bequest disappeared."

"Was any reason given for that change?" Frost asked.

"None. When I asked him specifically, he wouldn't answer; just ignored my question," Lincoln said. "But you've got to understand that Clifton was threatening to change his will all the time, even though he never did anything about it. He started doing it as soon as he made his first real money. It was all ridiculous—a young, healthy man talking about his will—but he seemed to get some weird satisfaction out of his dramatic threats."

"It is pretty strange, though I suppose it was still another way of torturing Teresa—and Jack," Frost said. "And we were supposed to run this damn foundation?" Frost went on, pointing to the operative clause in the draft.

"Yes," Lincoln replied. "Might have been kind of fun. We could have been the new Shuberts."

"Well, there's no chance of that, right? I mean, the old will still governs," Frost said.

"Absolutely. Thank God, for Teresa's sake. She's been through enough humiliations without the final one Holt was planning."

"Well, Melvin, I think I'd probably better go over to Holt's apartment and have a look around. What do you think?"

"I agree."

"But how can I get in, do you know?"

"I think Clifton's maid is there every day. A Miss Fleiss, I believe."

"Do you mind if I call and see?"

"Not at all. My secretary has the number, I'm sure." Lincoln got the number for Frost, who placed a call.

"Miss Fleiss is expecting me," Frost said, as he put down the telephone. "So I'll be on my way."

"One thing, Reuben, before you go," Lincoln said. "I assume your firm will want to take over representation of the estate, with you as executor and all. . . ."

"No, no, Melvin," Frost said. "Were I still active in the firm, I might have felt I had to say yes. But I'm not, and besides, you've always represented Holt's activities and I want you to continue. You know all about Clifton's affairs and are much more experienced than anyone at my firm in copyright and artistic-property matters. I'm going to need your help to straighten things out."

"That's very generous of you, Reuben. But I assure you I'll abide by your wishes either way," Lincoln said.

"My wishes are that you stay on," Frost replied. He genuinely did want Lincoln to continue representing the estate, though there was no way he could transfer to Lincoln & Gold the fee he would earn as executor (which he had already decided he would donate to NatBallet).

"Fine. Just let me know what I can do to help," Melvin Lincoln said as they parted.

Frost walked from West Fifty-seventh Street to Holt's apartment house on East Sixty-sixth Street, off Madison Avenue. Before leaving home, he had talked briefly to a young trusts-and-estates partner at Chase & Ward about what he should be doing at Holt's residence. Frost had been advised to look things over in general and to make sure that there were no obvious valuables left around that might be stolen. A formal inventory of the property could follow in due course.

After being announced by the doorman, Frost was admitted to Holt's apartment by Miss Fleiss, a retainer of uncertain age, but certainly not young. Frost introduced himself, explained his role, and said that he wanted to inspect the apartment.

"Very good, Mr. Frost," the woman said. "You'll find everything the way Mr. Holt left it yesterday. Except for a little tidying up I did."

Frost had visited the apartment often—Holt, despite his stinginess, did entertain, if not particularly lavishly—and he now went directly into the living room. The room was large, but decorated in a most conventional fashion. The miscellaneous pieces of furniture neither matched nor complemented each other, and there was too much chintz in the curtains and the slip coverings of the larger pieces. Holt had never hired a decorator to do the room; or if he had, he had been badly taken.

A grand piano in the corner and tables about the room were covered with photographs, all in silver frames, showing the apartment's owner posing at various times at various places with various friends. Frost thought that a skillful editor could take all the pictures from the room and with very little effort construct a pictorial biography of Holt; the only periods that seemed to be missing were childhood and early adolescence.

Nothing seemed amiss; nor were there objects crying out to be stored away for safekeeping. So Frost continued on into Holt's study. Here there were more photographs, this time autographed pictures of virtually every important figure in the dance world for the past generation. These were hung haphazardly on the walls, amid framed posters for Holt's movies.

A large antique desk was covered with stacks of

papers. Frost began to examine them. There was little of interest—bills, a letter to Bloomingdale's about an undelivered chair, a sheaf of invitations (with a notation of acceptance or regret on each in Holt's meticulous handwriting), a letter from a doctoral candidate at a Midwestern university asking a series of questions about Holt's choreography.

But there was a copy of Holt's note to Melvin Lincoln outlining the shocking proposed changes in his will. And there was one other surprise, a major one: a manila folder labeled "MATTISON." Inside was a copy of a letter to the critic Arthur Mattison, written in early March. It read:

Dear Arthur:

This is a very painful letter for me to write, but I feel it is important that I do so. Before I go further, rest assured that I have not discussed this letter with anyone, nor shown it to anyone. Nor will I do so, so long as you cease at once the practices I am about to describe.

I am afraid that the conclusion is inescapable that much of your recent dance criticism in the *Press* has been plagiarized from Edwin Denby's early writings. Three examples are enclosed, showing quotations from recent columns of yours in the *Press* and the related excerpts from the old Denby reviews in the *Herald-Tribune*. (Several years ago, an admirer gave me a scrapbook of Denby's pieces from the *Tribune*; hence my familiarity with even the most obscure of his writings.)

This is disgraceful conduct. It dishonors one of our greatest dance critics. And it insults the artists of today whom you purport to be evaluating, while in reality recycling old criticism irrelevant to these artists and their work.

As I say, if your conduct ceases, neither you nor

anyone else will hear from me again on this subject. But if you are caught once more, I shall expose your plagiarism to the world.

Frost could scarcely believe what he read. New York's most influential cultural arbiter a plagiarist? So it appeared if Holt's letter was to be believed—and the photocopies attached left little doubt.

The first was an excerpt from a Denby review in the September 17, 1945, *Herald-Tribune*:

> And Franklin's personal achievement this season as a classic dancer is striking, too. His line is large and open, his deportment is convincing, his execution is clean, his support is sure and easy. He has variety of attack and he ends with assurance. Though he has no startling brilliance or Slavic subtlety, he dances with a continuity of rhythm and a clarity of phrasing that are rare indeed. Franklin's dancing always makes perfect sense; like a true artist, he is completely at the service of the role he takes, and his straight delight in dancing, his forthright presence and openhearted nature give his version of the great classic roles a lyric grace that is fresh and sweet.
>
> Excellent he was as Danilova's partner in two traditional classic ballets, in *Coppelia* yesterday afternoon and in last Wednesday's *Nutcracker*. Danilova, who is again magnificent this fall, was particularly so in both of these pieces.

On the same page, facing the *Herald-Tribune* piece, was an excerpt from a recent Mattison column in the *Press*:

> Gerald Hazard's personal achievement this season as a classic dancer is striking. His line is large

and open, his deportment is convincing, his execution is clean, his support is sure and easy. He has variety of attack and he ends with assurance. Though he has no startling brilliance or Slavic subtlety, and is not yet a principal in the Company, he dances with a continuity of rhythm and a clarity of phrasing that are rare indeed. Hazard's dancing always makes perfect sense; like a true artist, he is completely at the service of the role he takes, and his straight delight in dancing, his forthright presence and openhearted nature give his version of the great classic roles a lyric grace that is fresh and sweet.

Excellent he was as Veronica Maywood's partner in *Paganini Variations* on Tuesday. Maywood, who is again magnificent this winter, was particularly so in this piece.

Good for Holt! Frost thought. Sometimes being a bastard paid off. Many, with their professional reputations at stake, would have been afraid to challenge Arthur Mattison, the *Press*'s heavy-hitting columnist. But Holt had not been so afraid (assuming, as there was no reason not to, that the original of the letter had been sent).

With some amusement Frost thought of what Cynthia's reaction would be. Nothing short of jubilation, he believed, in light of Mattison's recent attacks on the Brigham Foundation. Frost decided to take the folder with him.

Nothing else on or in Holt's desk came near to the interest of the Mattison file. While he was rummaging through the desk, he heard footsteps on the stairs and turned to face Jack Navikoff.

"Oh, hello, Jack," Frost said, trying to conceal his lack of enthusiasm for the producer.

"Hello, Reuben. What you doing?"

"Just seeing what's here. I'm Clifton's executor, you know."

"Yes, he told me that once."

"You are, by the way, a major beneficiary of his will."

"Really?" Navikoff said, dubiously.

"Yes. He left you five million dollars."

"You have checked this out?"

"Yes. I talked to Melvin Lincoln less than an hour ago."

"Well, I guess I should be grateful. I *am* grateful," Navikoff said, no longer doubting and scarcely able to conceal what seemed to be his relief.

"You're very lucky. I may as well tell you. Clifton had ordered a new will drawn up—in which he cut you out except for forgiveness of some outstanding debt."

"He did that?" Navikoff said, at least feigning incredulity.

"Yes. He was going to sign the new version tomorrow."

"My God—you mean if Clifton had died two days from now . . ." Navikoff's voice dropped and he did not finish the sentence.

"That's right. Assuming he signed the new will, you would have been out almost the full five million."

"Jesus Christ," Navikoff said. He was obviously stunned, and there was a pause before he spoke further. "Is there anything I can do to help?" he finally asked.

"I don't think so. I'm just taking a look around," Frost said. Then, after another pause, he asked Navikoff directly if he lived there.

"Off and on. I've got my own place over on Central Park West. And another place in Beverly Hills. But yes, since you ask, I did live here. Whenever Clifton and I were getting along."

"Which was most of the time?"

"Used to be, but not lately. We didn't see that much of each other in recent months."

"But you obviously have the run of the place."

"Yes, I suppose so," Navikoff said, after a noticeable pause.

"I want to take a look upstairs," Frost said.

"There's nothing up there," Navikoff said quickly. "Just Clifton's bedroom and the guest bedroom."

"That's all right. I won't be long."

Frost thought for a moment that Navikoff was going to block the way. But he moved aside and allowed the older man to pass up the stairs. Frost went first into the smaller bedroom, which had an adjoining bath. There were clothes in the closet and a bathrobe and shaving gear in the bathroom.

"These yours?" Frost asked.

"Yes."

Frost then went into the master bedroom, its king-size bed made up with black sheets. Opposite the bed were a television set and a videocassette recorder. And next to it a bookcase of cassettes. Frost went to the dresser in the room, examined the top, and pulled open the upper drawers, looking for jewelry or other valuables. He found only several pairs of gold cuff links, which he put back where he found them.

Navikoff watched Frost as he moved about the room, now focusing on the bookcase of tapes. Frost examined the titles for a moment, then removed one of them from the shelf. He looked the cover over and quickly put it back. Then he repeated the procedure with a second, after which he turned away in disgust. The two tapes he had picked out were homosexual pornography, as he suspected the whole collection was. He did not speak to Navikoff as he went down the stairs. In the study he retrieved the Mattison file and then sought out Miss Fleiss.

Frost instructed the maid to continue coming to the Holt residence on a daily basis, assuring her that she would be paid. He gave her his telephone number and went out, leaving an embarrassed Jack Navikoff behind.

Why was Navikoff so patently untruthful? Frost wondered to himself as he went down in the elevator. There was every indication he lived there on a full-time basis; yet he denied it. And had he not known about the change Holt proposed in his will? Melvin Lincoln had said Holt was always threatening those around him about his estate; and the copy of the letter outlining the changes was readily available to anyone who was the least bit nosy—as he would be willing to bet Navikoff was.

Oh, well, what does it matter? Frost thought as he went out into the street. Petty and irrelevant details best forgotten.

7

IT WAS ONE O'CLOCK WHEN FROST LEFT THE HOLT APART-
ment. Normally he would have gone to the Gotham
Club for lunch. But he had been unable to find an
envelope at Holt's big enough to hold the damning
Mattison file, so he was carrying it loose. Given its
explosive contents, he felt it would be imprudent to
take it to the Gotham, so he decided to take the file
home.

Once there, he fixed his own lunch—a clumsily made
tunafish sandwich and a bowl of Campbell's tomato
soup. As was his custom, he left his dirty dishes on the
kitchen table—after all, wasn't the maid meant to pick
them up and wash them? He then retired to the master bedroom, where he began reading the copy of the
afternoon *Press* he had bought at the corner newsstand.

The *Press*'s coverage of Holt's murder was extensive, including an extraordinarily effusive piece on his
career by Arthur Mattison. He found the article very
odd in light of Holt's devastating letter to Mattison.
Was Mattison perhaps so glad to have his accuser dead
that he wrote about him with delirious relief?

Frost would never have acknowledged that he took

a nap in the afternoon. But as often happened nowadays, he fell asleep soon after he sprawled out on the bed, dropping the *Press* to the floor as he did so. (Unlike a couple of his clubmates, he did not fall asleep while sitting around the Gotham after lunch; he napped only in the dignity—and privacy—of his own home.)

He was awakened more than an hour later by a ringing telephone. Before he could answer it, the ringing stopped, which led him to think that Cynthia had returned and picked up on one of the extensions downstairs.

Several minutes later, his wife came into the bedroom.

"I didn't realize you were here," she said.

"Yes, I must have fallen asleep. I got back from Holt's place—oh, my God—two hours ago."

"That was Teresa. She's back from California and wants to talk to you whenever you're available."

Reuben groaned. "Can she come over here, or do I have to traipse over there?"

"We didn't discuss it," Cynthia replied.

"She's a very lucky woman," Frost said.

"What do you mean?"

"I started the day having a long talk with Melvin Lincoln," Frost said. "Clifton was about to cut Teresa out of his will, but he was murdered before he could sign the new version that tried to do it."

"I can't say I'm surprised," Cynthia said. "How long has it been since they stopped living together? Seven years? At least that, I think."

"Holt wanted to set up a foundation with Melvin and me as trustees."

"To do what?"

"Dance education, basically. And funding for developing choreographers."

"And you and Melvin Lincoln were to run it? I love you dearly, Reuben, and Melvin is a sweet old soul, but do you think that would have been wise?"

"Cynthia, I do know a fair amount about the dance—thanks in large part to you. So I think we would have done just fine, thank you," Frost said. "Besides, we could have gotten expert help," he added defensively.

"I know, dear. I was only joking. You and Melvin would have been fabulous. But Teresa gets all the marbles instead?"

"Except for one or two of the ballets. And five million to Jack Navikoff."

"That's pretty hefty! How much did Clifton leave, for heaven's sake?"

"Melvin estimates about fifteen million. Plus whatever royalties are earned from now on on the ballets . . ."

"And the old movies?"

"Yes, I think so."

"Pretty good for an ex-chorus gypsy from Idaho," Cynthia said.

"That's where he was from? I'd forgotten."

"Yes. I remember him well. Lucia Chase at American Ballet Theatre had seen him dance somewhere and hired him on the spot. He showed up at ABT wearing cowboy boots—a totally unsophisticated hick."

"I remember all that."

"He never was the greatest dancer in the world. But then he got the choreographing bug and turned out to be really good at it. After that, Hollywood and finally dear National Ballet. Quite a record, when you think about it."

"Indeed. But right now I must go see the widow. Don't you envy me?"

"I can't say that I do."

"Oh, I almost forgot. A little bit of information that

will please you," Frost said. "Let me get it." He went to the library and brought back the copy of Holt's letter to Mattison.

Cynthia read the letter and its attachments avidly, smiling at first and then hooting.

"Why that big, fat fake! I've always known he was a phony—but it's never been proved in such a delicious way before," she declared. "Do you think I can use this to shut him up about the Foundation?"

"I'm not sure you can go that far," Reuben said. "But I thought you'd be interested."

"Interested! It's the best thing I've read in weeks. And I'm sure there's a way I can use it."

"Now, now, my dear. What you just read is confidential, something I learned as Holt's executor. I wouldn't have shown it to you at all if I thought you were going to make trouble."

"Oh, Reuben, don't worry. Have I ever told one of your lawyer's secrets out of school?"

"No, you haven't," Frost admitted. "And I suggest you treat this tidbit about Mattison the same way."

"Yes, dear. You don't want to have Teresa over here for dinner, do you?"

"I don't think so. Let me go see her, and then we can go out. I don't think I should be very long."

"Call me when you're ready," his wife replied.

Reuben called Teresa Holt and arranged to meet her at her apartment in the Dakota, at Central Park West and Seventy-second Street. She had lived at her fancy address, surrounded in her cooperative apartment by glamorous show-business neighbors, ever since she and Clifton Holt had broken up.

Frost considered himself a good but not intimate friend of Holt's widow. Holt had married her in the mid-1960s in Hollywood and had lived with her there until the couple returned to New York in the early 1970s. Teresa had been around during the time when Cynthia and Clifton had had endless conversations about NatBallet, often with Reuben and herself present. They came to like each other as they patiently indulged their spouses' almost uncontainable enthusiasm for the NatBallet project. And several years later, when it became known that the Holts had separated, Reuben had felt great sympathy for Teresa as the wronged woman.

Getting out of his taxi, Frost went to the entrance of the Dakota, identified himself, and then walked to the corner of the interior courtyard where Teresa's apartment was located. Ever since John Lennon's death, he had become uneasy walking through the Dakota entrance—it was where the unsuspecting Beatle had been gunned down—and this evening—only a day after Holt's violent and unexpected assassination—he felt even more apprehensive than usual.

Frost took the elevator to the fourth floor. Teresa was waiting for him and after an affectionate kiss, escorted him inside. As always, Frost was struck by the woman's irredeemable plainness. It was not only that she didn't use makeup; her face was just not interesting. And her slightly drawn-down mouth and the horn-rimmed glasses she wore made her look forbiddingly prissy.

What had Holt seen in his wife? She was barely twenty-one, a recent graduate of Bryn Mawr, when he had married her. She had gone to Hollywood right after college and taken a job as a production assistant at American Pictures, where she was assigned to the second of Holt's musical productions. Fresh from the smash success of his first movie, Holt was king of the roost (or cock of the walk, as one gossip columnist had mischievously expressed it at the time) at American.

To those who thought of Holt as a hyperactive Don Juan, his marriage to the plain Teresa Graves came as a great surprise; so did it to those who had known Holt in the gay underground in Hollywood.

For a decade after their marriage in 1966, Clifton and Teresa at least acted the part of husband and wife—despite Holt's insatiable desire for sex with those who attracted him, male or female. But, to the outside world at least, Teresa appeared oblivious to her husband's exploits, and their friends, taking their cue from her, did likewise.

"Reuben, dear friend, come in," Teresa said, propelling Frost by the arm toward the large, high-ceilinged living room of the apartment. "I got all the papers at Kennedy on the way in. Is there anything to add?"

"I don't think so. The whole thing is a depressing, outrageous New York saga—vital, successful citizen murdered by desperate, no-account junkie."

"I know, Reuben, that's what you said last night. And it's what the newspapers and the TV say today. It's just that I find it ironic."

"Ironic, Teresa?"

"Yes, ironic. You read the *Press,* Reuben. You know that every night there is a stabbing, or a garroting, or a shooting, or some terrible sort of violence, as if the underside of the City times its violence for the convenience of that creepy little Limey who owns the *Press.* And the victim is always innocent—hardworking teen-age student, diligent laborer and father of ten, nun about to take her final vows. Clifton really didn't fit that category of innocence, Reuben, so I find it ironic that he is the *Press*'s unsullied martyr for the day."

"Teresa, Clifton was a difficult man and was not very nice to a lot of people. But he had done nothing to the young punk who murdered him."

"True enough. I guess I was thinking in more poetic terms."

"Did you hate him, Teresa?" Frost asked.

"Hate? Yes, I suppose I did, in some ways at least. Being constantly assaulted with Clifton's sexual infidelities was pretty hard to take. I did hate him for that. Hated him profoundly. But while I despised the nasty little sex rat, I always remained in love with the genius, with the brilliant choreographer. Can you understand that?"

"I think so," Frost replied. "I'm not so sure a lot of others didn't feel the same way—myself included."

"You are his executor, aren't you?"

"Yes, I am. I am because he asked me and I had no good reason to refuse."

"So you've seen his will, then?"

"Yes. He sent me a copy years ago, and I confirmed with Melvin Lincoln this morning that the version I saw was still in effect. Everything is left to you, except some of the ballets and five million that he left outright to Jack Navikoff."

"Are you sure about that, Reuben?" There was the same question, for the second time that day.

"I'm certain of it."

"I get everything except what the other woman gets?" Teresa said. "Excuse me, that was bitchy."

"Yes. That's right," Frost answered. He saw no reason to tell the woman how close Holt had come to changing his will.

"Lord above," the woman said, nervously lighting a cigarette. "I need a drink."

"Let me get it," Frost said.

"Scotch and soda."

Frost went to a side table of liquor bottles just inside the adjoining dining room.

"There's ice in the bucket. I put it there before you came."

Frost made two drinks—a gin and tonic for himself—and returned to the living room, where Teresa appeared to be deep in thought.

"Do you have any idea how much the estate is worth?" she asked.

"Melvin Lincoln thinks about fifteen million."

"So that's ten for me and five for Jack."

"Correct," Frost said. Then, after a pause, he asked the widow whether Jack and Clifton had been lovers.

"Oh, yes. Good heavens, yes. I'll tell you about it sometime."

"I'm not sure I want to hear."

"You're right. But good old Jack can use the money," Teresa said.

"What do you mean?"

"Well, some of my friends in California say he was all but wiped out with that last movie he produced. That awful bomb, *Sister Ellen*."

"I didn't see it."

"Very few people did. Supposed to be simply terrible. But anyway, he violated Hollywood's cardinal rule by investing his own money, and losing the nice little fortune he had built up from Clifton's movies. I just assumed he was living off Clifton."

"That's very interesting," Frost replied, thinking of how Teresa's version of things failed to square with the impression Navikoff had tried to give Frost earlier in the day.

"Do you want to have supper, Reuben?" his hostess asked.

"I'd love to, but I'm afraid Cynthia and I are already committed," Frost said, telling a white lie. "Actually, I have to go soon, but before I do we should discuss a funeral."

"Are you asking me? If so, the answer is no. Clifton had no religion other than the dance, or maybe sex. It would be a mockery to have a religious funeral."

"But surely there should be a memorial service?"

"No, I don't think so. Nobody's going to want to get up and talk about Clifton's personal life. And you know how he hated people talking about his work. 'Let it speak for itself,' he always said. If you do anything, Reuben, I would suggest a performance at NatBallet dedicated to him."

"That's an excellent idea, and I think sooner rather than later." Frost pulled out his pocket engagement calendar. "How about next Tuesday, a week from today? If Arne Petersen wants to do anything special, that should be time enough. You will come, won't you?"

"I don't know. What's the difference? Everybody knows about us. But I suppose, in view of my good luck, that I should continue the charade for one more week."

"Okay. Is Tuesday all right with you?"

"Fine. I'll come, Reuben. Having played the dutiful wife for so many years, I may as well play the dutiful widow."

FROSTS' NIGHT OUT

8

FROST CALLED HIS WIFE FROM A TELEPHONE BOOTH ON Central Park West and arranged a rendezvous for dinner. He then strolled leisurely to the agreed spot—Patricia's Café, on Columbus Avenue. Patricia—no one knew her last name—was the presiding eminence at a relatively new, gentrified storefront that specialized in *nouvelle cuisine*, California style. Like every other spot of its type on the Upper West Side, it was too small to accommodate the yuppie hordes that had taken it up; its tables along narrow bare-brick walls, closely spaced though they were, were insufficient in number, and the bar at best could accommodate six people comfortably.

Patricia, in common with the other chic new restaurateurs about New York, did not take reservations. Normally this alone would have been enough to put Frost off.

"I suppose all restaurants will end up like the Eastern shuttle, with no reservations," he had once told his wife. "But when I go out to dinner, I want to eat. I am not interested in picking up a chic young Citibank vice president at the bar, or sipping Perrier with the upwardly mobile regulars."

"Meat and potatoes, you mean, Reuben," Cynthia had said.

"In effect, yes," he had answered. "If I want to socialize, I'll do it at one of those countless cocktail parties we, or at least you, get invited to. Drinking is fine in its place. But so is eating, and I still maintain that's what a restaurant's for."

Patricia, however, had taken a liking to the Frosts. Was it their eminence? Probably not; Reuben did not have the feeling that the woman had the faintest idea who the Frosts were. He was terribly afraid that their status at the restaurant, which usually led to prompt seating regardless of any line waiting for tables, was much more prosaic: he suspected that Patricia liked to have the occasional older couple in her dining room so that her restaurant would not be tagged as exclusively a yuppie playpen.

This night the magic worked again, and the tanned but nearly anorectic Patricia showed him to a table as soon as he arrived. Cynthia joined him almost immediately and they ordered drinks, a Kir Royale for her and another gin and tonic for him.

Both were hungry, so they ordered at once. The place's food was good, despite a tendency to put goat cheese on everything—what is it with these Californians? —from salads to steaks to (almost) desserts. Reuben ordered lamb chops with a creamed mint sauce—"On the side, please," he demanded—and Cynthia asked for the pasta of the day, ziti with smoked salmon and cream.

"How did it go?" she asked, their ordering completed.

"All right. Not much grief there, not many tears. And the fact that she was going to inherit ten million dollars seemed to cheer Teresa up immensely."

"I can understand that."

"We talked about a funeral, and she said it would not be appropriate to have one. Clifton had no religion, according to her."

"There I think she's right. As far as religion went, I don't think poor Clifton could ever quite bring himself to acknowledge the existence of a higher being."

"Waiter, I forgot, could I see the wine list?" Frost interrupted, flagging one of the young men in the standard Patricia's uniform—pink shirt, bow tie and butcher's apron—who passed by the table. Cynthia fell silent as her husband looked at the list.

"Thank God, they're off the California kick," he said, scanning the handwritten (in italic penmanship) list. "My complaints to Patricia bore some fruit."

"I know, dear: one vat for red, another for white," Cynthia said, quoting her husband's frequently uttered opinion of the California vineyards.

"Well, dammit, it's true. Here, waiter, let's have the Haut-Bailly 1981. I assume red is okay with your pasta?"

"It doesn't matter, dear—whatever you want."

"Good. That's what we'll have. Number fourteen. Haut-Bailly 1981."

The waiter went away and returned almost instantly to report that number fourteen (he did not pronounce the name) was out.

"Not surprised," Frost muttered. "Too good a price to be true."

"How about the Médoc, sir?" pink-shirt said, pronouncing the word "*mee*-dock." "It's very nice."

"Let's see, that's number sixteen. Coufran '81. *Haut*-Médoc, actually. Fine."

"Thank you, sir," the waiter said as he ran off again.

"Too young, indifferent year, high-priced. But still

better than Blue Ridge, or Stillwater, or whatever that dreadful stuff was we had the other night."

"I'm sure it will be fine, dear," Cynthia said, temporizing. (She realized that, as lawyers go, her husband was relatively well behaved in restaurants. She had spent years watching Reuben's partner Harry Brinsley insult waiters, flirt with waitresses, and generally display an impatience that must have made him dyspeptic. She was grateful that Reuben confined himself to low rumbles of discontent, projected neither to the staff nor to the dining room as a whole. And while he knew a good deal about wine, he did not flaunt his knowledge in the all-too-typical wine-bore fashion.)

"So you think there shouldn't be a funeral?" Reuben said.

"Yes."

"What about a memorial service? Or a memorial performance?"

"That's what should be done. A performance dedicated to Clifton's memory. It's the most he would have wanted," Cynthia answered.

"And shouldn't it be right away?"

"Probably."

"You mean a regular performance, don't you? Not some special event?"

"No, just a regular performance. Perhaps with some special work performed."

"I suggested next Tuesday to Teresa."

"Why not?" Cynthia said.

"Tuesday is also the weakest subscription night, so there will be plenty of available seats for the dance worthies who want to attend."

"Isn't that the night Luis Bautista and Francisca are going to the ballet with us?"

"Yes, I believe it is. But that doesn't matter, does it?"

"No, certainly not. But it won't be the happiest occasion in the world, that's all," Cynthia said.

Pink-shirt interrupted with their order, all served correctly except that the creamed mint sauce enveloped Reuben's lamb chops. He did not, however, object. Still another pink-shirt arrived simultaneously with the Coufran, which he opened lovingly, treating the youthful bottle with a respect more properly reserved for the aged.

"This should be *very* good, sir," he said. In the best Californian, pro-feminist tradition, he poured out a sampling for both Reuben and Cynthia to taste.

"Mmn," Frost grumped, as he tried the wine. "Fine."

"And you, ma'am?" the waiter asked.

"Me? Oh, yes. Fine," Cynthia said.

"I knew you'd like it. Nothing like the good old French wines, is there, sir?"

"Mmn," Frost grumped again, but still restraining himself. "Thank you very much." He wondered what the pink-shirt with the wine, now pouring full glasses, would have done if one—but not both—of them had pronounced the Coufran unsatisfactory. He supposed there was some California protocol governing this.

"How shall we arrange it?" Frost said, as the waiter left and he and his wife began eating. "Should I talk to Arne or should you?"

"Why don't I do it? I'll be taking class in the morning, and I can talk to him then. What about the Board? I assume this will be all right with them?" Cynthia asked.

"I think so. Except for those like Andrea Turnbull, who, if asked, would probably preside over a voodoo rite for Clifton."

"That awful woman."

"Awful rich woman, unfortunately."

"She really loathed Clifton, didn't she?"

"Clearly. But Clifton was correct on that one. By what right did this ugly, self-centered, spoiled rich monster from Syracuse think she could dictate how NatBallet should be run? You know what she's like, Cynthia. Artistic views on everything, and most of them appalling. NatBallet would have been inferior to the local ballet company in Podunk if she—and not you and Clifton—had been around from the beginning."

"Yes," Cynthia sighed, "it's true. Andrea's taste is in her left toe—and though I've never seen her barefoot, probably an unattractive left toe at that."

"Exactly. Being the widow of an upstate car dealer does not automatically make you Diaghilev. Andrea's never learned that, and I fear for what's going to happen now."

"Don't you think your Board will promote Arne? See what he can do?" Cynthia asked.

"I hope so. But as he said the other night, the likes of Andrea or Ken Franklin—*Ambassador* Franklin, for heaven's sake—will probably discover some rustic genius who wouldn't know a *pas de deux* from a do-si-do."

"I don't think so, Reuben," she said. "There are still people like Bartlett Empson around, who are not going to allow anything crazy to happen. And there's you."

"Me? Perhaps. Sure, I'm Chairman of the Board. But there are a lot of directors that think I'm an old fuddy-duddy and that Andrea, with her bottomless wallet, and others like her, are the wave of the future."

"Nonsense. I think the Board is grateful that you

spend the time you do on Company affairs. And they're not going to go against you."

"I'm not so sure."

"And if they do, they'll have someone else to contend with as well."

"Meaning?"

"Meaning me. If you think I'm going to let a gang of used-car heiresses and real estate speculators destroy National Ballet, you're wrong. I've worked too hard, Clifton worked too hard, everybody has worked too hard—the dancers, Jeb Crosby, everyone—to let that happen." Uncharacteristically, Cynthia took a long gulp of wine as she finished speaking.

"I hope you're right."

"Look, this isn't like naming the theatre for Everett Zacklin. That was just silly, and as you've often said, temporary. What we're talking about is the heart and soul of a great and important ballet company. The Huns and the Visigoths are simply not going to destroy that." Cynthia's voice rose as she spoke, and a slight red splotch—visible proof of great agitation—appeared on her forehead.

"No, dear, I agree," Frost said, quietly. "It's not going to happen. And your poor, sweet, senile husband will do everything he can to prevent it." He reached across the table as he spoke and clasped Cynthia's arm. Just as he did so, their waiter reappeared.

"How's everything?" he jauntily asked.

"Fine, thank you," Reuben replied.

"Finished?"

"Yes."

"Let me clear some of this away," pink-shirt replied. He painstakingly removed the couple's plates and wine glasses and then, even more painstakingly, scraped crumbs from the table.

"You know, that creamed mint sauce wasn't bad," Frost said, after the cleanup chores were over and the waiter had disappeared again. "These new restaurants are so peculiar; half the things they tout on the menu sound perfectly awful. But once they come, they're usually okay."

"I know. There should be a Culinary Institute course in menu writing," Cynthia replied. "It's a wonder people order anything in these places, based on the way they're described."

Pink-shirt returned and asked if they wanted anything else. Frost said no and asked for the check. To his surprise, the waiter produced it from the pocket of his butcher's apron and put it down. He was about to ask how pink-shirt had known in advance that they didn't want dessert or coffee—let alone brandy or the drink Reuben had noticed on the menu, an old-fashioned stinger. Then he realized that the same pink-shirt had waited on them on occasion before and knew that they did not take either dessert or coffee; he also realized, glancing toward the door, that there was an even more formidable line than usual for tables.

Frost examined the check and began pulling bills from his pocket to pay it.

"Ninety-six dollars," he said, as he did so. "Do you remember, dear, that other Patricia's we used to go to? Back when we were first married?"

"Patricia's? Oh, yes, Patricia Murphy's," she replied.

"That's it. Patricia Murphy's Candlelight Restaurants."

"Yes, yes, yes. Patricia Murphy's Candlelight Restaurants. We used to go to the one on East Sixtieth Street. Hot popovers and broiled chicken."

"And checks of twelve dollars for two. Three ninety-nine apiece for dinner and two drinks."

"No wine."

"Wine? Who knew about wine in those days?"

"Well, anyway, this dinner was very nice. And Patricia Murphy's didn't have pink walls and attire for adorable waiters to match."

"I'm not complaining, my dear," Reuben said. "Just living in the past as we old people do."

The couple left with a flurry of thanks from the waiter, the wine waiter and Patricia herself. And an admonition from the hatcheck attendant to "have a nice evening."

PREPARATIONS

CYNTHIA FROST, LIKE EVERY BALLERINA PAST OR PRESent, had mixed feelings about taking class, about stretching, pushing and exhausting her body in the daily routine universally thought necessary to maintain the rigorous and arcane skills necessary to be a dancer. Class had been a part of her life as a youngster in Kansas City, Missouri, and ever since. She was, of course, no longer a performer; she had last appeared on stage with the American Ballet Theatre in the 1950s. Then why did she continue the punishment, the exposure to sore and twisted muscles and hairline fractures in the bones of her feet? Was she compulsively in thrall to a masochistic habit she could not break? She didn't think so, and was sure she could quit at will anytime.

The justification she gave, when asked, was that it was the best way to keep up with the Company, to judge the quality of instruction and the progress of the dancers. But that was not the only reason; secretly she knew that she intrepidly continued class to maintain a link—outside of performing, the most important link—with the profession she had known, loved and practiced all her life. And to prove to herself that she was not getting old. (Class also had the added virtue of preserving her lithe, spare figure, but that was a dividend, since she knew preservation could be attained through a short regimen of calisthenics in the morning or periodic visits to a health club.)

She had often thought recently about quitting, but had never been able to bring herself to do it. She thought of how she teased her husband about going to the office, even when it was clear that as a retired partner of Chase & Ward, he often had little or nothing to do once he got there. But she was sure going to the office prevented an emptiness in his retirement that he might otherwise have felt, even given his enormous self-sufficiency. Despite her teasing, she understood why Reuben continued his lifelong routine; at bottom the reasons were little different from her own.

She had recently cut down, going to the Zacklin only for an hour from Tuesday through Friday, leaving the weekends and Mondays (the one day when the Company's classes were suspended during the season) free of the physical stresses and strains. And when she and her husband were traveling or in the country, or when the Company was on vacation, she did not try to find substitute classes. Compulsion might be compulsion, but there was a limit to it.

This particular morning, Arne Petersen led the women's class. There were the usual moans and groans as the dancers started on the first round of their daily punishment. (More classes, rehearsals and the evening's performance would, in some varying combination for each of the regular dancers, make up the next rounds.)

An ornithologist viewing the scene would have concluded that the male species was a drab one, compared, at least, with the plumage in which the females were arrayed. The only male in the room, other than Kirk Drinan, the rehearsal pianist for the day, Petersen wore gray warm-up pants, a gray sweat shirt and gray leggings. His charges, by contrast, wore every hue and color of pants, leotards, sweat shirts, T-shirts, stockings, and other garments and swatches of cloth that defied classification. There was no elegance here—no cygnets in immaculate tutus, no beautiful silks or elaborate brocades. Just forty highly individualistic and often eccentrically chosen outfits. And none more unique than Veronica Maywood's: a shocking purple leotard with an orange overskirt, red leg warmers and what appeared to be a herringbone-tweed vest from a man's suit.

Petersen took the class through a relatively easy routine of *pliés, tendus* and *battements* at the barre, all accompanied by Drinan's barrelhouse renditions of *Blue Skies* and *Oh, What a Beautiful Morning,* the pianist's wry tribute to the gray and dark skies outside that Wednesday morning.

Cynthia held her own through these preliminaries, but did retreat as the class moved from the barre to the center of the room and its members were commanded by the Acting Artistic Director through twirling *fouettés* and *ronds de jambe en l'air.* As far as Cynthia was concerned, *ronds de jambe à terre* were fine, but she really was too old to go airborne in any serious way. She nevertheless did her best to keep up, and was as exhausted as the youngsters when the fifty-minute hour came to an end.

After the traditional *révérences* that ended the class, Cynthia went up to Arne and asked if she could see him for a few minutes.

"Certainly, my dear. Here? Or in the office?" he asked.

"In your office," Cynthia said. "Do I have time to change my clothes or not?"

"No rush. I was planning to be there at least until noon."

Petersen was seated at his desk in Clifton Holt's old office when Cynthia joined him twenty minutes later. He seemed to be working his way through a stack of papers, like any busy executive, although he was still dressed in his gray rehearsal clothes.

"How is it going, Arne?" Cynthia asked. "All settled in?"

Petersen sighed. "Settled in, I guess, but doing two jobs as near as I can tell. I always had to do the dirty work that Clifton loathed. So I've still got that, plus all his other duties. *Mr. Petersen, could you please speak to John Miller about getting makeup on his partner's costume every time he lifts her? He has no conception of the damage he does to our costumes!* That from Madame Roubinsky, harridan of the costume department. I'm used to that. That's always been part of my job. But now it's *Arne, when can I learn the lead in 'Mostly Mozart'?* from ambitious little ones like Dorothy Maxwell. Or calls from Mrs. Turnbull saying that she has heard that I am considering using Dorothy in *Mozart* and letting me know in no uncertain terms that she thinks that's a mistake. In one week I really have learned why Clifton hated that woman so much."

"I'm afraid it goes with the territory, Arne. Besides, I'm sure you'll be able to handle her better than Clifton ever did."

"It's like commando training, I can tell you."

"Well, *I've* let you alone, at least," Cynthia said.

"Oh, yes, I've heard nothing from Cynthia Frost, the manipulative dowager who runs NatBallet from behind the scenes."

"It's too soon for that, Arne. The manipulative dowager is very democratic. She only strikes after dreadful mistakes have been made."

"Well, I'm glad to hear that, Cynthia," Petersen said, laughing. "I'm not sure I could really face all this if I didn't know you were on my side. Or are you here to tell me that you've defected already?"

"No, no. I wanted to talk about a memorial for Clifton. Reuben and I have been discussing it—and Reuben has also talked to Teresa Holt—and we thought what would be most appropriate would be a Company performance dedicated to his memory. All things considered, we thought a regular performance, with perhaps a very short speech or two, and maybe a work with special meaning for Clifton, would be the best."

"That's a good thought," Petersen said. "Clifton was a great believer in the show-must-go-on tradition, and he would have liked the idea of nothing special being done for him. When do you think we should do it?"

"We thought it should be soon—and Reuben suggested Tuesday."

Petersen picked up the master schedule for the Company on his desk and studied it.

"That might work out all right," he said. "There are three short ballets—two Holts, one Sara Schroff—scheduled for that night. Maybe we could change one of them to fit the occasion."

"Like the Sara Schroff?" Cynthia asked.

"Cynthia, please. Sara's *Hoagy's Dust* is one of our most popular works."

"Arne, dear, as I have said before, if I want to see

people dance to *Stardust* I can go to Roseland," Cynthia replied with asperity.

"I don't know what I'm going to do with you. Can I talk seriously to you about Sara sometime?"

"Of course. She's very clever, Arne, and she's brought a bit of fresh air to us, the same way she has to other companies. But *Hoagy's Dust* is dreadful, concede me that."

"No comment. But I agree it can go from the memorial program. But what would you do instead?"

"How about that little *Requiem* Clifton did a few years back? What was it? Piano music by Lennie Tristano."

"Oh, yes. A requiem for Charlie Parker, as I recall. With Veronica Maywood dancing her heart out in grief for the dead saxophonist."

"That's it," Cynthia said. "It really was quite beautiful and haunting. Do you think Veronica would do it?"

"Oh, God, Cynthia, I don't know. She's been so difficult. First the rehearsal where she blew up at Clifton. Then the most histrionic grief I have ever seen. Tears upon tears. It's a wonder the place hasn't washed away, it's been so wet backstage. All as if she were compensating for her guilt."

"Guilt?" Cynthia asked, startled.

"For carrying on so at the *Chávez Concerto* rehearsal. It turned out to be Clifton's last meeting with the Company, after all."

"I suppose. Though I've never seen Veronica show any remorse for any other tantrum she's ever had."

"Well, she's been acting quite mad, even for her," Petersen said. "But would she do *Requiem*? I'm sure she would."

"Should I ask her or will you?"

"Let me do it. If she refuses, then I can bring you in as reserve ammunition."

"What about speeches?"

"Short."

"I know, but how many?" Cynthïa asked.

"I would vote for just one."

"You?"

"No. I didn't know Clifton that long. You."

"Me? Shouldn't it be Reuben? He's Chairman of the Board, after all."

"I know, dear, but this is an artistic occasion—no offense to Reuben. He's as sensitive as you could ask. But you were Clifton's colleague from the beginning of this Company."

"Well, I'll accept your judgment," Cynthia said. Would Reuben object? Of course not, she thought. Would he be disappointed? Perhaps, though he would never admit it. But Arne was right; she really should give the speech. So on with the arrangements. "You'll ask Veronica, then? And if it's okay, you'll have Moira Burgess send out a press release right away. And—oh, my God, what about the Board? Don't worry about it. Reuben and I will call them between us. Except it takes so many phone calls to do it diplomatically."

"I don't understand," Petersen said.

"Well, take your self-important pal Ms. Turnbull. Her hatred of Clifton was almost pathological, yet she would consider it the highest form of insult if she weren't consulted about the memorial performance. So you have to call and say, 'Andrea, dear, we want to dedicate a NatBallet performance to Clifton Holt and were thinking about next Tuesday. Would that be convenient for you?' Andrea being Andrea, it naturally isn't. 'Then what would be convenient, dear?

Wednesday, Thursday or Friday? Splendid. Let me talk to the others and get back to you.' "

By this time Cynthia was standing in front of Petersen's desk and punctuating her monologue with mimicking gestures. Petersen was laughing hard.

"So then, dear Arne, you call the others, several of whom object to Tuesday as well. That's when you begin Round Two."

"What happens then?"

"Hello, Andrea? Dear, I don't know what to tell you. I've talked to *everyone* and I'm terribly afraid Tuesday comes up as the most convenient day. Is there any way you could change your plans? No? Well, I'm very sorry, but I'm afraid we have to go with Tuesday; it's the best night for weeks to come, and we must have the ceremony soon. We've got to change it, you say? Well, I don't see how we can; it's everyone's best night but yours. . . . I understand, and you certainly should be there. . . . But no, I'm afraid we can't change now, otherwise we'll never get this done. . . . No, Andrea, TOO BAD, ANDREA, WE'RE GOING AHEAD WITH TUESDAY!" Cynthia poked Petersen in the ribs as she raised her voice. They both were laughing as they kissed on the cheek and parted.

A NEW TWIST

REUBEN FROST WAS GLAD FOR THE PEACE AND QUIET
that prevailed for the next several days. The shock of
Clifton Holt's murder had begun to dissipate. Frost
had abided by Teresa Holt's instinctive feeling that a
funeral would have been a mistake. Holt's body was
cremated without ceremony or incident, and the memorial performance by NatBallet that Cynthia and
Arne Petersen were arranging was the only obsequy
remaining to be observed.

Holt's estate had to be settled, but Melvin Lincoln
and his firm seemed to have the matter well in hand; if
lucky, Frost would have nothing more to do than sign
the necessary papers prepared by Lincoln & Gold. He
had neither seen nor talked to Teresa since the day
after the murder. Except for insistent calls from Andrea Turnbull, he had really had little to do with
NatBallet business, other than long conversations with
his wife about the Company's future.

Turnbull had finally been successful in trapping him,
and he had reluctantly agreed to see her at her apartment this Monday afternoon, a week after Holt's death.
Aside from this meeting, which he dreaded, he looked

forward, as he drank the morning orange juice Cynthia had squeezed for him, to a quiet day. He would spend the morning in his office at Chase & Ward with, to his satisfaction, some actual legal work to do. An old-time client, Earle Ambler, had called the week before with a thousand questions about "leveraged buy-outs," "poison pills" and the like, and requested a meeting to discuss them. As always, Ambler had insisted that the meeting be in Portland, Oregon, where Frost's crusty old client presided over his prosperous empire of radio and television stations.

Frost knew it was futile to argue for a meeting in New York; Ambler hated the City, and Frost was sure that he derived secret pleasure from bringing the mountain (Chase & Ward, or more particularly, Frost) to Mahomet (Ambler Broadcasting Company, or more particularly, Earle Ambler). Frost knew that Ambler was at least a year or so younger than he was, but that carried no weight either. But Ambler, however unreasonable and complaining in other respects, always paid his bills, and his insistence on having Frost do his legal work, even though Frost was retired as a partner of Chase & Ward, gave him greater standing, as far as Frost was concerned, to make demands that might not have been agreed to so readily by the younger, active partners in the firm.

The first mutually convenient date the two men could arrange was the upcoming Wednesday, April 13. Frost would fly to Portland that morning, meet with Ambler the same day, and return to New York on Thursday. But this morning he felt that he had to do a bit of homework at the office. He recalled the observation an astute senior partner in one of the Big Eight accounting firms had made to him years before: "When we send a young man out to a client, we want him to be knowledgeable—and if we can't succeed in doing that, at least we want him to give the *appearance* of being knowledgeable." Frost realized that the same was at least partially true for lawyers and, in the present circumstances, could even be applied to himself.

Frost knew very little about the mysterious new world of "M&A"—mergers and acquisitions—that had become such an important part of Chase & Ward's practice, just as it had in other major New York firms. He knew in general terms about tender offers, friendly and unfriendly, for the shares of public companies; colossal mergers of industrial giants under the benign and passive eye of the Reagan Justice Department; leveraged buy-outs, or "LBOs" as they were known for short; going private; and all the other M&A techniques.

Discussions among the partners at the Chase & Ward lunch table and in informal conversations around the office had given Frost at least a surface degree of familiarity with these new legal tricks. But M&A was a game for young and ambitious investment bankers and lawyers willing to work impossible hours with intense and high-pressure dedication. As an older lawyer nearing the end of his career, Frost would need to ask a few discreet questions of the firm's go-getting younger partners in order to give Ambler the benefit of his knowledge—or the appearance of his knowledge.

Frost had toyed with the idea of taking one of these partners with him to Portland. But that had seemed a waste of money—Ambler probably had nothing concrete in mind at all and just wanted to talk things over. (Ambler was always alert to every trend, and Frost suspected that the old man probably felt he was not part of the hectic corporate landscape if he did not at least think about taking over someone else—or, possibly but not likely, having Ambler Broadcasting bought out by someone else.)

As usual, Frost took the subway to One Metropolitan Plaza, then the elevator to Chase & Ward's offices on the fifty-first floor. He greeted Dorothea Cowden, the firm's receptionist, and made his way to his modest office overlooking New York harbor. (In earlier times, as Chase & Ward's Executive Partner, Frost had had a corner office with a sweeping and breathtaking view of downtown New York; now he had only a slice of that view, albeit an attractive one.) Having not been in the office for several days, he turned to the pile of mail his secretary, Miss O'Hara, had placed in the center of his desk. He soon discovered to his disappointment that it consisted largely of fund-raising appeals. Where do these obscure charities get the money to make such elaborate mailings? he ruminated as he turned irritably from the pile.

Frost was about to begin his homework for Earle Ambler when the intercom rang. Luis Bautista, his detective friend, was on the phone.

"Reuben, can I come over?" the detective asked, without any preliminaries.

"Certainly, Luis," Frost answered. "What's up?"

"I'll tell you when I get there. Can I come right now?"

"Yes, yes. Come as soon as you like. But what's going on?"

"I'll be there in ten minutes," Bautista said, ignoring Frost's question a second time. "All I can say is, we're back in business."

"We're what?" Frost asked incredulously. But Bautista had already hung up.

Frost was stunned. What did the detective mean— "back in business"? It had to be murder. Holt's? But his murderer had already been caught, and caught red-handed. Frost simply could not imagine what Bautista had been talking about and resigned himself to waiting, however impatiently, for the detective's arrival.

Bautista found Frost pacing the floor in his office. They had barely shaken hands when the lawyer began bombarding his visitor with questions.

"Sit down, Reuben," Bautista interrupted. "I'll tell you all about it."

"All right, let's hear it."

"I wanted to tell you before you read about it in the afternoon *Press*. The long and the short of it is that Jimmy Wilson has been murdered."

"Murdered? How? Where?"

"He was stabbed by another prisoner at the Men's Detention House on Rikers Island last night. He'd been acting crazy ever since he was arrested—not surprising, since he's probably been cold turkey since he went into the Detention House, which makes any junkie crazy."

"Cold turkey—that means no dope?"

"Yes. Unless he'd bribed his way into a supply, and I doubt he'd been there long enough to do that. Anyway, he'd caused a lot of trouble, though the other prisoners in his area seemed to be afraid of him—he was in on a body, after all—and kept their distance. But last night he got into a fight with a white prisoner and the white guy stabbed him with a sharpened table knife."

"Incredible," Frost said. "Poetic justice, I guess. Wilson stabs Holt, then gets stabbed himself."

"Yes, I suppose it is," Bautista replied.

"But how does this make more business for us,

Luis?" Frost asked, after a pause. "I would have thought young Mr. Wilson's death closed the case once and for all."

"There's more to the story, Reuben."

"Go on."

"Before he was killed, Wilson was bragging to anyone who would listen that he had killed Clifton Holt for money."

"Oh, my God!" Frost said quietly, slumping in his desk chair.

"And it seems to check out. After Wilson was arrested, the policemen who went to his apartment on Tenth Avenue found twelve thousand dollars in new hundred-dollar bills. They thought at the time it was probably linked to his drug operation—which was fairly extensive, judging by the address book and the records they found. Wilson was an addict himself, but he was a sharp little dealer as well, with some fancy connections."

"Couldn't he have been just bragging about being hired to murder Clifton?"

"Sure. But the sum he mentioned—twenty-four thousand dollars, twelve thousand down and twelve thousand after the murder—agrees with the twelve thousand the police found."

"Who did he say paid him?"

"He didn't."

"Man or woman?"

"He didn't say that either."

"Damn," Frost said, hitting his desk with his fist. "Will all this be in the papers?"

"Wilson's murder will be—it's probably on the radio already. But the other part, the murder-for-hire angle, I think we can keep the lid on, at least for a while."

"Will you be handling the case?"

"Yes, thanks to you. Because of your call to me the night of Holt's murder, I claimed it and I got it."

"Thank God for that."

"I don't know, Reuben. Cases involving famous people can be tricky. But they're more interesting than guys shooting their brothers-in-law. And besides, it means we can work together again."

"Mmn," Frost said. "So what do we do?"

"You remember the drill, Reuben. We need a list of suspects to start working on."

"That's very hard in Clifton's case. He was a genius, but he certainly wasn't well liked. For example, Luis, look at this." Frost picked up a NatBallet program from his desk and turned to the roster of Company dancers. "See this list? Eighty-plus dancers. All dependent on Holt for the advancement of their careers. Ballet masters are always dictators at heart, but Holt was a true martinet. Nobody got a part, or got promoted, without his say-so. So right there you've probably got eighty grievances, eighty motives for killing him. Plus all the backstage crew that he was more than capable of insulting."

"But just because they had reasons for disliking the man doesn't mean they would have him murdered. If that were the case, at least half the Police Department would be dead."

"True enough."

"And besides, how many of those dancers would have access to twenty-four thousand dollars?" Bautista asked.

"Maybe they took up a collection," Frost answered. "No, Luis, you're right. Twenty-four thousand dollars is more than a year's salary for most of the younger ones."

"Surely, Reuben, there must be some obvious suspects."

Frost turned and stared out the window without answering. "You know," he said, finally, "I was thinking about something Cynthia said the night Holt was murdered."

"Like what?"

"She said she was glad Clifton's murderer had been found because otherwise the number of suspects would have been very large. When I pressed her, she named four obvious ones without even trying."

"Who were they?" Bautista asked, pulling out his notebook.

"Luis, I will tell you, but it's going to be difficult. Some of them are good friends of ours, and I mention them only because they are suspects in theory only."

"I understand, Reuben, but we have to begin somewhere."

Frost gave the detective the four names mentioned by Cynthia—Arne Petersen, Teresa Holt, Andrea Turnbull and Veronica Maywood, adding in each case a short description of who they were, and why they might have wanted Holt dead. Then he added two more—Jack Navikoff and Arthur Mattison.

When Frost had finished, Bautista put down his notebook.

"I see what you mean—six people with real motives, but not an obvious killer among them. So I guess we'll just have to start digging."

"Where will you start?"

"The money looks the sexiest to me. From the way you describe them, Teresa Holt, and certainly Andrea Turnbull, could put their hands on twenty-four grand easily. How about Petersen?"

"Possibly. He's a bachelor and I don't think a high

liver. He probably has some savings. But understand, Luis, this man lived under our roof for almost a year. We are practically his adoptive parents."

"Reuben, I do understand. But as you yourself admit, he did have a motive for getting rid of Holt at NatBallet. Now, to go on, what about Navikoff?"

"Being the Hollywood operator he is, I'm sure he could have gotten the money too, even though he's supposed to be in financial trouble, as I told you."

"Maywood?"

"No problem there, I'd guess. She can command pretty big fees—three or four thousand—for guest appearances."

"Let's see, that leaves Mattison."

"I don't know about him. He's a notorious free-loader, always looking to pick up a quick buck. I suspect the money goes out just as fast—or faster—than it comes in. But I can't really be sure."

"Well, that's a start," Bautista said.

"Can you trace the money?"

"Maybe. The police report said it was in new bills. I've got to retrieve it from the Property Clerk's office—assuming they haven't lost it."

"Is that possible?"

"Unfortunately, yes. I'm sure the investigating officers bagged the money and that it was logged in with the Department's Property Clerk. But that doesn't mean the dimwits who run that office can find it again. But if we do find it, maybe we can trace the serial numbers to a local bank."

"What about the forty-seven eighty-nines? Isn't that what they're called?" Frost asked.

"That's right, form forty-seven eighty-nine. To register large cash transactions. Designed to thwart drug dealers and tax evaders—if the form is filled out. But how do you know about forty-seven eighty-nines?"

"Just run-of-the-mill law practice, Luis," Frost answered, smiling. "Some years ago, after the Feds put in that reporting requirement, a bank out West that we do work for got caught not filing the reports. There was a branch in Los Angeles, I recall, where the little-old-lady tellers were 'accommodating' their customers by taking in bagfuls of fives and tens and giving back brand-new hundreds. And accepting little twenty-dollar tips for the trouble of counting the dirty small bills. What they were really doing was laundering dope money from the streets, and getting bribed for it in the process—and not filing the forty-seven eighty-nines with the Internal Revenue Service. But they thought they were just being nice to their customers, hard as that may be to believe."

"What did you do?"

"We advised the bank to plead guilty, pay a fine—and revise its internal controls."

The two men laughed.

"I remember that every transaction involving ten thousand dollars or more has to be reported. That amount hasn't gone up, has it?"

"I don't think so."

"It's easy enough to check," Frost said, pressing the intercom. "Miss O'Hara, have the library send me the *CCH Banking Law Reporter*," he asked, then added, turning to Bautista, "If you're lucky, you'll be able to trace the money to a nice branch bank and then find a form forty-seven eighty-nine with a familiar name on it."

"If I'm lucky. If I'm very lucky," Bautista said.

"And if you're not?"

"Well, maybe Wilson's address book, or his customer records, will yield up a name."

"I certainly hope so. Oh, thank you, Miss O'Hara," Frost said, as his secretary brought in the bulky black Commerce Clearing House loose-leaf volumes. Frost looked in the index and quickly found what he wanted. "The Bank Secrecy Act of 1970, designed quote to require certain reports or records where they have a high degree of usefulness in criminal, tax, or regulatory investigations or proceedings unquote. Yes, here it is. Ten thousand dollars."

"Well, at least the Feds aren't against us and didn't raise the floor for making currency reports."

"Let's hope that's a good sign."

"Reuben, I'm going off now and chase down some of these leads. Can we talk later this afternoon or tonight?"

"Yes. I'm headed up to my club now, and then, believe it or not, I'm seeing one of the suspects. Andrea Turnbull. So you can call me at home later in the afternoon."

"Good. And we'll see you tomorrow anyway, right?"

"That's right. You know that tomorrow's performance is a memorial to Clifton Holt, don't you?"

"No, I didn't."

"It is. It was just an ordinary performance when Cynthia invited you and Francisca. But now, just think, by traveling with us in the rarefied atmosphere of NatBallet, you and Francisca may just get to meet a murderer."

AN INTERESTING LUNCH

11

AFTER BAUTISTA'S NEWS, FROST KNEW IT WOULD BE useless to continue his preparations for his meeting with Earle Ambler; he could not concentrate on the legal niceties of mergers and acquisitions after what the detective had told him. What he most needed, Frost decided, was a Gotham martini, the *specialita della casa* of the Gotham Club. (Frost realized that martinis are martinis, and the difference between the good and the superlative is very fine. Yet he clung to the myth that certain bartenders in certain bars—Claudio, at Harry's Bar in Venice, for example—worked a special magic with gin and vermouth. He was also realist enough to know that the special attraction of the Gotham martini was the discreet dividend that Renato, the head bartender, retained in the mixing pitcher. If pressed under close interrogation by Cynthia —"Reuben, how much did you have to drink?" —he could always answer, honestly, "one martini," though a Gotham martini would have passed for at least two in any commercial saloon.)

Frost left the office soon after Bautista's departure, instructing Miss O'Hara that he would be reachable at home after lunch—and after his dreaded confrontation with Andrea Turnbull. He took the Seventh Avenue subway to Fifty-ninth Street and then walked back to the Club at Fifth Avenue and Fifty-sixth.

As he approached the Club, Frost marveled at how it had stayed out of the clutches of Everett Zacklin or some other developer ready, willing and able to exploit its choice site. The Club, a Beaux-Arts pile designed by Warren & Wetmore at the turn of the century, had been designated a City landmark, but he knew very well that even this protection had a way of dissolving in the face of a large mound of cold cash. But several of the more generous and prosperous early members—the Club had been founded in the palmy 1890s—had contributed a generous endowment that, prudently invested, had enabled the Club to survive with both its independence and its building intact.

Frost enjoyed the Gotham. Before his retirement, he had not been a terribly active member. Coming uptown from Wall Street for lunch had been a chore, creating an unseemly and inconvenient break in the workday. But now that he had more time to spare (more than he cared to admit, if the truth be known) he enjoyed the camaraderie of the Club and, like the other members, discreetly ignored the generally execrable quality of the food.

Given his interest in cultural matters, Frost had been approached, in middle age, about becoming a member of the Century, New York's legendary men's club for those connected with, or at least patrons of, the arts. He had declined, in large part because his candidacy for membership in the Gotham was already moving forward, at the behest of a classmate and old friend from Princeton. He had also declined membership in at least two of the more strictly social clubs. A

WASP and an establishment figure, Frost nonetheless felt uncomfortable with those whose status rested purely on social position—old money, old St. Paul's, old Yale; while he never flaunted it, there was still more than a trace in Frost of the barefoot orphan from Upstate New York. He desired more than comfortable superficialities in his associations, and in the Gotham he had found a congenial "tree house" (as Cynthia mockingly called the all-male club). As a fellow Gothamite had once put it, its members were "quiet doers" in their fields, both intellectual (the universities and the foundations) and commercial (though the number of publishing-house executives and editors well outnumbered the oil wildcatters), and in each case had at least some small measure of prestige and influence in their chosen fields. (At any given time, the President of Columbia University would be a member; the shy and drily academic chairman of an obscure department at the University would not.) Flamboyance was the cardinal sin among the members; Everett Zacklin might someday raze the place to erect the City's tallest building, but he would not be a member.

As he got to the front door of the Club, Frost wondered again at its quaint locked-door custom. Even on the hottest summer day, one had to ring the bell for admittance by John Darmes, the genial old black man who guarded the entrance. No one had ever explained the custom to Frost's satisfaction, and he knew of no other institution, with the possible exception of the Federal Reserve Bank, that had a comparable practice. Was it to underscore to the members, distracted by other thoughts and busy lives, that they were entering the sanctum of a club and should, while within its precincts, conduct themselves as Gothamites, not as busy men of affairs? Or was the practice meant to recall the speakeasies of Prohibition, giving a small *frisson* of adventure to those crossing its doorstep?

Frost rang the bell and was admitted by the faithful Darmes, who, as always, greeted him by name. Frost proceeded directly to the small mahogany slab in the first-floor bar where Renato presided.

"Hello, Mr. Frost. Haven't seen you in a while," the bartender said. "The usual?"

Frost nodded slightly, and Renato began pouring the gin into a pitcher, while Frost greeted his colleagues at the bar: a nervous foundation executive who always seemed to need the comfort of a midday drink; a retired banker slightly older than Frost, who invariably sought conversation and companionship at Renato's bar; and a young (at least, by Gotham standards) literary agent waiting for his author client.

Only the literary agent, Frank Lewis, had seen the predicted headline in the afternoon *Press* about Wilson's murder in prison, and connected it to Frost's association with NatBallet.

"I guess justice was done," he said to Frost. "Probably more justice than if he had come to trial."

"That's true, I'm afraid," Frost answered. "I'm told Wilson was a severe drug addict, so he probably would have gotten off on an insanity plea, or a reduced charge of some kind."

"Shocking, isn't it?" Miles Trapp, the retired banker, interjected. It was clear he desperately wanted to join the conversation but was rather muddled—he was on his second Gotham martini—about how to do so.

"What's more shocking," Lewis said, "is that someone like Clifton Holt can be murdered in cold blood on the streets of this city. There has to be some way the hoodlums can be controlled."

Frost almost said that Holt's murder was no ordinary street crime, but checked himself in time.

"It's the frontier," the banker said. "People getting killed all around the town. It's like a Western movie. Don't you agree, Renato?" He sought support from the bartender, his best friend at the bar.

"Is bad, Mr. Trapp. Is very bad. Little punks everywhere. They should put them all in jail."

Frost was not uplifted by the conversation, and he was nervous about his own knowledge of the crime. He drained the pitcher, left discreetly in front of him at the bar, drank the dividend to his martini, and headed off for the dining room.

"Anyone else going to eat?" he said. The response was negative; the midday happy hour was not yet over.

Frost entered the dining room and went over to the common table, which seated twenty strays who did not have their own engagements for lunch. Some members ate there regularly, claiming that both the company and the conversation rivaled Dr. Johnson's circle at the Cheshire Cheese. Others, like Frost, found the table a serviceable way of having lunch when at the Club alone. The conversation could be erudite or witty, but more often than not was small talk of a fairly high order, though perhaps slightly pallid by Dr. Johnson's standards.

Frost sat down next to a man he did not know and introduced himself. (He had always understood that at the Century the members never did this—it was assumed that each and every one of the members was so eminent that introductions would be superfluous. The Gotham had more modest pretensions.) His companion turned out to be an amiable enough editor from a large publishing house. As they exchanged pleasantries about the April weather and joked about the day's special lunch (chipped beef on toast), Frost looked around the room. As usual there were groupings to excite anyone with the vaguest sense of conspiracy: a *Time* editor and a *Newsweek* writer; the presidents of three major New York banks (did their lawyers think that the Gotham automatically conferred some sort of immunity from the antitrust laws? Frost wondered); a university president and a local realtor; a major editor with a famous author *not* on his list. The variety was great, lacking only women. (Frost believed firmly in the tree-house theory—that men should have the right duly to assemble and to keep the ladies out. But was it perhaps unfair to exclude them from the tree-house? He wasn't sure, though he certainly did not have the rabid antifeminist feelings of many of the Gothamites of his own age. He guessed admitting women would be all right, except that the first applicants would probably be the likes of Andrea Turnbull and Jeanine Saperstein.)

No sooner had Frost ordered than Arthur Mattison came and sat beside him. Mattison was a regular at the common table and was a firm believer that the traditions of Dr. Johnson were nobly being carried on there, in no small part because of his own verbal contributions. Mattison, almost as round as he was tall, filled not only the chair next to Frost but most of the territory surrounding it. His suits were British, but no one could say he was "impeccably tailored." The trousers, held up by suspenders decorated with circus acrobats, came almost to his throat, or at east to the middle of what would have been a chest on a man of normal proportions. His tie was too long, extending well down his large *poitrine,* and one had the impression that there was no way that his jacket, ample as it was, could ever be buttoned across his stomach. Both the tie and jacket were stained with the remnants of meals past.

"Hello, Reuben, how are you?" Mattison asked jovially. "And the dear Cynthia, how is she?"

Frost felt like replying that the dear Cynthia would be a good bit better if Mattison stopped attacking the Brigham Foundation in print. But he did not, acknowledging only that he and his wife were fine. Mattison scarcely heard the reply, having turned to the more serious business of ordering lunch.

"What are you having today?" the fat critic asked.

"My usual, Arthur. Safe, sensible and boring Welsh rarebit."

"What first?"

"Nothing."

"Good grief, my good man, you'll starve to death." Then, to the waiter standing at his back, Mattison inquired about the oysters.

"Very good bluepoints, sir. Very fresh," the waiter answered.

"Let's see. April. An 'r.' That means they're all right. Or does anyone pay attention to that old saw about months with an 'r' anymore?"

"I think not, Arthur," said Mattison's companion on the other side, a retired surgeon named Willard Stowe.

"I'll keep that in mind when May comes," Mattison said. "But Willard, is it because the waters are so polluted you can get hepatitis in any month, or because oyster beds are safer these days?"

"I'd hate to speculate," Dr. Stowe replied.

"Well whatever, I should be as safe as I'll ever be in mid-April. So, waiter, bring me a dozen bluepoints, with extra lemon. Then the club steak rare and a half-bottle of that delicious Simard you've got on the wine list."

Priority business finished, Mattison turned to Frost and began questioning him about NatBallet. But only after delivering a paean of praise for Clifton Holt, in which he quoted liberally from his own column on the subject. (Probably stolen from an old obituary of Massine or Fokine, Frost thought scornfully.)

"I wish I'd known Holt better," Mattison said. "I met him a number of times, of course, but we never did have what you might call an intimate talk—an interview or two, but always very formal and very guarded. He was a very private person, wasn't he, Reuben?"

"Yes, you could say that."

"I was really crushed by his death, the circumstances and all that. We don't have that many certified geniuses in this City and can't afford to lose any of them."

Frost observed Mattison, and observed him hard, as he talked. There were no telltale signs, no quavers of voice, that indicated to Frost that the man was lying. But he clearly was—how could Mattison say that he wished he had known Holt better after Holt's devastating letter to him? Mattison was calculating and clever and, it now became clear to Frost, nerveless. Nerveless enough, at least, to lie about his attitude toward Holt. But nerveless enough to have Holt killed? There was the question.

Conversation ceased as Mattison's oysters were presented. After dousing them (and Frost and Dr. Stowe) with lemon juice, he attacked them voraciously, loudly sipping the juice from the shells after devouring the oysters themselves.

Frost silently reflected on his luncheon partner during the process. Little was known about Mattison's past. He had been a theatre critic in Chicago before the *Press* had made a big splash about stealing him away. He was installed at the *Press* with great fanfare and given a prominently placed thrice-weekly column in the front of the newspaper as its critic-at-large with, apparently, a brief to say anything he wanted about any subject. He was a clever writer and quick with the amusing phrase—his theatre, movie, and literary commentaries were the delight of those who made up ads containing short, punchy—and favorable—quotations.

He was also the delight of producers, museum directors and publishers, for he was an appreciator. His pieces nearly always boosted the institution or individuals responsible for an event; if he could not praise, he remained silent in print. However, in order to balance the ledger somewhat, and probably to assist the *Press*'s publisher in his naked appeal to lower-class (and non-Manhattan) readers, he occasionally launched populist and basically anti-intellectual attacks—always on lesser-known organizations like the Brigham Foundation, which he accused of being elitist and unreceptive to the needs of "little" projects—attacks he would never make on the Metropolitan Museum, or the Nederlanders or the Shuberts.

The arts establishment of the City quoted him widely and professed pleasure at his unashamed boosterism, though in private the more discerning recognized the shallowness of his criticism. A prolific writer, he not only turned out his three newspaper columns each week, but articles for the *Press*'s Sunday magazine and free-lance pieces for a half-dozen other magazines as well. Frost had often thought that a bitchy observation about another acquaintance, a prolific but hardly profound literary critic, to the effect that he had written more books than he had read, applied equally well to Mattison.

Frost had once been curious enough about Mattison to look him up in *Who's Who*. What he found was that Mattison, born in Chicago, had attended the University of Iowa and, after two years as an enlisted man in the Army, had gone to work for one of the Chicago dailies. But then the *Press* attempted to make him New York's preeminent critic, whether discussing Robert Redford, Robert Motherwell, Robert Venturi or Robert Merrill. Not to mention Robert Browning, Robert Burns or Robert Benchley.

The prominence given Mattison's prose by the *Press*, and the grateful acceptance of his boosting praise by those who mattered, had achieved the *Press*'s aim of making his name known not only to its readers but also to the public at large, and better known than any of the critics and culture writers at the City's other newspapers.

But did this make him a critic who really could relate a new production of *Hamlet* to those that had gone before? No, it did not, and the man's reviews seldom went beyond describing what he had seen on stage or in the gallery; there was little or no linkage of the present event to past history.

Frost also recalled that his companion, now attacking his steak, had started writing about the dance only fairly late on, and well after it had become an established part of the City's cultural life. But by then Mattison was supposed to be an omnicompetent expert, and rather than let his deficient knowledge of the dance show, he had evidently resorted to the plagiarizing tactics uncovered by Holt.

Frost had finished his Welsh rarebit and a cup of

coffee and was about to leave when a new conversation drew his interest. Donald Jeffries, another book editor sitting across the table and down two places from Frost, asked Mattison about writing a book.

"I understand you've signed up with Darnall & Chapman," Jeffries said.

"That's old news, Donald. Did that a month ago," Mattison replied.

"And a pretty healthy advance, I hear," Jeffries said.

"I guess, for a bunch of recycled columns," Mattison answered. "Let's just say a quite comfortable five figures."

Five figures, Frost thought. At least ten thousand dollars. Quite comfortable five figures. At least twenty-four thousand dollars, and enough to pay Mr. Jimmy Wilson?

Frost got up from the table quickly, mumbling his goodbyes to those around him and trying not to show his inner turmoil at the discovery that Arthur Mattison not only had a motive for hiring Holt's killer, but probably had the money to pay him as well.

A BOLD DEMAND

12

As he left the Gotham Club, Frost looked at his watch and realized that he was running slightly late for his three-o'clock appointment with Andrea Turnbull. He sighed to himself—he was in no way eager for the meeting—and hailed a cab heading crosstown. In minutes he was standing inside the lobby of her Beekman Place apartment house, where he was directed to the fifth floor.

There was no response when Frost first rang the bell of her apartment, though there was the pulsing sound of rock music coming from inside. After the second ring, a tall, sullen teenaged boy opened the door. He towered over Frost by a good six inches, his spiky hair dyed punk-yellow and a small gold earring piercing one ear.

"Yeah?" the hulk said.

"I was looking for Mrs. Turnbull," Frost replied. He introduced himself and put out his hand.

The young man shook hands without enthusiasm. "Mark," he said simply, presumably by way of identification.

"Is Mrs. Turnbull in?"

"Yeah. Come in."

The music in the hallway was deafening. "I'll go get her," Mark said, raising his voice to be heard over the music. He disappeared down a side hallway, a figure clad in jeans, a baggy oversized sweat shirt and torn black sneakers.

Unbidden, Frost went into what he took to be the living room, moving toward the windows along one wall to behold a magnificent view of the East River. The apartment was on a low enough floor that there was an immediacy to the waterway outside, giving the illusion that the busy barge traffic was passing by only feet away from the apartment.

The only distraction from the view was the grime on the windows, both inside and out. As he turned around to survey the living room, Frost realized that the entire apartment was filthy—dust everywhere, piles of old newspapers and magazines in odd corners, a floor-to-ceiling bookshelf in disarray. The place was nothing short of squalid, and at least two pieces of furniture, a straight-backed chair and a small end table, were broken. An offending human—or perhaps a pet—had also made two large and visible spots on the rug.

The apartment looked like the home of an eccentric and slovenly recluse, the kind of quarters where the body of its deceased occupant molders for days before being discovered. There was a peculiar odor in the air also, which Frost identified—or thought he identified—as stale marijuana smoke.

While he continued to look around, Andrea Turnbull appeared and greeted him grandly, as if they were in immaculate surroundings. She seemed quite oblivious to the dirt and disorder, and certainly made no apologies for it. Her cheap print dress—large orange flowers on a beige background—was the brightest thing in the room, but as usual, did not fit her bulky figure particularly well. (And, as usual, her slight mustache bothered Frost—though he always tried very hard not to let it do so.)

"Is the music too loud?" she asked.

"It is a little hard to hear over it," Frost said.

"I'll ask him to turn it down," she said as she went toward the door to the side hallway and shouted to her son. After a long wait, the volume diminished.

"You met Mark?" she asked.

"Yes."

"He can be something of a trial, but I'm glad to see him. He's here on vacation from the University of Maine."

Frost wondered at this statement, knowing that spring vacations were already over at schools with which he was familiar. Had Mark perhaps been suspended from the University instead?

"He's my only child, you know," Mrs. Turnbull went on.

"I see."

"Sit down over here, Reuben," she said, motioning to the threadbare couch at the side of the room. Frost did so, if a trifle gingerly.

"Would you like some tea? Or a drink?"

"No, thanks. I just finished a big lunch."

As he spoke the music suddenly stopped and the son was standing in the doorway.

"I'm going out," he announced.

"Where to, dear?" his mother asked.

"Just out. See some friends maybe."

"Will you be back for supper?"

"I dunno. Like, I've got no big plans, so I dunno."

"Well, will you let me know? We could go out for dinner if you want."

"I probably won't be back."

"As you wish, dear. It's your vacation."

"Say, Ma, can I have some money?"

"What for, dear? I gave you quite a bit yesterday."

"I spent it. You got fifty?"

"That seems a lot."

"Yeah, I know. But it goes pretty fast."

"In my purse, dear. But only fifty."

"Sure. Thanks. Goodbye." He put a pair of Walkman earphones in his ears as he left, turning up the volume so high that the bass rhythms could be heard in the living room.

Mark appeared to make quick work of extracting money from his mother's purse, since the outside door slammed resoundingly almost at once.

"What year is your son in college?" Frost asked.

"A junior. He's just twenty-one."

"What's he majoring in?"

"Oh, he's told me, but I've forgotten. Journalism perhaps. He's changed his mind several times."

"They often do at his age," Frost said, tempted to add "but their mothers usually know from what to what." He did not.

"Reuben, I'm sorry to have dogged you this past week, but I simply had to talk to you about the future of NatBallet, and I wanted to get to you before any decisions were made."

"I don't think anything drastic is going to happen very soon," Frost replied. "Everybody's too shocked right at the moment to make any permanent decisions. Besides, I think the Company is in good hands with Arne."

"You think he should be given a chance?"

"Yes, I do. Not that we really have any alternative in the short run. But I would be quite surprised if the

Board did not pick him as the Artistic Director on a permanent basis.''

"I agree. And he probably would be a good choice. He was always under Holt's thumb, but he sometimes showed some independence. Welcome independence, I might add. Arne has a mind of his own. And one can also talk to him. Which is more than one could ever say about the great Clifton Holt."

"I'm glad we're in agreement on Arne," Frost said, trying to deflect a tirade about Holt. "But is that the real reason you wanted to talk to me?"

"No, it isn't," Andrea Turnbull said. "Since Clifton's death—a nasty death for a nasty man, in my view—I've been doing a lot of thinking about NatBallet. And about my part in it. As you well know, Reuben, I've given almost two million dollars to the Company in the last two years. That's more than any of those fancy ladies who think they own the place, or any of those *men* who think the same thing."

"There's no doubt that you've been very generous, Andrea," Frost interjected.

"But what do I have to show for it? A seat on the Board? Wonderful! Absolutely no one there listens to me or cares what I think. A new production bearing my name? What a waste that. Paying the production costs of *Chávez Concerto,* an ill-conceived piece that will never be put on stage? And finally, Reuben, the continued humiliation of Clifton Holt's rudeness, ignoring or ridiculing every suggestion I ever made."

"I'm sorry you feel this way, Andrea," Frost said.

"That may be. But now that Clifton Holt is gone, things are going to change. You probably didn't know, Reuben, that I spent a fortune trying to start a decent ballet company in Syracuse. We tried—or at least, I tried—very hard for ten years to create my dream—my dream of a ballet company that I started and kept going. But everything was against me. The cheap public wouldn't pay the ticket prices. The local newspapers gave us less coverage than the stock-car races. The stingy banks wouldn't lend money. The rich wouldn't give to it—they were too jealous of me. The University thought I was treading on its turf. The State Council on the Arts thought we were pretentious and wouldn't help. And no dancer worth anything wanted to suffer through the upstate winters in a pretty dull town. No dancer in his right mind wants to spend five months of every year with his precious limbs exposed to freezing weather."

"I didn't know all this, Andrea."

"There's no reason why you should. But I've loved the dance ever since I was at Sarah Lawrence. It was the only thing that interested me there. I used to come to the City all the time, to see every performance I could see. I did so much of it that I never graduated, to tell the truth. Then I went to Syracuse, where Emery, my husband, made a lot of money and gave me the freedom to spend it. I spent it all right, but it ended in failure. Total, disastrous failure."

"Is that why you came to New York?"

"Yes. Emery died very suddenly just when the ballet was going broke. It was a terrible time for me. I left Syracuse two weeks after the funeral and have never been back. And never will go back. Which brings me to the present, Reuben, and what I want. I'm determined to make an impact on the ballet, and NatBallet in particular."

"What do you have in mind?" Frost asked, almost visibly holding his breath.

"Let me be very direct. I realize that Arne, or another dancer or choreographer, will always be the

Director of NatBallet. That won't change. But I want to be his co-Director. His equal. His partner."

Frost was stunned. Could this absurd woman be serious? The Company would be the laughingstock of the dance world if it sold out in such a bizarre way. Did Andrea Turnbull not realize there were certain prerogatives that money couldn't buy?

"Reuben, you're silent," the woman said. "I'm sure what I've said comes as a surprise, maybe even as a shock. But I'm as qualified as anyone for the job. I grant you I'm not a choreographer and I've never been a dancer, but I've got taste; I know the history of the dance." Then she added, after a pause, "And I've got money."

"I would have thought, Andrea, that if there were such a position as co-Director—and certainly no one has ever suggested it before now—the job would go to someone with actual experience as a dancer, or as a choreographer."

"Maybe. But there is no earthly reason why there has to be a hard-and-fast rule on the subject. Diaghilev was not a dancer or choreographer. Neither was Lincoln Kirstein. Neither was Oliver Smith."

"Well, you've certainly given me something to think about."

"You bet I have. And I want to make it absolutely clear that there's no give on my part. I want to be Arne Petersen's co-Director. Period. Clifton Holt's death has given me a chance to prove what I can do—to prove to the good people of Syracuse that they were wrong. And I'm going to have that chance, or else. . . ."

"Or else?"

"Or else my support for NatBallet will stop just as fast as it began."

Frost got up from the decrepit sofa. "You've certainly made your position clear, Andrea. I'll think about it. Yes, I'll do that much."

"Good. Do think about it—and about the consequences. And I'd like an answer soon. I want to get started on the job as soon as possible—or, if the answer is no, to consider where I can spend my money to greater effect."

"Give me a week."

"Fine."

"Good day, Andrea."

Frost felt downright unsteady as he walked out into Beekman Place. His disoriented thoughts were in contrast to the clipped, trimmed and polished neatness around him as he walked the length of the exclusive Beekman enclave, then out to First Avenue and toward home. He would definitely walk; the sunny weather and the fresh air would do him good—and give him time to think about Mrs. Turnbull's outrageous proposition. What a mess! NatBallet had an annual budget of twenty million dollars and a deficit, before gifts, of six. Andrea Turnbull made up a significant part of that deficit and had been immensely helpful in getting the Company onto a sound footing. But her terms for continuing her support were impossible. Outlandish.

As he sometimes did when agitated, Frost talked to himself as he walked up Second Avenue, oblivious to the occasional stares of those observing his eccentricity. How could that ugly woman think she could run NatBallet, alone or with others? he wondered. Despite his anger, he laughed to himself as he made up an imaginary conversation with Cynthia:

"Cynthia, dear, I've found a way to get your beloved

ballet company out of the woods. A sure way to make it secure and prosperous for years to come."

"Oh, Reuben, I knew you would. But what is it, darling?"

"We've decided to make Andrea Turnbull Arne Petersen's co-Director. And she's agreed to pick up the deficits for ever and ever."

"Reuben, you're crazy and a bastard."

The conversation faded out there. The whole thing was totally absurd. Cynthia wouldn't hear of it, and no one on the Board would either. Nor would Arne himself. Saddled with Andrea Turnbull? He would be on the next plane to Tucson.

Andrea Turnbull was certifiably crazy. There was no doubt about it. Sitting there in her untidy apartment she had ranted like a mad slattern. And then the ominous thought struck him: was she so crazy, so mad for power and recognition, that she had had Clifton Holt murdered? After the performance he had just witnessed he certainly could not rule out the possibility.

Frost walked faster as he approached his town house. He had to talk to Luis Bautista. He unlocked his front door and went immediately to the telephone in the library. On his way he called out to Cynthia, and was relieved when he got no answer. He could tell his wonderful news to his wife later, but now he had to talk to the detective.

Once Frost reached him, Bautista himself had no news to report, although the blood money had not been lost and was in the Property Clerk's custody. As it had been described, it was in new one-hundred-dollar bills, though the police laboratory had reported that there were no identifiable fingerprints on any of it. But efforts were still being made to trace the money through its serial numbers.

"And what have *you* found out?" Bautista asked.

"Plenty," Frost answered. He told the detective about his lunch with Mattison, and the unexpected revelation of the royalty advance on the critic's book. And then about Andrea Turnbull, the crazed, threatening Andrea Turnbull. And about sweet little Mark, who might well have done some playing in the streets with Jimmy Wilson.

13

THE NIGHT OF THE MEMORIAL PERFORMANCE, REUBEN tried to hurry his wife along as they were dressing at home. His nervous remonstrances were quite unnecessary; Cynthia had never been late for a performance in her entire career and seldom for a social engagement. But Reuben, perhaps aware that he no longer moved as fast as he once did, projected his own anxieties onto his wife.

"You know what the traffic is like through Central Park before eight o'clock. You have Lincoln Center and Broadway . . ."

"Yes, dear, of course I know. Will you snap my necklace for me, please? I want to wear these pearls, but I never can work the clasp." She came and stood with her back to her husband, who, awkwardly and with a mild curse word or two, performed the requested task.

"You look very nice," Reuben said, surveying her rose-colored silk Givenchy (a Christmas present from him the year before).

"Thanks. I hope this is all right. You don't think I should wear black, do you?"

141

"No, no, no. It's a memorial, but not a wake. You look just fine. The Mayor will love it."

"Oh, God, the Mayor. He can't resist showing up when there's publicity to be had, can he?"

"That's part of his job, Cynthia. He is, in his way—his very peculiar way—our Lord Mayor. Half the things he does are symbolic. He loves them for their publicity value. But he could be like his predecessor, who never went anywhere. Except, I guess, to Brighton Beach."

"I was stunned when his office called," Cynthia said. "He *hates* the ballet. Thinks it's snobbish and all that. You know as well as I do it bores him to tears."

"But look, as usual, he isn't going to watch the performance. A 'drop-in' I believe they call it at City Hall. He'll come backstage, make a few remarks to the audience, and then leave for his Chinese dinner."

"I hope you're right," Cynthia said doubtfully.

"Too bad he isn't coming for the performance. We could put him next to Andrea Turnbull."

"Oh, Reuben, I never want to hear that deranged woman's name again. Co-Director of the Company. Imagine! I hope we can avoid her tonight. I'll have quite enough on my mind without trying to be nice to her."

"She's certain to be there, I'm afraid," Frost said.

"The Bautistas are meeting us at the theatre?"

"Yes."

"Do you think Luis will learn anything tonight?"

"About the murder, you mean?"

"Yes."

"We'll see. Now come on."

"Just let me get my purse, Mr. Jitters, and we're off."

Luis Bautista and Francisca Ribiero, the Frosts' guests for the evening, were waiting in the lobby of the

Zacklin. Reuben spotted them in the crowd, thinking again what an attractive couple they were. On the basis of knowing Bautista for several months now, it was clear that Ms. Ribiero was his steady girlfriend, though neither Reuben nor Cynthia could tell whether they were simply friends or if Francisca was a "live-in." Whatever their living status, each seemed very fond of the other.

Frost guessed—and Cynthia agreed—that Francisca, who worked as a secretary for the vice chairman of a large investment-banking firm, must spend a large part of her salary on clothes. They were always in the latest trendy fashion, yet always in good taste and not bargains off the racks of the Canal Street Jeans Company. For this evening's outing she was wearing a jet-black silk dress with a jagged, revealing neckline, set off with a multicolored sash at the waist that matched a large scarf thrown around her shoulders. Her makeup, in less deft hands, would have looked grotesque, if not cheap—her already dark eyes heavily mascaraed, her high cheekbones touched up with bright rouge and her downright sensuous lips swathed in luminescent ruby-red lipstick. On her the effect was not cheap at all, but instead absolutely stunning. As he often did when meeting her, Reuben envied her boss: why didn't beauties like this, and seemingly competent ones at that, work at Chase & Ward?

Francisca enthusiastically embraced Cynthia and then, with perhaps even more enthusiasm, Reuben. Bautista, wearing his best *Miami Vice* pinstripe, shook hands with both of them. Smiling his slightly imperfect smile, all six feet of Bautista leaned over to kiss Cynthia, completely overshadowing her petite dancer's body in the process.

"Anything new?" Frost asked Bautista.

"Not really. They're still trying to trace the money," Bautista answered. "We haven't given up on that."

"Well, let's try to forget our little problem and enjoy the performance," Reuben said.

"Thank you for asking us," Francisca said to Reuben. "You've really got us hooked on the ballet. Do you know we came last week without you? Paid for the tickets and everything!" The woman laughed easily as she spoke.

"She's right," Bautista added, speaking to Cynthia. "Between the job and night law school, I've got about an evening and a half free every week. And it looks like we may be spending them right here—for one reason or another."

"I'm delighted, Luis," Cynthia said. "In my opinion there is no better place."

"We've got a rather special program for Clifton Holt's memorial," Reuben said, as they went upstairs to the mezzanine. "The ballet being done in Holt's honor is very beautiful. There will also be an added treat. Cynthia is going to speak."

"Great! Are you nervous?" Francisca asked, turning to Cynthia.

"Well I am, a little," Cynthia answered. "Speeches aren't really my forte, and eulogies certainly aren't."

"It doesn't matter," Reuben said. "The Mayor is speaking first, so whatever Cynthia says, she'll sound good."

"The Mayor? Wow! Is he a ballet nut too?" Francisca asked.

"Publicity," Cynthia replied.

"Publicity?"

"Publicity nut."

"Oh, I see," Francisca said, laughing once again.

The Frosts' seats were on the aisle in the front row

of the mezzanine and were, arguably, the best seats in the house. As NatBallet's Chairman of the Board, Reuben held the four seats by right. Opposite them on the side aisle were those reserved for Peter Howard, the Company President, and in the corresponding location on the other side of the house were the Artistic Director's seats. Arrayed behind them on the aisles were the seats reserved for the critics from the daily press, various magazines and television. Another twelve places were always reserved until the very last minute for other members of the Board and staff—and just in case Mrs. Reagan, or Colonel Qaddafi, or Nureyev, or a leading dancer's mother, decided that NatBallet must be seen, and seen at the very next performance.

All in all, a substantial block of the choicest mezzanine seats—among the dance cognoscenti, sitting below in the orchestra was decidedly *infra-dig*—were taken up to meet the many high-powered demands on the Company. But in practice, many of these prize tickets were placed on sale at the box office just before the performance began. Reuben and Cynthia, for example, by no means attended all performances, and often used only two of their four tickets when they did. (The result was that many lucky tourists, unfamiliar with this Byzantine ticket allocation, went back to the hinterland to tell the neighbors that they "didn't understand all this business about the National Ballet being always sold out. Why, we just walked in off the street at the very last minute and had the most beautiful seats you could imagine!")

Before they reached the mezzanine door, Cynthia's luck ran out. Andrea Turnbull and her son Mark were dead ahead of them. Reuben, Cynthia and Andrea were all stiffly polite, and no mention, of course, was made of the heiress's recent threat. Only Mark, again in his punk raiment, was surly. He did not change his expression as he was introduced to Cynthia and the Frosts' guests.

"I don't believe I've seen you here before," Andrea said to Bautista.

"We don't come that often," Bautista explained. "Usually only when the Frosts invite us."

"Are you in Mr. Frost's firm?" Andrea asked.

"No, no. I work for the City."

"Oh, politics. The Mayor's office?"

"No. Police Department."

"How interesting. But you've known the Frosts for a long time?"

"Not really. Just since last year."

"Well, it's nice to meet you." The curious Andrea and her glum son went to the right and the Frost party to the left.

"Curious, isn't she?" Frost said to Bautista. "She's the one I told you about yesterday. And that's the kid with her."

"I figured as much," the detective replied.

Bautista and Ms. Ribiero were by now used to the Frosts' seating plan—Cynthia four seats in from the aisle, then Bautista, then Francisca, then Reuben on the aisle itself. It was a placement Reuben had devised after some trial and error, giving one Frost access to one guest, and allowing their guests to huddle together (if necessary) for security.

The foursome sat down, but since they were early, Reuben was soon up greeting the familiar faces around him. Peter Howard (by much-discussed prearrangement) was sitting with Teresa Holt. Frost greeted the pair and said meaningfully to Holt's widow, "I'm so glad you could come, Teresa. I think it's going to be a fine occasion."

As he chatted in the aisle, Arthur Mattison put his hand on Reuben's shoulder and then shook hands. Mattison waved at Cynthia, oblivious to her strong feelings about his commentary on the Brigham Foundation, and looked Bautista and his date over with journalistic curiosity.

"Arthur, this is Francisca Ribiero and Luis Bautista. They're old friends that we're trying to convert into ballet fans," Frost explained.

"Good for you, Reuben. Are you in the arts, Mr. Bautista?"

"No, I'm a detective for the City."

"Oh, I see! Hanging out with the police, are you, Reuben?" Mattison asked.

"Mmn, we had some professional involvement a few months ago," Frost answered.

"Well, at least you didn't end up in jail. Good to meet you," Mattison said, and departed, with perhaps some haste.

Just before the lights went down, Frost looked across at the other side of the mezzanine to see Arne Petersen and Jack Navikoff in Clifton Holt's old seats. All very cozy, all one happy family, Reuben thought, as Cyrus Richter, the Company's principal conductor, led the orchestra in the syncopated overture to Clifton Holt's *Jazz Café*.

The ballet, made on three male dancers moving about in a smoky, checkered-tablecloth dive—was it New Orleans, the old Fifty-second Street in New York or just a spot in Holt's imagination?—was a great success with the audience, as it always was. The individual turns of the dancers drew more and more applause as the routines they danced, to the music of Duke Ellington, grew more and more intricate.

Holt had always insisted that the cast of *Jazz Café* be integrated—either one black and two white dancers, or two blacks and a white. The mix did not matter, but the importance of it did. In this performance Regan Isham, a promising, regally statuesque black in the corps, paired off with Aaron Cassidy and Tom Dunning in the kaleidoscopic series of solos, duets and trios that made up the ballet.

Frost remembered Holt's lament as he watched Cassidy bend and twist to the insistent jazz rhythms of the music. He did all the steps absolutely correctly; impeccably, in fact. But that was the problem, as Holt had frequently observed. Cassidy and his contemporaries, weaned on rock and blaring sound, simply did not have jazz in their bones and had to be meticulously taught each and every move. The result was "academically" correct, but lacked the spontaneity and sinuousness that was required. Dunning, a young corps dancer, had the same problem, though he tried—sweated and tried—to achieve the gritty, down-to-earth effect that Holt had sought in the work. Only Isham had the moves, and he took to Holt's choreography as if it had been made on him. He made the steps look easy, and connected them up with an elastic and fluid languidity that made one understand what jazz was all about.

Jazz Café, one of the first ballets Holt had done for NatBallet, was a wonderful work, combining the traditional classicism of ballet with solid American rhythms. That was one of Holt's greatest talents, Frost thought; the man had married unlikely opposites in an effective piece of stagecraft, moving the magical combination of jazz and classical dance beyond what those brilliant pioneers George Balanchine and Jerome Robbins had done.

Frost surreptitiously glanced at Francisca Ribiero beside him as the ballet unfolded. He had no doubt that Francisca had an innate sense of rhythm—not because of some ethnic stereotype, but because of the graceful way in which she moved, responded and talked. (Frost had a secret hope that some evening his friend Bautista would invite the Frosts, on one of Bautista's one-and-a-half nights out, to a discotheque. The idea of ear-shattering dance clubs did not appeal to him in general, but he was sure it would be quite marvelous to watch Francisca moving gracefully to the pounding sounds that these days passed for dance music.)

As the ballet progressed, Frost's thoughts turned more and more to its creator. What a despicable man Holt had been! Yet here was a work that gave unalloyed pleasure and was, quite possibly, touched with genius. The proof was not just in his own mind, he thought, but in the public response to *Jazz Café*, now a staple in the repertoires of dance companies across the country. In fact, Frost concluded, his mind wandering, *Jazz Café* was probably a nice little nest egg. What were the royalties? Five hundred dollars a performance, perhaps. Fifteen companies doing the ballet six times a year—a conservative guess: let's see, fifteen times six is ninety, times five hundred is $45,000. Not bad. It would keep Teresa in pin money.

Frost's meanderings were brought to a halt as the ballet ended. Waves and waves of applause followed—they always did, but given the circumstances, they were deafening this time.

"Did you like that?" Frost asked, as he accompanied Francisca up the aisle.

"Oh, yes. It was fantastic!"

"Who did you think was best?"

"Hmm, they were all good. But the black boy was

really with it! He's got the moves!" Francisca squeezed Reuben's arm as she spoke, moving a bit herself as she did so.

"What did you think, Cynthia?" Frost asked.

"Very good performance. Aaron and Tom will get there yet. But they've got to catch up to Regan. Clifton would have been proud of them all."

"How about a drink?" Reuben asked. "Francisca, Luis?"

"Sure. Let me get them," Bautista said. He quickly took orders and, with lynxlike precision, moved to the shortest line at the long bar in the lobby outside the mezzanine. He soon returned, somehow deftly balancing four plastic cups and dispensing them without spilling a drop.

"Thank you, Luis. You're much more agile than I am," Frost said. "Usually the intermission is half over before I can crowd to the bar."

"It's youth, Reuben, that's all. Youth and a powerful thirst," Bautista responded confidently.

"Cynthia, what are you going to do?" Frost asked, as the group drank its theatre-bar-minuscule drinks. "Are you going backstage now, or after the next number?"

"I don't know," she replied. "If I go back now, I'll only get nervous. But I suppose someone should be there to greet the Mayor."

"Can't Arne do that?" Frost asked.

"Good idea. In fact, there he is now. Let me ask him."

Cynthia went across the lobby and spoke briefly with the Acting Artistic Director. She had made up her mind by the time she returned to her husband and their guests.

"Yes. Arne is going backstage. Which means I can watch *Passacaglia,* which I very much want to do."

Cynthia's plans decided, the group returned to their seats.

"This ballet is quite different," Frost explained to Francisca after they were seated. "Very quiet Bach music, with a nice ensemble of eight dancers. It's very special for us, too. Mr. Holt dedicated it to Cynthia on her birthday a few years ago."

"Oh, that's nice," Francisca said. "No one's ever dedicated a ballet to *me.*"

"Oh, they will, Francisca, they will," Frost replied.

"You're a dreamer, Reuben," she replied. "But who knows? Maybe." She smiled, then laughed, then lapsed into a pose of close attention as the lights went down.

Passacaglia was the most serene of all Holt's ballets, written after what he himself called his "jazz phase" —and written after the likes of Arthur Mattison had questioned in print whether he could do anything notable outside the American idiom. The result was classical dance at its most sublime—slow and flowing and utterly enhancing of the beautiful Bach score. It had been written at perhaps the best time of Holt's tenure at NatBallet, after he himself had become fully reconciled to his career at the Company—no more looking back at the Hollywood days—and when, financially and artistically, it seemed certain that the Company would both survive and grow. And the *hommage* to Cynthia had been very touching. She had championed Holt, defended him against all criticism and insisted that he be given freedom to do just what he wanted as the Company's Artistic Director. The public had never known that the ballet was a birthday present—Cynthia was, like all vain dancers, at least a trifle sensitive about birthdays—though the program that opening night in 1973 (and all programs since) had noted that it was dedicated to her.

The original performance of *Passacaglia* had occurred at the height of Holt's immensely fruitful artistic collaboration with Veronica Maywood. (Only later would their sexual fling begin, and then abruptly end in bitterness.) But tonight, since Maywood was to dance *Requiem* to end the program, her nemesis, Laura Russell, danced her part. And danced it, at least in Reuben's eyes, very well, bringing her characteristic image of ethereal softness to the role.

When the ballet ended, again to tumultuous applause, Reuben offered encouragement to his wife before she went backstage.

"Good luck, dear," he said. "Just remember you're talking about the man who dedicated *Passacaglia* to you and you'll do just fine."

"Say, Reuben, do you think it would be all right if I went with Cynthia?" Bautista asked. "I'd like to see the backstage." Implicit in his request was a desire to see where Clifton Holt had been murdered.

"Of course. It's a good idea," Frost replied.

"Do you mind, Cynthia?"

"Not at all, Luis. I'll be glad for the moral support. Where shall we meet up afterward?"

"I hate to say it, but why not at the stage door? We'll wait outside for you," Frost said.

"Fine. Kiss me."

Frost did, and his wife and Bautista left.

Cynthia Frost and her detective companion went down the main stairs of the Zacklin to the ground floor, then moved against the crowd emerging for the intermission to the door at the front of the orchestra that led backstage. The usher standing by this door knew Cynthia well and unlocked it.

As the pair went up the metal stairs to stage level, Bautista announced that he was going to look around.

"Feel free," Cynthia said. "If anyone asks, just say you're with me. You can watch the performance from the wings. It's sort of fun if you've never done it."

"Okay. I'll be around here when it's over. And good luck."

"Thanks, Luis. Thank you very much."

The dancers from *Passacaglia* were now wandering around backstage somewhat aimlessly. The curtain calls were over, but they were not yet ready to return to the dressing rooms. They were not waiting in hopeful expectation that the applause would begin again, Cynthia knew. They were simply getting their breath back after their strenuous execution of Holt's flowing, legato choreography.

How did I do it all those years? Cynthia asked herself. And how do they do it? The laws of nature dictate that one gasps for breath to provide the oxygen necessary for strenuous physical activity. But the laws of the ballet require that there be no gasping mouths and no heaving chests—the natural physical consequences of great exertion must be concealed. Indeed, not only concealed, but hidden behind a mask—usually a disarming smile—in keeping with the emotional tone of the work being danced.

This conflict of inexorable principles was to be resolved in one way, and one way only—in favor of beauty and artistry and totally against the body's natural urge to fill the lungs. The result, somehow achieved through disciplined practice and a dedicated set of mind, meant that the gasping and heaving must be postponed—not wished away, but postponed—until the dancer was offstage, until beauty and artistry no longer needed to be projected.

Cynthia and Luis were now seeing the dancers making their delayed obeisance to nature's inexorable demands—gasping, heaving, retching, coughing or simply remaining quiet until their bodies, and especially their lungs, functioned normally again. Then too, there was the matter of flushing the echoes of Bach's music, and the related counting of the steps by means of which they executed Holt's choreography, out of their heads. Theirs was a form of ear-ringing tinnitus cured only by quietly walking around until something in their brains said "ERASE" and they could once again talk, think and breathe like normal human beings.

Cynthia went over to Laura Russell, who was standing in the wings talking to one of the corps dancers.

"A beautiful performance," Cynthia said, addressing Laura, now swathed in a knee-length turtleneck and leg warmers.

"Thanks, Cynthia. I'm glad it was good, for Clifton."

Cynthia then saw Arne Petersen and Moira Burgess quietly conversing while keeping anxious eyes on the door that led to the outside stage entrance.

"I take it Himself is not here yet?" Cynthia said to them.

"Correct," Petersen answered, looking at his watch. "They called from his car about ten minutes ago and said he was on his way."

"He'll get here; he always does," Cynthia said.

"By the way, who is that fellow you came in with?" Petersen asked.

"Oh, I'm sorry, I should have introduced you. He's a friend of ours from the Police Department."

"You have some strange friends, Cynthia. Oh, oh, here comes the Mayor."

The Mayor appeared in the door, his detective bodyguard directly behind him. He looked around hesitantly, then spotted Cynthia and strode toward her. His bodyguard, meanwhile, recognized Bautista and shook hands with him. The two stood at the side and talked several feet from where the Mayor stood.

"Hello, Mrs. Frost," the Mayor said, leaning over to kiss her.

"Hello, Norman. Do you know Moira Burgess, our public relations director, and Arne Petersen, our Acting Artistic Director?"

"Pleased to meet you," the Mayor said perfunctorily, before turning quickly to the business at hand. "What's the drill here?"

"Well, Mr. Mayor," Burgess said, "we've set up a microphone outside the curtain. Mr. Petersen will introduce you. When you are finished, Mrs. Frost will speak briefly. You can introduce her or Arne can, as you see fit."

"I'll be happy to," said the Mayor. "Always a pleasure to introduce Cynthia, even on a sad occasion like this."

"Fine."

"I have no set remarks," the Mayor said. "I thought I would just say what an important person Mr. Holt had been to New York—winner of the Handel Medallion, et cetera, et cetera. But I'll let Cynthia take care of the nitty-gritty. Does that sound all right?"

"Yes, Mr. Mayor," Petersen said. "Cynthia can handle the details about Clifton."

"What a sad event," the Mayor repeated. "Absolutely senseless crime."

As the Mayor talked, Cynthia noticed that he was looking over the heads of Arne and Moira to watch the spectacle of Veronica Maywood doing her warm-up exercises at the barre. Cynthia had seen Veronica warm up hundreds of times, but never with the energy she now displayed, bending her back forward so that her head almost touched the floor, then vigorously shaking her head from side to side in the utterly impossible position in which she had placed her body.

She has seen the Mayor, Cynthia thought, and can't resist a little showing off. Once a ballerina, always a ballerina, Cynthia sighed resignedly.

"Would you like to meet Miss Maywood, who will be dancing after we speak?" Cynthia asked. "She is going to do a solo, called *Requiem*, that Clifton Holt choreographed in honor of Charlie Parker some years ago."

"Yes, I would like that," the Mayor said, showing a scintilla of enthusiasm for the first time.

The group moved over to the barre, and Cynthia introduced the ballerina to the Mayor.

"Quite a workout there," the Mayor said. "I was watching you."

Maywood demurred becomingly. "Just trying to get my old bones in shape for what's coming," she responded.

Jeb Crosby, the stage manager, approached. "We're all ready if you are, Cynthia," he said.

"Are you ready, Norman?" Cynthia asked the Mayor.

"Fine. Anytime."

"Good," Crosby said. "This way, folks."

Crosby led them across the stage. At the side, a Steinway had been wheeled in. Kirk Drinan sat waiting at the keyboard, the Lennie Tristano score on the piano music rack in front of him.

Crosby held the curtain open and Petersen went out before the crowd. Cynthia hastily introduced the Mayor to Drinan, and then it was the Mayor's turn to speak. After polite applause he began, and Cynthia heard him over the backstage amplification system:

"This is a very sad occasion for me. Coming here to pay tribute to a man who meant so much to the cultural life of this City. Clifford Holt . . ."

"Clifford!" Cynthia whispered to Moira Burgess. "Where did he get that from? We must have called him *Clifton* at least five times in the last two minutes!"

"I remember three years ago giving Clifford Holt the Handel Medallion," the Mayor went on. "As I am sure you know, this is the City's highest award for arts and culture. I was proud to select Holt for this honor, because I knew what he meant to the dance life of this City, and the world."

"Dance life?" Cynthia said, backstage. "What the hell is that?"

"Now he has been struck down on our streets, by a petty crook with a long criminal record. One of the brightest lights in our cultural firmament has been blown out. But I say to you here tonight, this crime, this lawlessness, is going to stop . . ."

"My Lord, we're going to get his crime-in-the-streets speech!" Cynthia said. And sure enough, the Mayor repeated several paragraphs from the stock speech on crime he had given over and over again in his campaign for reelection the year before.

The applause at the end of the Mayor's remarks was less enthusiastic than at the beginning. As he came back through the curtain—having introduced Cynthia as "Mrs. National Ballet"—Cynthia quickly shook his hand, but did not offer any comment on his remarks.

Then it was her turn, and she spoke briefly, succinctly and eloquently:

"As the Mayor has said, this is a sad evening. One of the greatest choreographers in America, and the man who shaped the soul of this Company, is dead. We will always remember him and, fortunately, we will have many beautiful things to remember him by: the movies he made—the most wondrous musicals ever to illuminate the screen—and the brilliant dances he made for this Company and ballet companies around the world.

"I had the privilege of working with Clifton Holt since before our wonderful National Ballet was formed. We worked together, as artists and as friends, to get this Company started. We saw it grow and prosper; we saw its rank in the hierarchy of ballet companies soar upward.

"Clifton is gone, but his greatest memorial—this Company—remains. And I say to you tonight that it will continue, because of the exceptional legacy he has left to it, and also because of the dedication of all of us, from a faded old dancer like me to the newest member of the corps. National Ballet will go on, and it will go on as a creative, living memorial to the genius whose memory we honor this evening.

"I know the Company will continue to bring the most beautiful dance that can be created to audiences here in New York and around the country. We like to think, and I believe we are right, that dance, the ballet, is among the highest forms of civilized behavior. It is important, when there is so much violence around us, that such civilized endeavors flourish and prosper.

"I believe that the dance can save souls. And I like to think that someday, somewhere, at one of the Company's performances, some young woman or man will be touched, and that another Clifton Holt—rather than a pathetic, desperate, outcast street killer—will emerge to inspire and enthrall us all."

Cynthia, overcome with emotion, left the stage to ringing applause and fell into the arms of Arne Petersen, who was just inside the curtain.

"It was perfect, Cynthia," he said. "Just right."

"Thank you, Arne. It wasn't easy."

She then went to the center of the stage, where Veronica Maywood was poised for the beginning of *Requiem.* Cynthia embraced her, whispering into her ear the traditional and unlikely dancer's word for good luck: *merde.* Then she darted into the wings just as the electric motor began reeling up the curtain.

Cynthia watched the ballet from the wings, with Luis Bautista at her side. It was less than five minutes long, but gave the solo ballerina scarce repose. The sad blues line of Tristano's music seemed to be seamless, and the execution of the ballet required disciplined adagio dancing. It reminded Cynthia of some of Isadora Duncan's quieter solos, but the movements were distinctively Clifton's.

Requiem had not been done often, Cynthia recalled. Indeed, Clifton had retired it after one season. It had not been a popular favorite; good as it was, it was too heartrendingly sad to achieve audience popularity. Now Veronica Maywood was dancing brilliantly, with a ferocity of concentration that Cynthia found fascinating to watch.

When the piece ended, curtain call followed curtain call as the audience expressed a tribute both to Clifton Holt and to the ballerina who had inspired his best work. In between curtain calls, Cynthia congratulated the star performer again, this time embracing her.

Other members of the Company, gathered in the wings for this last, secular requiem to their late Artistic Director, embraced her as well, many crying as they did so.

Clifton Holt had been laid to rest.

SUPPER

14

CYNTHIA FROST LEFT THE ZACKLIN THEATRE WITH RE-lief. She shivered slightly as she realized she was standing near the very site of Clifton Holt's murder, but took comfort from Luis Bautista's strong and masculine presence at her side.

"That was a nice tribute," the detective said. "Holt must have been quite a guy."

"In many ways he was, Luis," she said.

"But pretty complicated, though."

"He certainly was," Cynthia said. "Did you see anything interesting tonight? Any clues?"

"I'm thinking about it," Bautista said. "I seemed to meet, or at least I saw, a good many of the suspects."

"Yes, I guess you did at that. Did you get any ideas?"

"Not really. But as I said, I'm thinking about it."

"There are Reuben and Francisca," she said, pointing to the entrance to the street. "Let's go; I'm starved."

Francisca and Reuben joined the pair, extending effusive congratulations to Cynthia.

"Where shall we eat?" Reuben asked.

"We could go back to the house," Cynthia said.

"I've got a cold chicken, if that's enough to satisfy everyone."

"You're sure?" Reuben said. "Not to a restaurant?"

"No, really, I'd prefer it," Cynthia answered. "But what about you two? It won't be very exciting."

"It's fine with us," Bautista said. "You're a better hostess than any restaurant."

"All right, you're stuck," Cynthia replied.

Bautista hailed a cab and the four set off for the Frost town house.

"Francisca, you come with me," Cynthia said, once they were inside the Frost residence. "We'll have supper ready in no time. What would you like to drink while you're working?"

"Oh, wine, I guess," Francisca said.

"Red or white?" Reuben asked.

"White would be fine."

"Good. Same for you, Cynthia?"

"No. I want and need a martini after that ordeal. Not Gotham size, but a good strong one," Cynthia said.

"Gotham?" Bautista asked.

"You know, my club," Frost said. "Cynthia is referring to the indecent size of its martinis. And what do you want?"

"I'll have a martini too," Bautista replied. "Any size will do for me."

Frost went about making the drinks as the women went to the kitchen. After delivering their drinks, he returned with martinis for himself and Bautista.

"Well, Luis, you met most of the cast of characters tonight," Frost said.

"That's what I told Cynthia. It was interesting."

"I hope it wasn't a mistake identifying you as a police officer."

"I don't think so," Bautista said. "You didn't have much choice anyway, the way they sniffed around to find out who I was. But don't worry about it. After all, no one knows what we know about Jimmy Wilson. They may have thought it was funny, the Wall Street lawyer and the cop, but—"

"The hell with them," Frost interjected. "What did you think of the rogues' gallery?"

"Hard to say. Mrs. Turnbull was a pretty determined number, and her son looked like a Class A delinquent. But you can't tell much from the way kids look these days."

"True enough," Frost replied. "But I didn't like him yesterday and I didn't like him tonight."

"You said on the phone you could imagine him knowing Jimmy Wilson. I've got no doubts about that."

"So we have a possible link between Andrea Turnbull and the murderer. What bothers me is, how could any of the other suspects have gotten in touch with Wilson?"

"That's easy, Reuben," Bautista said.

"I know you say that, Luis, but how would a respectable, or even famous, person like Arthur Mattison, or a naive little mouse like Teresa Holt, find a killer? Navikoff I could imagine, maybe. But even in his case I'm not sure I understand how it would work," Frost said.

"Look at it this way, Reuben. Let's say you're at that club of yours, the Gotham. You have maybe one too many of their martinis and you get really angry at some other guy at the bar. You decide you want him killed. Okay? Crazy, but just bear with me. If you walk out of that club and go just a little bit further west than you usually do, and start asking around, in a bar or on the street, you could be in touch with a hired killer by the end of the day. Assuming you had the money, and assuming you didn't get too eager, or indiscreet, and just kept cool. New York is a city of the greatest and the lowest, and all you gotta remember is that they exist side by side, about five feet from each other."

"It's very convenient to forget what you say," Frost said, with a sigh. "But of course it's true."

"And besides, Jimmy Wilson was a special case. He was a junkie, but he was also a clever small-time peddler, with some pretty respectable clients. Since we started going through his records, and trying to contact those clients, there've been some red faces in some pretty high-up places. Nothing to hook him up with Holt's friends yet, but young advertising executives and bankers—and even a lawyer or two."

"I suppose you're going to tell me half the young lawyers at Chase & Ward are cokeheads."

"No, but I'll bet the percentage is a lot higher than you think."

"I'm sure it is, since I would say it's zero."

"Then your firm is a very, very special place," Bautista said.

The men's conversation was interrupted by Cynthia.

"Soup's on," she said. "Let's eat before we all faint."

The group gathered at the marble dining-room table, the two couples sitting across from each other at one end.

"You forgot the wine, Reuben," Cynthia reminded her husband.

"Good Lord, so I did." Frost got up and quickly returned with a new bottle of Chablis and a corkscrew.

"You know, I can't get over the Mayor's getting Clifton's name wrong," Cynthia said, as they started eating. "We had been talking with him before he spoke and it seems to me every other word was Clifton, Clifton. Then he gets out there and calls him *Clifford*."

"Maybe he's shy," Francisca said.

"Fat chance," Cynthia replied. "He's got an ego the size of the World Trade Center. I think it's his staff. They must be morons not to brief him better than they do."

"I've got a theory," Reuben said. "We've known Norman one way or another for years. Knew him when he first got into politics. Back then, he made all the right moves. Met everybody, remembered who they were—and remembered their names. He's worked hard for what he's got—getting to be Mayor was not easy for him—and he paid good attention to details on the way up. But now that he's where he is, and not going to go any higher, he doesn't care anymore. He was just reelected with only that Republican brassiere maker running against him and, if he doesn't screw up too badly, he can get reelected for as long as he wants the job. What's the point of getting names straight if it doesn't matter anymore?"

"Well, for one thing it's polite and for another it's slightly classy to come across as something other than a clumsy oaf," Cynthia said emphatically.

"Norman the Nerd," Bautista said.

"I've never heard that, Luis," Frost said.

"Then you haven't been around the police much. It's his nickname in the Department."

"It's a shame," Cynthia added. "He's really a pretty good Mayor, but he must make the outside world think this is a city of shoe clerks."

"I shouldn't tell you this, but his bodyguard said he really didn't want to come tonight," Bautista said.

"Hizzoner told him it would just be a bunch of rich women and their fag gigolos."

"The nerve!" Cynthia exploded. "Imagine the Mayor of this City talking like that!"

"Besides, I believe they are now called walkers, not gigolos," Frost observed.

"Reuben, sometimes you're as bad as the Mayor," Cynthia shot back. "The nice thing about the ballet is nobody gives a damn about people's sexuality, on either side of the footlights. The audience is filled with plenty of perfectly normal people, a lot of them kids, and we really don't need Norman's stupid social observations."

"Well, it's over, anyway," Frost said. "Clifton has been suitably memorialized. Now all we have to do is find out who paid for his murder. How are we going to do that, Luis?"

The detective shook his head. "I'm going to put Francisca in charge," he said, taking his date's hand.

"No! No!" Francisca answered. "None of your cop stuff for me! I've got better things to do than that." She squeezed Bautista's hand as she talked. He disengaged it and turned serious as he spoke to the others.

"We're working to get a break as soon as possible. God knows how long it will be before word gets around that Wilson was a hired killer. Rumors like that have a way of spreading and then showing up in print. But let's hope we've got a little time before the perpetrator knows the secret is out. Our biggest hope is that we can trace the money; we should know about that tomorrow. Then, if we hit the daily double, we'll find a record of the cash transfer that incriminates someone. We're also checking each entry in Wilson's little black book, trying to find a link not just to a dope sale but to the murder. But tonight, I got interested in two people.

"First is that Maywood woman. She's one determined lady," Bautista went on. "It may not make her a murderess, but the way she tried to get the Mayor's attention backstage—*that* was real determination."

"You noticed that, Luis?" Cynthia said. "You're very observant." She described for Reuben and Francisca Maywood's gymnastic bid for attention in front of the Mayor.

"As I say," Bautista said, "it doesn't make her a murderess, but seeing her operate, I'd sure hate to cross her."

"You really are shrewd," Cynthia said. "Veronica is the most delicate woman imaginable on stage. And about as tough as they come off it. You must understand, Luis, that all ballerinas, if they're any good, are tough, willful and demanding. But Veronica Maywood has always been right up at the top of the list in those categories."

"You said you had two ideas," Frost interjected.

"Yeah. The other one is that Turnbull woman. All you tell me about her, Reuben, intrigues me. But was she mad enough to hire Wilson? I want to know more about her. For instance, what was she like up in Syracuse? How did she behave up there? I may just go upstate and do some checking around."

"Yes, it might be worth it," Frost said. "Besides, you'll love Syracuse."

"I'm sure," Bautista said glumly. "In and out real fast is what I have in mind."

"There are only two things you need to know about Syracuse," Frost said. "You're too young for this to have much meaning, but Syracuse was the largest city in the United States to vote for Alf Landon in 1936."

Bautista looked puzzled, so Frost explained further. "That was the year Franklin Roosevelt won every state except Maine. There were damn few cities anywhere that voted for Landon, but just remember Syracuse was the biggest one."

"Okay, what's the second thing I need to know?"

"Some years ago, a fellow tried to start a first-rate jazz club up there—real stars, real musicians. But the place went broke inside of a year. The local paper, the *Herald* as I recall, interviewed him and asked what went wrong. 'I learned my lesson,' he said. 'If I put on the *Last Supper* in my club with the original cast, these cheap bastards in Syracuse wouldn't pay a fifty-cent cover charge to see it.' "

"You sure make it sound attractive," Bautista said, laughing. "No wonder Mrs. Turnbull wanted to get out of there."

"I wish you luck," Frost said. "As I told you the other night, I'm off to Portland, Oregon, tomorrow and will be back Thursday. When will you go upstate?"

"Probably Thursday."

Realizing that Frost had a morning flight, Luis and Francisca got up to leave. As they did so, Frost said to Bautista, "Let's talk Thursday night to see what's new. Though I can't imagine I'll have any news after my day in Portland."

15

WEDNESDAY MORNING, FROST HAILED A CAB IN FRONT of his house to take him to LaGuardia Airport and the ten-fifteen United flight to Portland. On the way he noted with satisfaction that the *Times* gave full coverage to the NatBallet performance in honor of Clifton Holt, including liberal quotations from Cynthia's remarks. Her speech really had been very gracious and he was pleased to see it accurately quoted.

At LaGuardia, he proceeded directly to the gate, as he carried only a small overnight bag for his brief trip. It was all rather silly, he thought—traveling almost across the country to have a meeting with Earle Ambler. All to discuss corporate maneuvers that he was sure had little relevance to Ambler's broadcasting company.

But inconvenient as the trip was, Frost was not entirely ungrateful for the chance to get away from the investigation of Holt's murder. Besides, Ambler had been a good client and if now, as a lonely widower (his wife Sarah having died two years earlier), he wanted to have Frost keep him company, Frost couldn't complain too much.

There was a short wait at the gate until Frost was issued his first-class boarding pass. (He knew the first-class fare probably violated Chase & Ward's guidelines, which said that travel should be in accordance with the client's policies. Knowing how close Ambler was with his money, and how tightly he operated Ambler Broadcasting Company, he suspected Ambler policy might well be to travel by Greyhound bus. Frost had never actually bothered to ask what Ambler's travel rules were. At his age, if he was going to make a transcontinental overnight trip, he was going first class, thank you. The new business class, or whatever they called it, probably would have done nicely, but too bad. He had always traveled first class before, and Ambler had never made a fuss when the disbursement showed up on the Chase & Ward bill.)

The Boeing 727 was not crowded, and Frost had a window seat with an empty aisle seat beside him, for which he was grateful. The plane left the gate on time, and there was no delay in leaving the ground. Almost instantly the rather bookish-looking young stewardess came around offering drinks.

Frost was always taken aback at the prospect of drinking in the morning and refused the woman's offer. He asked instead for a plain tomato juice and was told he would have to settle for something called "Snappy Tom," which he knew from past experience was a thoroughly vile concoction purveyed by the airlines as a base for Bloody Marys.

"It's very good," the stewardess said.

"No, it isn't," Frost snapped. "Give me a Perrier."

"Will club soda do?"

"I suppose so," he replied grumpily.

Several of those around him did not share his compunction about morning drinking, and dipped eagerly into the bourbon and Scotch. Why did they do it? Were they trying to drink up their fares? Or were they simply incapable of saying "no" when a drink was offered, whatever the hour? He had never known how to explain the phenomenon.

Frost drank his soda water gloomily. He regretted again that he had not had a chance to talk to the M&A experts in his office before this trip, but he was confident, as he had been on Monday, that he could field the expected barrage of Ambler's questions. He was sure that Ambler was seeking "country-club" advice, the term Frost had once invented for legal advice that was probably not going to be used in a client's business, but would stand the recipient in good stead at his country club when talking with other captains of industry.

A decade earlier, country-club advice had centered on "going public." Ambler Broadcasting, after much agonizing on Earle Ambler's part, had done so in the 1960s, selling off forty percent of its common stock to public shareholders, though leaving Earle Ambler firmly in control. But the subject had been discussed incessantly before the decision had been made and Frost knew that Ambler talked over going public with other prosperous company owners at his golf club and, indeed, had heard him do so on more than one occasion.

Now, Frost was sure, the subject would be "going private"—getting rid of the Ambler public shareholders by some sort of buy-out, or perhaps by a sale of the whole company. This was the craze of the 1980s —the investment bankers' way of earning fees (shared to a lesser extent by lawyers) now that every business except the corner hash house had "gone public"—and Frost was sure Ambler wanted to be up-to-date. As a result of Frost's brief trip, Ambler would be able to pepper his nineteenth-hole conversations at the Oswego Lake Country Club with references to "my lawyers in New York think" or "Chase & Ward thinks" when the subject of "going private" came up.

Frost's thoughts were interrupted by the arrival of lunch—a dark brown lump of steak with mysterious gravy, underdone sliced potatoes and overcooked carrots. He found eating steak before noon almost as repellent as having a drink, but he picked at the plate put before him, while declining the proffered California red wine.

At the end of the meal, the stewardess brought coffee with what she chose to call "cream." Frost was ready. Always loyal to his roots in the dairy country of Upstate New York, he knew at a glance that the little vial of "nondairy creamer" had almost every ingredient known to man except any that had ever been near a cow. Besides, he was convinced that oily dairy substitutes were bad for his stomach.

"Could I have some regular milk, please?" he asked. The stewardess smiled tightly—he had interrupted the flow of the coffee-serving routine—but brought him the milk he had requested when she finished her coffee rounds. (In times past, Frost had sometimes explicitly pointed out that the dairy substitute being served was *not* milk, let alone "cream." But this had on occasion led to his being treated like an unwelcome vacuum-cleaner salesman, or at least being subjected to a pained expression on the flight attendant's face that had "crank" written all over it. The compromise was to ask, as he had done, for milk, hoping that the message of the downtrodden dairy farmer would get through nonetheless.)

Lunch over, Frost napped until the plane landed in Denver. There was to be an hour's wait, so he left the plane to stretch his legs in the airport. He had no wish to buy anything, but looked over the "native handicrafts" in the gift shop. His short foray proved his theory that the telltale sign that one had left New York was the hats of the men. Clothing and accessories in airports, in New York or anywhere else, were not that different—lots of blue jeans, bright-colored composition slacks on most of the women (usually the ones with the broadest bottoms, too), backpacks—but men's hats were. Once one saw big Stetsons with bands of feathers, one knew that he was west of the Hudson River (maybe only as far as Albany or Harrisburg, but definitely west).

Once Frost had reboarded the plane, he declined United's kind invitation to have a second lunch. Although the hop from Denver to Portland was short, he napped once again, awakening only when the seat-belt announcement was made as the plane approached the Rose City.

Frost took a cab directly to the Ambler Broadcasting offices on Broadway, hearing a detailed recital from the driver as they went about the severity of the recently ended winter. But the ride was pleasant enough, since the driver spoke English, knew where he was going, did not play the radio and drove a car that might even have been cleaned recently (all signs, Frost thought, just like the feathered Stetsons, that one had left New York).

It was now three-thirty local time, and Frost knew Ambler was expecting him. The friendly receptionist confirmed this—she recognized Frost from earlier visits and greeted him warmly—and told him to go straight in to Ambler's office.

"Reuben! Good to see you. You must have been

right on time," Ambler said by way of welcome. He got up from behind his desk and shook hands with enthusiasm. He was a stocky, ruddy man about a head shorter than Frost and dressed, as he usually was in the office, in a blue blazer and gray flannel slacks (no three-piece banker's uniform here). "Your flight okay?"

"Fine, except they wanted to feed me too much—and to start me drinking at dawn," Frost replied.

"I know, I know. But that's how they keep you strapped in and not making trouble."

"I suppose."

"Put your bag and coat over there," Ambler said. "I thought we could talk for a while; then we'll take you over to the Benson. Are you free for dinner, by the way?"

"Of course."

"Good. I've made a reservation at the Couch Street Fish House. We've been there before."

"Yes. I remember it well."

"Is that okay? Maybe you'd like something fancier. Or Prima Donna, perhaps." Ambler guffawed.

"Prima Donna?"

"A good, noisy jazz joint over by the University. Very popular. But I don't think it's for two old geezers like us."

"It doesn't sound it."

"How about some coffee, Reuben? Or a soda? We'll save the serious drinking for later."

"Thanks, Earle, coffee would be fine."

Ambler went to the door and asked his secretary to bring coffee. She did—and it came with a small pitcher of real cream.

"So what kind of trouble are you in, Earle?" Frost asked after the secretary had left.

Ambler guffawed again. "No trouble, Reuben. No

trouble at all. I just need some advice on a couple of things, and besides I wanted to see you. How's Cynthia, by the way?"

"She's just fine, thanks. She sends her love."

"Good. Wonderful wife you've got there, Reuben. Hold on to her."

"I do my best," Frost said, smiling.

"How old are you, Reuben?" Ambler asked, changing the subject. "Seventy-three?"

"Seventy-five, I'm afraid."

"You look good for such an old fellow, you know."

"Thanks, Earle. You don't do so badly yourself."

"Well, I'm a mere kid compared to you—seventy-two. And that's really why I wanted to see you. I've got to get my affairs in order so that this outfit isn't a complete wreck when I die. Got to take care of ABC." (Ambler had always facetiously called his Company "ABC"; it was not as large or as well known as American Broadcasting but was, for its size, even more profitable.)

"It doesn't look like that's about to happen," Frost said.

"I hope you're right. I love this business and I'm going to keep going as long as I've got my health and my marbles. That reminds me: there's an old fellow I see over at the Club—eighty-eight if he's a day, and still running his chain of department stores. Still the chief executive officer. He's been talking about dying for years—'When I die, when I die,' he's always saying. But he's still the CEO, and recently he's changed it—he now says '*If* I die, *if* I die.' Silly old fool, he's going to be six feet under just like the rest of us, but he thinks he'll live forever!"

"I know the type. And I hope I never get like that," Frost said.

"Me too," Ambler replied. "Anyway, everybody's got a lot of ideas about what I should do. I've got scarcely any family, you know. No children and now no wife. Just a sister and two nieces and two nephews. They're all very nice, and very nice to me. But none of them's interested in running this business. My sister, the mother of the other four, moved to California when she got married years ago and they all live there. I don't think any of 'em would want to move back to Portland now.

"The result of all this," the old man went on, "is that I've got one investment banker after another in here with all kinds of schemes for ABC. There must be one of them here once a week at least. From all over the country. And one crazier than the next."

"What do they think you should be doing?"

"Some of them want to find a buyer. They say that all the media giants would be delighted to buy ABC and then break it up. Sell off some of the stations and a lot of the cable TV operations. They say I could get a good price—well in excess of the current stock price. But I don't want to do that. I want to stay here and run what I've built. At least for a few more years."

"How many properties do you have now?" Frost asked.

"Well, there're the six television stations—you know all about them—and, let's see, eight radio: four AM and four FM. In cable, we've expanded a lot. We're now in twenty towns, some pretty big, others fairly small, but with about sixty thousand subscribers in all."

"That's a big increase."

"You're right. All in the last three years. And the going price to sell seems to be about fifteen hundred bucks for each subscriber. That's ninety million total for the whole cable operation. Not bad, heh?"

"Not bad at all," Frost replied. "What's your investment in cable?"

"Not much. Eighteen, twenty million tops. The thing's a money machine. Once you hook a town up, all you've got to do is get a girl to send out the bills and to cart the money to the bank when it comes in. It's even better than practicing law."

"Many things are, Earle."

"Anyway, I'm not going to sell the cable, or anything else."

"What other ideas do your banker friends have?" Frost asked.

"Oh, plenty. The one they all seem to be crazed about is a leveraged buy-out—'LBO,' isn't that what they call it? Get my managers and officers to buy out the public shares, and pick up part of mine. And, of course, the investment-banking boys—and girls, I might add—suggesting this usually want to buy a piece of the action themselves."

"At a special cheap price, I bet."

"Always," Ambler replied.

The two old men launched into a serious discussion of an LBO for ABC. How many employees would be involved? Could they ever hope to borrow the money? And if they did, was there any prospect that the company, however profitable it might be, could generate enough income to pay the loans back?

Then there was the question of Ambler himself. Would he stay on, or retire? Or gracefully and gradually remove himself from running things? He said he would only stay on long enough to effect an orderly transition, but Frost had his doubts.

The conversation went on for better than an hour

but ended, just as Frost had predicted, without any resolution as to Ambler's future, or his company's.

"One of these days—and very soon—I'm going to make up my mind what to do," Ambler said. "Then I'll need your help. Have you got people who can do these things?"

"Oh, yes. Many. In your case, matters are not too complicated. I think my young partner—former partner —Peter Denny would be good. I don't believe you've met him. And Keith Merritt, whom you do know, could do the tax work."

"Fine. I'll let you know as soon as I decide anything," Ambler said. "Now, you must be tired, so why don't I have one of the boys run you over to the hotel? I'll pick you up there about quarter of seven in the lobby. Our reservation's for seven. All right?"

"Fine, Earle. I look forward to it."

Frost took a nap after checking into the Benson. Fortunately, he remembered to leave a call, so he was awakened at six-fifteen, in time to prepare for Ambler's arrival. His client appeared in the ornate Benson lobby promptly at six-forty-five.

"Have a nap?" Ambler asked.

"Yes, I did," Frost replied, somewhat defensively. It was clear that Ambler had come directly from his office—or at least, he had not shaved. Was he now patronizing Frost, three years his senior? Frost chose to think not.

"Come on, my car's outside," Ambler said. They got in, and Ambler deftly maneuvered his Buick through the early-evening traffic. Frost was admiring; he had never learned to drive properly and felt that, behind the wheel, he would either kill or be killed.

The restaurant was not far away, and Frost and

Ambler soon were seated in a comfortable and relatively private corner table in the Couch Street Fish House.

"Martini, Reuben?" Ambler asked.

"If you insist," Frost answered.

"I'll have one too," Ambler said to the waiter.

"You know, Reuben," Ambler said, as they drank their cocktails, "fifty years ago I never thought I'd be sitting around with a high-powered—and high-priced—Wall Street lawyer talking about LBOs. I started out with one asset—one radio-broadcasting license—a few hundred dollars' worth of junk broadcasting equipment and a two-year lease on a two-room studio. The bank owned me, and we were a staff of two, Sarah and me. We did everything—sold ads, read the news, you name it. And then, like every other broadcaster, we got lucky. The station made good, and we kept buying more of them. Television came, and we were ready. Then cable. And now a corporation worth four hundred million. Not bad, would you say?"

"No."

"And a big public company. Listed on the New York Stock Exchange, with lots of widows and orphans doing very nicely with our stock."

"Lots of widows and orphans," Frost said, "but you were smart enough to keep control."

"Yes—and am I glad. If I didn't own sixty percent of the stock, I'd have even more investment bankers hanging around, telling me how to keep ABC from getting gobbled up."

"Indeed. I sometimes think that's become a full-time job for a lot of corporate executives. Trying to protect themselves from being taken over, instead of figuring out how to compete with the Japanese," Frost said.

"I know. I see it here. I'm on the board of an outfit here in town that spends all its time adopting gimmicks—'poison pills,' staggered terms for directors, loan agreements that go in default if control of the company changes. Endless. But a five-year research plan? Or even a sales plan? Forget it. Worry about the raider, who's probably never going to materialize anyway."

The waiter returned to take their order. Frost knew that Ambler would urge the salmon on him—which he did. But that was all right. Pacific Northwest salmon was delicious, and the restaurant prepared it very simply (no goat cheese).

"What do you want first, Reuben?" Ambler asked.

"I'm going to pass. Don't want to eat too much," Frost replied.

Ambler seemed disappointed, but did not order a first course himself. He did ask for the wine list.

"Reuben, I've got two choices about the wine. I can be a good local booster and offer you one of our local vintages—wine's big business up here these days. Or we can have a modest, overly priced Pouilly-Fuissé."

"The latter," Frost said.

"I knew it. But please bear in mind that we now have some pretty darn good local wines here."

Frost kept cagily silent as Ambler ordered the Pouilly-Fuissé.

"One thing I'm curious about, Earle," Frost asked, as they waited for their fish. "You've made a helluva lot of money. What are you going to do with it?"

"Well, one thing, I'm giving a big fund to the University of Oregon. That's where I went, you know. I was on full scholarship, and I'm going to pay them back. Sarah and I started a scholarship fund there some years ago, and I'm going to add to it. Then—this will knock you off your chair, Reuben—I'm giving some to Columbia and your alma mater, Princeton."

"Princeton? How come?" Frost asked incredulously.

"Well, we're such a big and fashionable company now, we recruit our people nationwide. And the very best people we've gotten have been from Princeton— what do they call it? the Woodrow Wilson School? —and the journalism school and the business school at Columbia. So I want to reward them."

"That's wonderful, Earle. Very generous. On behalf of Princeton, I thank you in advance," Frost said.

"Then there's the local art museum. Handsome place, and they do the best they can with what they've got. But what they've got is a miscellaneous collection of things left when people died. Everything from kayaks to Tiffany glass. Pathetic. I'm going to set up a modern-art fund—a *real* modern-art fund—so that we don't have to be ashamed any longer. I mean, it won't be like the Getty money, or anything like that, but it will be substantial."

The two men argued about modern art and which painters they liked—and disliked—as their dinner was served. They were in surprising agreement, though Frost had reservations about Jennifer Bartlett, for whom Ambler expressed great admiration.

"Maybe you could have her do one of her boat scenes with one of those surplus kayaks you've got at your museum," Frost said.

"Now, Reuben, don't be provincial. She's a fine artist. I'll probably be dead before the museum buys one, but I'm sure they will."

"This salmon is excellent, as always," Frost said.

"Good; I'm glad you like it. There's nothing as good anywhere else."

Both men finished their salmon and declined dessert. Frost glanced at his watch; it was well before nine.

"How about a brandy with your coffee?" Ambler asked.

"Fine."

"That we do not make locally. Have to go all the way to France for it."

"Good."

The two men sipped their brandy slowly when it was served. Both were quiet and reflective, when suddenly Ambler came to life once again.

"Oh, say, Reuben, there's something I wanted to tell you that I almost forgot," Ambler said.

"Yes?"

"You're still involved with Cynthia's ballet company, aren't you?"

"Yes, indeed."

"Good. That's how I first met Cynthia, you know, when she was here on tour."

"I know. And chased after her until she married me."

"Not quite—until I married Sarah."

"Be that as it may. The answer is, I'm still involved with NatBallet."

"My story is kind of complicated. You've heard of the Pacific Northwest Ballet?"

"Yes," Frost said. "I've heard good things about it. And Cynthia has said good things too."

"Well, anyway, they had a big benefit performance here a week ago, week ago Monday. One of my widow friends asked me to go—performance, big black-tie dinner dance afterwards, all that. So I did. And one of the people on the program was one of your dancers, appearing as a guest. Fellow named Gerald Hazard. Redhead."

"Yes. He's a very good dancer. One of our best," Frost said. "He's never been promoted to principal, but lots of us think he should be."

"He did that Tchaikovsky thing—the *pas de deux*—with one of the Pacific Northwest girls."

"That's their big number on tour," Frost said. "Short and showy."

"Right. Well, to get to the point, I went to this big party afterwards. A real dance crowd, and a lot of them were talking about your choreographer, the fellow who got murdered."

"Clifton Holt."

"Right. It had been on the news that night, and most everybody there either knew him or knew of him."

"Yes?"

"Anyway, your Mr. Hazard had not heard about it, and when he was told, he behaved in a very odd way."

"What did he do?"

"He got roaring drunk. Not out of grief, mind you, but seemingly out of unbounded joy. I've never seen anybody dance on someone's grave the way he did."

"Oh, dear. Did he say anything?"

"No, he just got exuberantly plastered. Didn't say anything bad, didn't say anything good. But he sure as hell seemed happy. Everybody was a little upset. Didn't know what to make of it."

"I'm sorry. I don't know what to make of it either," Frost said. He was lying. Ambler's news was most disturbing. God knows everyone connected with Nat-Ballet knew that Hazard was discontented with Holt, impatient at not being promoted, worried about supporting his wife and two children. But this kind of reaction—did it not betray a deeper hatred, a hatred Hazard could flaunt unobserved in a city so far from

New York? A hatred deep enough to result in a murder for hire?

Frost was suddenly weary. It had been a long day, complicated by a three-hour time loss. And now this, an unneeded twist to the riddle of Holt's murder.

"Earle, this meal was delicious," Frost said to his host. "But I'm afraid I'm getting tired."

"I understand. Sure you won't have another brandy?"

"No, I couldn't."

"Then I guess we should call it a night. Unless you want to go over to the Prima Donna," Ambler said, laughing.

"Next time. Next time when I bring out my troops to do your LBO."

Ambler paid the check and drove Frost back to the hotel.

"I hope you sleep well," he said.

"I will," Frost answered.

"I guess we've tired the sun with talking," Ambler said.

"Callimachus," Frost replied.

"Right," Ambler agreed.

"We certainly tried, Earle. Good night."

16

CYNTHIA FROST LEFT HOME MINUTES AFTER REUBEN'S departure for the airport. She looked forward to a calm day, after the inevitable tension involved in Clifton Holt's memorial. She was off to class, but then anticipated a quiet afternoon and a low-key evening with Arne Petersen, attending a private screening of *Glory Days,* the new movie starring Petersen's girlfriend, Vivian Brooks.

As her taxi inched its way through the traffic on Central Park South, she thought again, as she had constantly over the last ten days, of Holt's murder. At first her thoughts had been conflicted—shock at the sordid death of her long-time colleague yet, at the same time, guilt because she did not feel any overwhelming grief. She felt herself ungenerous for not sifting out her memories so that only the good ones remained—the recollections of their triumphs together in forming and building NatBallet. But the other memories, of an often quixotic and mean man, of his sexual excesses and his cruelty to wife and dancers alike, persisted and would not go away.

Then the focus had changed, with Bautista's shocking announcement that the murder had not been what it seemed. Her thoughts had been obsessed since then with identifying the true murderer, the one who had used Jimmy Wilson as a pawn. Bautista had said that it was inevitable that the press would find out the true circumstances of Holt's murder. When that happened, all hell would surely erupt within the NatBallet family. Suspicion would be rampant, morale would sink and the Company would be distracted—perhaps fatally— from its basic mission of performing with excellence.

Cynthia reviewed the possible suspects in her mind, discouraged to realize that they did not constitute a complete list, the number of Holt's enemies being as vast as it was. Perhaps there was some jilted lover of Holt's out there with nothing to do with NatBallet. Or a disgruntled dancer who had failed to get into the Company. Or an old enemy from Hollywood. But more than likely the NatBallet family was involved. All the people the Frosts had discussed with Bautista had been more or less from the family, other than Arthur Mattison. In a way she wished he were the guilty one, not because of his antipathy to the Brigham Foundation, she told herself, but because he was the most remote from the Company. But as much as she wished to believe it—God knows he had the motive—her instincts told her sadly that someone closer to NatBallet, someone more directly and openly hurt by Holt's nastiness, was more likely.

Who? She could not (or would not) speculate. But she had resolved to observe things as sharply as she could when around the Zacklin. (She liked Luis Bautista very much; he seemed very competent as a detective and he certainly had become a good friend. But she didn't think his money-tracing scheme sounded very promising, especially since nothing had happened in the days since Bautista had been on the case. And as for Reuben, he now fancied himself a great detective after he and Bautista had cracked the Graham Donovan murder together. But for all his good sense and shrewdness, could he be expected to come up with the solution? Maybe the two of them would do it again; but a third pair of eyes and ears certainly wouldn't hurt, even though the night before they had acted as if they regarded tracking down Holt's murderer as men's work.)

This was Cynthia's frame of mind as she entered the main rehearsal studio at the Zacklin. Veronica Maywood was conducting the day's class. This had happened occasionally in the past, but more frequently in recent months. It was most unusual for a leading ballerina to conduct class; even more unusual for one to want to, as she apparently did. Cynthia had been surprised at Veronica's interest in teaching; she decided that she must find out what had prompted it.

Cynthia did not fault Maywood as a teacher. She was quite good, and put her subjects through a grueling regimen. And Cynthia, while she often prudently "marked" the more difficult passages when others ran the class, now found herself straining to execute each new command Maywood called out. Did competition among ballerinas never end, even for one as long retired as Cynthia?

By the end of the hour, Cynthia was short of breath. As she stood leaning on the barre, she spoke to Maywood as she passed by.

"That was quite a session, Veronica," she said.

"But you did splendidly, Cynthia," the ballerina answered. "I watched you through the whole class—"

"—I know—"

"—and you were amazing. Perhaps you should come out of retirement."

Cynthia only laughed at such an absurd idea. Then she had an inspiration. Why not ask Veronica Maywood, leading ballerina and possible felon, to lunch? Maywood seemed surprised at the invitation, but accepted without hesitation.

"I usually don't, you know. I mostly have Fritos and Pepsi, like the kids. Keeps the weight down. But as it happens, I don't have any rehearsals this afternoon, so why not?"

The two women reassembled at the stage door, dressed in street clothes and carrying their dance bags. (If "street clothes" could be said to characterize Veronica Maywood's outfit. Glorious and elegant on stage, her shimmering beauty a pleasure to see, she now did all she could to conceal that beauty. She was wearing a revoltingly gaudy sweat shirt that read "Mykonos" and tight slacks one would be more likely to see on a woman soliciting afternoon tricks a few blocks from the Zacklin.)

"That's quite a shirt," Cynthia said. "Have you been to Mykonos?"

"No, I haven't. I hope you're not offended. One of the boys in the corps gave it to me. It's a popular vacation spot with some of them."

"I'm sure it is," Cynthia said. "Offended? Not at all. It's . . . very colorful. Where shall we go?"

"Luigi's?"

"Fine."

Luigi's was a theatre-district bar with passable food. The charm was not in the food, however, but—assuming there was any charm at all—in Luigi himself, a confirmed show-biz addict who treated any entertainer, famous or not, as a valued customer, as did the young unemployed actors and dancers who waited on table there.

The two women walked the three blocks to the restaurant and were greeted on arrival by Luigi himself.

"Ah! La prima ballerina assoluta! E l'altra prima ballerina assoluta!" the restaurateur called out, noisily kissing both women on both cheeks. Although as American as Cynthia, he persisted in speaking fractured Italian, perhaps thereby creating an Italianate ambience that would not otherwise be divined from the humdrum decor of his restaurant.

"Oh, Luigi, cut it out," Cynthia said. "You know very well there can only be one *prima ballerina assoluta* at a time, and you'll make us both very angry if you suggest there can be two."

"Ah, *signore, belle signore,* let an old man indulge his whims! In my restaurant there can be two."

He showed them to a quiet table in the back, strewing compliments as he went.

Cynthia ordered a Campari and soda, Veronica a Bloody Mary.

"This is a *real* rarity for me, having a drink at lunch," Veronica said, as she lit a cigarette. "I don't usually break training this way."

"How about the smoking?" Cynthia said, with a slight air of disapproval. (She knew that many dancers smoked heavily, although she never had. The reason always given was that it cut down on appetite, but she had always thought the real motivation was that a dancer, restricted by the rigors of training and performance, had to show defiance in some way, and smoking was as good as any. It was much like otherwise model adolescents who brandish cigarettes in front of their parents.)

"I've tried to stop, Cynthia, I really have. But I love it too much. My addictive personality, I guess."

"Well, you're not the first dancer to do it, and certainly not the last. So I won't lecture you."

"Thank God. What are you going to have?"

Cynthia ordered a low-calorie hamburger (no roll, no French fries) and Veronica a chef's salad.

"I'm surprised restaurants put up with the likes of us," Veronica said. "They certainly don't make money off us."

"Don't be silly. Luigi is delighted to have us. And at six ninety-five for a hamburger he won't exactly starve."

The two women laughed and continued drinking.

"I thought you were splendid in *Requiem* last night," Cynthia said.

"Thank you. I wasn't sure I could get through it. My head was absolutely dizzy."

"Why?"

"Thinking about Clifton," she replied. "My thoughts are so complicated about that man I can't tell you."

"I'm sure they are. I think everyone's are."

"Did you ever love and hate a man at the same time?"

"No, I don't think I ever did," Cynthia answered. "But I think I can understand the feeling."

"It's happened to me twice. Certainly I felt about Clifton that way. On the one hand, he took me to the heights—all those beautiful ballets he made on me. That part was wonderful, and I loved him for it. But then there were the personal things. He was unspeakably cruel—ridiculing any idea you might have had, alternating between wild affection and cold avoidance. I never could love him for that."

"You two were very close at one time," Cynthia said noncommittally.

"Oh, yes. We were going to be married! He moved out on Teresa and moved in with me. Years ago now. He was going to get divorced and marry me. I was young and stupid and didn't know any better. And what could be greater for a ballerina than to be Mrs. Clifton Holt? To have the great American choreographer at work and in bed as well?" The ballerina paused to dig into her chef's salad.

"I can understand that," Cynthia said. "Clifton was a most compelling man back in those days."

"Then he changed his mind and left me. That hurt a lot, and his flaming around with every pretty-boy in sight hurt more. But we still worked together, he still did wonderful things for me, and I got over the hurt. If I couldn't have all of Clifton, at least I had the professional side almost to myself. Until . . . until he decided that Laura Russell was as good a dancer as I was."

"Did he ever say that?"

"All the time, constantly. Starting about six months ago. He made it a point to tell me how good he thought she was. It was clear I was losing the professional part of Clifton too. So we ended up with that awful scene just before he died. You certainly heard about that?"

"Yes," Cynthia said.

"I had had it," Veronica went on. "Clifton was being awful, and he was doing a new ballet that would make Laura look better than I did. My strong point is not that herky-jerky stuff that was required for *Chávez Concerto*. But it is Laura's. She looks like a drum majorette when she does it, but Clifton didn't think so."

"I'm just as glad the ballet will never be done. I never thought it showed any promise at all," Cynthia said.

"It didn't. But Clifton didn't care. He didn't care if it was a failure—as long as I failed with it."

"I'd like to think you're wrong, but I'm not sure I

can," Cynthia said. "But he let you conduct class," she added.

"Oh, yes. He kept telling me what a wonderful teacher I would be, as if he were pushing me right off the stage into the classroom."

"You've been leading the class a lot."

"Well, he did make me think. In my own mind, I see myself dancing forever. I know that's not realistic, but certainly I've got another ten years. But what then? Or what if I get injured? I've got to have something, and the ballet is all I know. Oh, sure, I learned how to milk cows as a little girl in Canada—I really did—but I sure as hell don't want to go back to that. Besides, they have milking machines now."

Veronica, finished with her salad, lit another cigarette. "I'll be a good teacher someday, I know it," she said, exhaling.

"You do very well right now, even though I'm still feeling the effects of this morning," Cynthia replied.

"Look, I admire you for taking class at all. I'm sure you'll be all right after a cup of coffee."

"Good idea. Oh, oh, here comes the *padrone*," Cynthia warned.

Luigi appeared at the table. "And what can I offer you beautiful ladies for dessert? Rum cake? Zabaglione?" he asked.

"Luigi, you silly old man," Cynthia said. "Tempting us like that. I just want an *espresso doppio*."

"*Subito, signora*. But you are missing a great treat. The rum cake is delicious."

"When I retire," Cynthia said. Then, gently, she asked Veronica about the second man with whom the young ballerina had had a love-hate relationship.

"Oh, God, Cynthia, it's so awful I don't want to talk about it," Veronica said.

"Something recent?" Cynthia pressed, gently.

"Yes. Very. But it's over."

"A dancer?"

"No. A man from another world—could have been from another planet. But you don't really want to hear about it."

"I'll be happy to listen, if it will be any help," Cynthia responded.

"I've never talked to anyone about him. I don't really have any close friends in the Company—*personal* friends, I mean—so no one knows about him. He was a very well-kept secret."

"What was his name?" Cynthia asked.

"Oh, God. Bernard Reyman. A stockbroker, of all things. Or investment banker, or whatever they call themselves. A partner in something called Hughes & Company. He started writing me notes about eighteen months ago. Saying how much he loved this or that performance, and how much he wanted to meet me. I didn't answer them for a while, then wrote him notes back saying no. Then I decided, what did I have to lose? He wanted to meet me like any other fan. So I agreed. Agreed to meet him after a performance and have supper."

"And?"

"We did. We had supper, all right, and went straight from there to bed. On the first date. He was gorgeous, Cynthia, absolutely gorgeous. Big, strong and handsome. A blond god, with the most wonderful icy blue eyes you ever saw. And he knew about all the things I'm totally ignorant of—business, politics, sports. And he made a million dollars a year."

"He told you that?"

"He told me that, and one night, after we'd been going together awhile, he showed me a copy of his income tax return. Can you imagine?" Maywood giggled.

"Sounds like a prize catch to me," Cynthia said.

"He was. For someone like me, who could go for months without talking to anyone except about the ballet, or without seeing anyone outside the Company, it was wonderful. We met all the time. Went to Europe together during the summer break—Venice, Rome, London, everywhere. It was a fantastic time."

"It sounds it," Cynthia said.

"I deliberately kept him away from the Company. I didn't need a Laura Russell or her kind stealing him away. And I didn't want the gossip columns to get wind of it. We were going to be married, and I didn't want to take any chances on competition or publicity. But then it all fell apart."

Maywood paused as the waiter—belatedly—cleared away the lunch dishes. Except for asking her companion, "How come?" Cynthia kept quiet.

"We'd been going together for six months. I guess I was so in love I didn't notice what was happening. Little mood changes. Paranoia every so often, that I took for jealousy of me as a ballerina. Then I discovered he was taking heroin. We had done coke a few times, but always on holiday, never during the season—I have seen enough nose problems with dancers that I wouldn't do that. But this was steady and constant. And heavy."

"Did you try to bring him out of it?"

"You bet I did. He said he'd try, and he did for a while. But he never would go to a clinic. I finally realized he wasn't serious, so I left him."

"I'm sorry. The dope thing really is awful, isn't it?" Cynthia said.

"Poison. Pure poison. A bloody damn curse on the unsuspecting."

"What happened to him, do you know?"

"Yes," Veronica said. She paused and wiped a tear from her eye. "After our quarrel I saw him a couple of times—he would show up and not go away unless I talked to him. Then, about two weeks ago, a friend from his office called. Bernard had died of an overdose. His firm hushed it up, of course, and there was nothing in the papers. But he died of an overdose."

"Awful. I'm very sorry, Veronica."

"Thank you, sweet Cynthia. It's been a pretty bad time for me."

"But you've kept on dancing and have been dancing marvelously."

"Thanks. I decided I'd better concentrate on what I know and forget about stockbroker millionaires."

Luigi once again broke into the conversation. "You ladies like an after-dinner drink?" he asked.

"No, Luigi. Besides, it's only lunch, not dinner," Cynthia said. "And you'd better bring us the check."

Cynthia insisted on paying, over Veronica's protests.

"Where are you headed?" Cynthia asked.

"Oh, I think I'll just take in a movie. It's a funny thing, you know. I was supposed to rehearse *Chávez Concerto* this afternoon. But now that the schedule's blank, I think I'll see my first movie in months."

"Well, I'm off to Saks myself," Cynthia said.

"Thanks for the lunch."

"My pleasure, Veronica. Be of good cheer."

The two women kissed and went their separate ways.

Cynthia Frost, once in Saks, took the escalator to the third floor. She needed time to digest all she had learned from Veronica Maywood. But she could think perfectly well looking at the designer summer dresses. There was nothing particular she had in mind buying; it was purely an impulse trip. Her instincts for an attractive new garment—be it a Saint Laurent linen suit, an Armani blouse or a Valentino summer evening dress—could function perfectly well as she sorted out what she had heard at Luigi's.

So Veronica Maywood was a coke user, she reflected, not believing for a minute the disclaimer about off-season use. She had known too many people who claimed to drink only at holiday time, or to smoke only after dinner, or to fornicate only when on the road, to believe that addictions could be channeled and neatly regulated. What did that prove? Maybe it worked in her favor. Maybe the famous scene at the last rehearsal of *Chávez Concerto* had been induced by coke. Or maybe coke—or worse, heroin—had fomented the madness in her that had led to Holt's murder? The discarded lover sounded like a bad lot, but as near as she could guess, his role, in his drug-induced state, would have been simply that of another negative goad propelling Veronica to desperate action.

"Can I help you, madame?" one of the Ruritanian saleswomen said to Cynthia, who was examining, with some hesitation, a bare-backed Ungaro evening dress.

"Is very beautiful, madame," the woman said.

Cynthia knew better than to ask the woman's advice; if a sale was in prospect, she and her kind would say anything to close it. She moved away from the backless dress and surveyed those beside it.

"Perhaps this would be more suitable," the saleswoman said, indicating a stark, black, full-throated horror. That did it; she would try the backless number, hoping that she could discreetly see whether the wrinkles of age were visible in the considerable areas it did not cover.

Cynthia tried on the dress and ignored the Mittel-European cluckings of the saleswoman as to its exquisite beauty on her slim dancer's figure. The mirror told her that it was all right, and she bought it. So much for the parody of widow's weeds that the saleswoman had tried to push on her. "More suitable" indeed.

With her new purchase in hand and her dance bag slung over her shoulder, Cynthia went out into Fiftieth Street, uncertain what to do next. Home, she thought. The walk would help the postclass stiffness in her right thigh. Walking up Madison Avenue, she encountered Teresa Holt, peering into the window of a jewelry store.

"Cynthia! I'm so glad to see you. I thought you were wonderful last night. Very appropriate remarks. Unlike the Mayor."

"You mean what I said about Clifford?" The two women laughed in mid-sidewalk. "I'm pleased that you're pleased," Cynthia went on. "It all went very well, I thought. Where are you going?"

"Oh, I'm just wandering around. Thinking of ways to spend my legacy, I guess. You know about that, surely?"

"Yes, Reuben told me. I'm glad the estate turned out all right."

"*You're* glad? Well, enough about that."

"Would you like to have a drink, or tea?" Cynthia asked. It was somewhat early for cocktails, but why not look over another candidate for arrest?

"Goodness, I don't know. Where could we go?"

"The St. Regis is right around the corner. They've absolutely ruined the King Cole Bar, but you still can get a drink there."

"You're on, Cynthia. What fun."

Teresa and Cynthia walked to the lobby entrance of the bar, where Cynthia was confronted by a stern headwaiter who insisted that she check her satchel of dance paraphernalia and Saks shopping bag.

When seated, she asked Teresa if she thought she would have had to check the shopping bag had she not also been saddled with her dance bag.

"I don't know," Teresa said.

"Well, I do," said Cynthia. "I'm sure you could come in here with enough shopping bags to rival Mrs. Santa Claus and they wouldn't say a thing. But carry a dance bag, and they somehow think you're going to spend the night. Society's discrimination against those artistically inclined."

"How is Reuben?" Teresa asked.

"He's off in Portland, Oregon, of all places. Off with one of his old clients. A lonely old dear who insists Reuben come out there to see him personally."

"Good heavens, I saw him last night at the theatre."

"He only left this morning. Back tomorrow."

"I see."

The women ordered daiquiris, both protesting that it was perhaps a bit early for such things, but . . .

"What are your plans, Teresa?" Cynthia asked.

"I don't know. I suppose I'll have to stay around here until the estate is settled. I must ask Reuben what's expected of me. Then I think I'll go back to California. I had a wonderful time there until this happened. An uninterrupted, very happy six weeks. San Francisco, or Sausalito, is not New York, but I have good friends there. The climate is fine, and the pace is fine. Reuben will be back tomorrow?"

"Yes. And I'm sure he'd be happy to talk to you," Cynthia answered.

"Cheers," Teresa said, holding up the stemmed glass the waiter had brought.

"Cheers to you, Teresa," said Cynthia, raising her own glass in reply.

"You know, Cynthia, I feel so odd about this inheritance business."

Cynthia did not comment, but only twisted her pearls and looked interested.

"I mean, here I am a widow, inheriting all this money from Clifton, yet our marriage ended years ago," Teresa went on.

"How long ago exactly, Teresa? I know that things were not good for a very long time, but just how long?"

"About seven months after we were married. When Clifton started seeing Doris White on the side."

"That was before Veronica?"

"Oh, yes. Amusing and jolly Doris White. ABT's great character ballerina, right? Not old enough to be Clifton's mother, but still old enough. He snuck off and had a fling with her while ABT was in Los Angeles. I was shocked, and we had a battle royal and he came back. Very penitent. Then there were all the other Hollywood stories. And then Veronica. But it all really had ended with Doris—cheap old tart turning Clifton's head."

"It must have been a trial. I've often wondered how I'd have reacted if Reuben had played around."

"A trial? Not really. After Doris, the marriage was over. Clifton Holt remained of interest to me for one reason and one reason only: he made regular deposits to my bank account. And even that was coming to an end."

"How do you mean?" Cynthia asked.

"For years, Cynthia, we had a deal—unstated, but nonetheless a deal. I kept quiet—no interviews, no speculating in public or private about Clifton's personal life, no flamboyant behavior to remind people that we were separated. In return, he supported me— not extravagantly, but certainly adequately. More than adequately, I suppose. Then last New Year's Day he called me. Told me I should enjoy the year ahead because it was the last one he was going to pick up the check for."

"Any reason given?"

"Clifton never gave reasons. No. He simply said I had a year to work things out before the money stopped."

"Did he ever talk about his will?"

"Oh, he mentioned that, all right. Said he was cutting me out completely. Going to use his money to start a foundation. I told him I didn't think he could do that, that I was sure I had some rights to the estate, or at least to a part of it. 'Not when I get through with you, you won't,' he told me. It was all so silly—who ever thought of Clifton dying? Talk about his will seemed very remote to me, but he did it all the time.

"I didn't know what he was thinking of," Teresa continued. "Was he going to get a divorce at last? Was he trying to provoke me into getting one? Or was he threatening me in some more ominous way? I couldn't tell. He sounded utterly mad. Mean and utterly mad."

"What did you do? Got a lawyer, I hope," Cynthia interjected.

"No, I just decided to wait and see what developed. Then went to Calfornia to try and forget it all."

Cynthia, intrigued by what she was hearing, had sipped continuously on her drink, which was now gone.

"Since we're violating the yardarm rule, shall we have another?" she asked Teresa.

"I suppose. No harm done."

The two sat in silence for a moment. Then Teresa

spoke again. "I'm so confused, Cynthia. I think of all the money I'm getting, then I think of all the hateful things Clifton did to me. But then in the next breath I'm figuring out ways to preserve his works and to perpetuate them. I've thought a lot about that these past few days."

"It's a worthy cause, Teresa, even if Clifton wasn't."

"You know, you take a ballet like *Summer Sonata*. One of the few great women's roles he did for someone other than Veronica. It's absolutely beautiful. And when that young Hailey Coles does it, it's absolute radiance."

"You're so right. It was one of his most magical creations. I think it's done all over the world now."

"So here I am. Ready to spend the money of the man who despised me. Still loving in some ways the man who made my life hell. Any advice, Cynthia?"

"I'm not very good at such advice, I'm afraid. If I were you, I'd take the money and run; let it make up for all the years he made you miserable. But remembering him, helping to preserve his body of work, that would be very noble and very generous."

"That's about where I'm coming out. Split right down the middle once again."

"I'm afraid I've got to go. I have a date tonight with Arne Petersen," Cynthia said.

"Good for you. He will carry things on the right way, won't he?"

"I think so."

"Let's hope. The bad things about Clifton have been killed. The good things must not die."

17

THE MOVIE CYNTHIA WAS SEEING THAT EVENING IN PRE-
view was *Glory Days*, the latest starring vehicle for
Vivian Brooks. A startlingly beautful and sexy redhead, Brooks had recently had a string of critical successes and was at the moment one of the most
sought-after actresses in the movie business. She was
also Arne Petersen's girlfriend.

She had first come to public attention for her sheer
beauty. No one really cared whether she could act; the
public was quite willing to buy tickets just to view her
beautiful body and face on the screen. She could have
made a long and successful career simply by displaying
herself, but she had wanted more than that. So, after
much persuasion, her studio had gingerly allowed her
to appear in roles of substance, where she revealed a
knack for sophisticated comedy not seen in Hollywood
since the 1930's.

Now advance word had it that, discontented again,
she had insisted on playing against type in *Glory Days*,
billed as an epic of the American frontier as filtered
through the 1980s sensibilities of Kris Housenman, a
hot young director whose "relevant" pictures had al-

ready made him, at the ripe age of thirty-two, a cult
figure in campus film societies around the country.

Vivian Brooks preferred Los Angeles to New York,
which greatly complicated her relationship with Arne
Petersen. On a regular basis he was in Los Angeles
each year only for the brief two weeks when NatBallet
was there on tour. At other times he was always
frantically juggling his schedule to be with the actress
as often as possible.

Both Frosts, at Arne's urging, had seen Brooks's
most recent movies and liked them. They had met her
on several occasions and had enjoyed the experience
each time, since she was an intelligent, down-to-earth
all-American girl and not at all "actressy." Both had
encouraged Arne in his pursuit of her, but somehow
the transcontinental romance had not yet blossomed
into marriage.

Having heard advance descriptions of Vivian's new
movie, Cynthia was apprehensive as she approached
the office building at Forty-sixth Street and Broadway
where the screening of *Glory Days* was to take place.
She understood that Vivian in the film played a tough
woman cattle rancher who tangled successfully with
her male competitors, the local authorities and a band
of outlaws. It did not sound precisely right for the
beautiful comedienne.

Cynthia tried not to convey her feelings to Petersen
when she met him outside the screening room. She did
not need to; he was quite nervous enough in his own
right.

"Look, Cynthia," he said, glancing at his watch,
"this thing isn't scheduled to start for another ten
minutes. I need a drink badly."

"Then let's go have one," she said. "You look
terrible."

"I always get this way when I go to Viv's movies. I love to watch her, but it's torture at the same time."

The two went back down in the elevator and to the bar at the steak house next door. Petersen had a double vodka, Cynthia a Perrier.

"I seem to have been drinking all day," she explained. "I really couldn't have another."

"This is my first, and I sure as hell need it," Petersen said.

"What kind of screening is this?" Cynthia asked.

"I don't know. But I think some of the critics will be there. It's very small, the publicity woman told me."

"Well, Arne, as we say at the ballet, *merde*."

The two returned to the screening room, which was occupied by perhaps a dozen people, including critics whom Cynthia recognized from the *Times* and *New York*. She and Arne took seats on the aisle halfway back.

"This really is the way to see movies, isn't it, Arne?" Cynthia said. "Comfortable seats and no waiting lines. And free, besides."

Petersen was still too distracted to reply coherently. It was as if the large screen in front of them were about to expose new, and unwelcome, personal revelations about the woman he loved.

"Yes, yes, you're right, Cynthia," he said distractedly.

The small audience sat in silence until well after the announced starting time of six o'olock. Finally, the young woman press agent for the studio came to the front.

"Ladies and gentlemen, I'm terribly sorry about the delay," she announced. "We are waiting for Arthur Mattison, who just left his office and should be here in a few minutes. I know you will understand our reluctance to start."

The audience laughed appreciatively.

"While I'm up here," the woman continued, "I should say that what you will be seeing is a complete print of *Glory Days,* except that the credits are not yet finished. The finished credits will be done over a panoramic shot of the Badlands. Please bear this in mind when you watch the film."

The delay set Cynthia to thinking. Mattison could delay a screening, or a Broadway curtain, because of his power. Such was that power, she thought, that cultural events did not really seem to occur unless and until Mattison saw them with his own eyes. Oh, yes, the film unspooled or the actors said their lines, but until Mattison observed the event, the film or the play did not really exist. The *Press*'s critic was at the height of his powers. Mere movie reviewers or theatre critics, however intelligent or eminent, and no matter what the circulation and reputation of their publications, no longer mattered in New York. Mattison, the all-purpose critic, the cultural polymath, was the man to listen to. However threadbare or uninformed his criticism—or how larcenous—it was the commentary that sold tickets and got the public up from their videocassettes and into paid seats. Or at least, that was the folklore.

As she thought about this, Mattison appeared, huffing and puffing, and settled his ample girth into an aisle seat toward the front. He offered scattered "Hallos" to those he recognized—including Cynthia—but no apologies. He carried with him a delicatessen bag containing a paper cup of iced coffee and a sandwich, which he began eating as soon as he was seated.

Cynthia could not help reflecting on the man's plagiarism. His career would be over if his journalistic peccadilloes became known. She could not get out of her mind the logical theorem: Holt knew. Mattison

knew he knew. Therefore, Mattison had to destroy
Holt. Too simple? Perhaps. But Mattison's entire life
had become the role-playing one of being the City's
unquestioned cultural arbiter, a role he manifestly enjoyed. Perhaps murder was not too large a price to
pay to keep it.

The lights went down, and Cynthia reached over
and squeezed Arne's hand as the unfinished credits
appeared. He was already mesmerized and did not
take his eyes off the screen.

The movie was a disaster. All the critics, including
Mattison, shifted about in their seats, though they did
not laugh aloud. Others in the audience—presumably
friends of the film company, at that—did so, guffawing
loudly at each new clumsiness. Cynthia, out of respect
for Arne, did not join in. He watched in stunned
silence as his beloved took a bullwhip to a recalcitrant
ranch hand, shot through her front window at a band
of rustlers—and curled up nude in her bed with a
deputy sheriff.

The nude scene agitated Petersen greatly. Finally,
as the covers were pulled over the courageous ranch
owner and the lawman, and the bed on screen began
thumping violently, he averted his eyes and put his
head in his hands. There was nothing Cynthia could
do but tough it out—no laughing, no sighing, just
(pretended) absorption in the hanky-panky on the
screen.

Finally—after almost three hours—the movie was
over. The crowd filed out without a word. The publicist and the studio representative accompanying her
had disappeared, sparing the audience the problem of
either saying something deeply hypocritical or avoiding them.

Cynthia recalled the various all-purpose lines for

such occasions: "My, that *was* a movie," and "How did you do it?"—but did not have to use them.

She and her escort left in silence. Petersen's distress was apparent.

"How about some dinner, Arne?" Cynthia asked, once they were out on Broadway.

"I'm afraid I'm not hungry after that," he replied. "But you probably are. Can we get something quick?"

"That's fine with me."

"How about a hamburger?"

"Oh, dear, I had one for lunch."

"Oh."

"Look, I can fix something at home for myself. But why don't we walk a little ways?" Cynthia did not want to leave him without a few consoling words.

"Let's do. I want to stop at Doubleday's on Fifty-seventh, so I'll walk that far with you."

"Well, dear, Vivian was the best thing in it," Cynthia said as they strolled toward Fifth Avenue. "But who wrote that screenplay? Someone who didn't have the faintest idea either about the Wild West or how women—then or now—behave."

"I know," Petersen said. "Poor Viv, she gets sucked into these things. She wanted to do something other than comedy—desperately. So she demanded other parts, and when this came along, she felt she had to take it. It's too sad—that beautiful creature up there crawling through the mud."

"Or writhing around in bed."

"Or writhing around in bed. Jesus! That was awful!"

"The more I see of movies lately, the more I'm convinced 'R' stands for raunchy."

"Imagine," Petersen exploded, gesturing widely with both arms as he walked. "Imagine going to bed with that goon, that television pretty-boy who played the deputy sheriff."

"It's only a movie, Arne," Cynthia said. "And besides, it was about as unbelievable a love scene as I've ever seen. It must have been designed for the pimply kids who sneak into the 'R' movies."

"I suppose. But, dammit, Viv deserves better. She's a *good actress,* Cynthia."

"I know she is."

"This never would have happened except for Clifton Holt," Petersen said.

"Why on earth do you say that?"

"Well, you know—or maybe you don't know—that every time I ever planned to go to L.A. to see Viv, or every time I *had* to go to see her, Clifton always managed to keep me in New York, or wherever we were on the road. Always a plausible reason, and being the agreeable guy that I am, I always gave in. Was he jealous, or just being a prick? I'll never know, but whenever he found out I was taking off for California for a couple of days he would do anything to screw it up."

"This is all news to me, Arne," Cynthia said quietly.

"He also made it more expensive. I never could plan ahead for a cheap fare. It was always full freight, because Clifton kept me on the hook until the last possible minute. I haven't saved a dime, Cynthia, in two years, with all the air fares—expensive air fares—to L.A."

"I'm sorry to hear this," Cynthia said sympathetically.

"Let me give you a good example," Petersen said, halting on the street as he talked. "A year ago, Viv called and said she'd been given a script to read. Just the sort of new departure she was looking for. But she had doubts about it. I told her to send it on, I'd read it. She said there wasn't time, she had to give an answer immediately. I asked if it couldn't wait till I got there. She said yes if I came right away. I told Clifton it was an emergency, but he found a reason to keep me around for a week. You know what that reason was?"

"No, what?"

"He wanted to put Roberta Shaw in *Summer Sonata*."

"You've got to be kidding! That's a role for a young girl, and Roberta's forty-five if she's a day."

"I know, Cynthia, I know. It was crazy. Roberta hasn't the stamina for the part—let alone the looks. She's retired, for Christ's sake! But Clifton insisted. Said I had to teach her the part—he was too busy. So I did. Clifton saw the result and decided not to go ahead with it. So it wasn't performed until Hailey Coles learned the part this season."

"I never heard this before. It's about the craziest thing I've ever heard about Clifton," Cynthia said as they resumed walking.

"You're telling me. But it meant I didn't get to California and Viv signed up for that piece of crap you saw tonight."

"That's terrible."

"It never, never would have happened if I'd been there to advise her. She listens to me. Most of the time, anyway. But that bastard made it impossible. They should dedicate *Glory Days* to Clifton, God rest his soul," Petersen went on, then lapsed into silence.

"Don't worry," Cynthia said. "Vivian will survive this movie."

"I know she will. It's just too damn bad she made it, that's all."

"It will be different now, anyway," Cynthia said.

"You're more your own man now. And your higher salary will help a little bit on those air fares."

"Yeah, I know. I've got to get Viv to move to New York, though. Bicoastal romance is rotten."

"How are things going, by the way?" Cynthia asked. "Still overwhelmed by the job?"

"It's better. But I'm really busy. Probably won't get to California for weeks."

"And how are all your problem children? How is Andrea?"

"You know, Cynthia, I'm not sure she's as bad as people say. I think she's tried to give me a break lately. At least, she hasn't been as imperious and demanding as she was before. If you smile at her a little bit—something Clifton never did—she can be all right."

Cynthia was appalled by what Petersen was saying. Had Andrea changed—could she change? She didn't believe it. No, Arne was becoming an unwitting pawn in her mad campaign to become co–Artistic Director. She was sure Petersen did not know about that, and this was neither the time nor the place to tell him. Instead, now that they had reached Doubleday's and Petersen was relatively calm, it was time to go home.

Arne Petersen put Cynthia in a taxi in front of the bookstore. There was little traffic, and she arrived home in no time. She paid the driver and walked to the front door, fumbling for the keys in her purse. As she did so, she had the feeling she was being watched. She looked around and was sure she saw a young man duck into the service entrance of the apartment building down the street after she had seen him. Fortunately, the cabdriver was one of those decent souls who waits until his fare is inside the building. Even so,

Cynthia hurriedly grabbed her key, opened the door and locked it as fast as she could. She had never, ever, seen anyone lurking around the Frost house like that before. She was both frightened and relieved as she threw the double lock.

18

LUIS BAUTISTA MET WITH HIS COLLEAGUES THURSDAY morning to review developments in the Holt case. There had been one breakthrough: the $12,000 found in Jimmy Wilson's apartment had been traced, through serial numbers, to the branch of First Fiduciary Bank at Second Avenue and Sixty-ninth Street. Unfortunately, the money trail appeared to end there. The bank manager had refused to produce his file of recent forms 4789 to the detective working on the money angle, although he had finally agreed, reluctantly, to check the list of names supplied by the detective against his files. The result was negative. And none of the people on the police list had an account at the branch.

Nor did the Upper East Side location logically point to any of the suspects; none lived in the immediate vicinity. The only possible hope seemed to be to get photographs—easy enough to do, given the prominence of those involved—from the NatBallet publicity office and the morgue of either the *Press* or the *Times* and see if the memory of any of the tellers at the Fiduciary branch could be jogged. The group meeting with Bautista was not optimistic that this painstaking step would produce results.

Efforts to tie Jimmy Wilson to one of the suspects through his list of customers were going forward, but again without results so far. The tedious process of interviewing his customers—most of them respectable yuppies shocked at being questioned by the police—had not uncovered any link that seemed to have any significance.

Bautista himself had been in touch with the Syracuse Police Department and had talked on the telephone with a seemingly agreeable man named McNeilly, who was chief of detectives in the upstate city. Bautista had told him he was interested in information about Andrea Turnbull and her late husband, Emery. McNeilly did not automatically say that he had never heard of her, and had no information, but told Bautista that he would be happy to see him if he wanted to come up.

Thus encouraged, Bautista was driven to LaGuardia to take the eleven-fifty-nine Piedmont flight to Syracuse. He barely made the plane at the airport. The cabin in the Fokker "Fellowship" aircraft was both crowded and cramped; he was glad the flight would be only an hour. He squeezed his well-developed body into a seat next to an attractive young girl who turned out to be a Syracuse University coed.

Why was he always on cramped and crowded flights? Bautista asked himself. As a boy, he had gone frequently with his parents to Puerto Rico. These trips meant months of advance saving by his father and mother and were always done at the lowest fare available, with seats so crowded together the planes made the Eastern shuttle to Washington seem luxurious by comparison.

Then, recently, he and Francisca had taken a couple of weekend trips together—once to Puerto Rico, once to Florida. At least the planes they took had a normal seat configuration, though the reality was that Bautista was simply too big to sit comfortably in economy.

The one time he had traveled first class was as a rookie detective, assigned to bringing a prisoner back from San Diego. The circumstances had not been exactly right for enjoying the amenities provided, but he still remembered the relative spaciousness of the first-class cabin. Once he became a lawyer, he resolved, that would sure be the way to go.

The trip to Syracuse was short, austere and uneventful. He declined to buy a drink, but did take the proffered apple juice, reflecting, as he did so, why the beverage was so prominently featured. Having heard others in the Department refer to upstaters as "apple knockers," he assumed it represented the airline's attempt to help business in its service area.

Drinking his apple juice, he realized that this trip would—once again—keep him away from his night law-school classes. The work of the N.Y.P.D. without question came first, he realized that, but he still hated disruptions like this that made his law-school work that much more difficult. He would be missing the commercial-law class; maybe Reuben could help him. Article Nine of the Uniform Commercial Code—secured transactions. Would Reuben know about that? He would have to ask him.

Just before landing, Bautista speculated on what kind of reception he would get at the Syracuse Police Department. Had the locals ever seen a Puerto Rican? He was sure they had, but guessed—correctly—that the Hispanic population of Syracuse was minute. Menial employees mostly, he assumed sadly. Would they be ready for a Puerto Rican homicide detective from the Big City? Well, he would be polite and hope for the best. And after the verbal racist assaults he had endured as a patrolman in New York, how bad could it be?

At the airport he rented a Ford from Hertz. He felt something of an invader when he had to ask where Syracuse was in relation to the airport. The young woman behind the counter pulled out a map and directed him to his destination on South State Street.

Bautista decided not to stop for lunch and went straight to police headquarters. Lawrence McNeilly, chief of detectives, was in when he got there, and came out of his modest office to meet Bautista when his arrival was announced. McNeilly was a tall, erect Irishman with steely gray hair. He was polite, in a reserved way, and seemed businesslike; there was no trace of the loutish hick sheriff Bautista had half expected. McNeilly and his guest settled down behind the closed door of the former's office.

"What can I do for you, Officer?" Bautista's host asked.

"I'm in charge of the investigation of the murder of Clifton Holt. Maybe you read about it. Holt was a choreographer at the National Ballet in New York. A pretty famous guy," Bautista explained.

"Yes, I think I saw something on the TV about it," McNeilly replied.

"He was stabbed in the street by a young kid who was caught on the spot. Seemed open-and-shut, and then it came wide open. The kid himself was killed in prison, but not before telling his buddies that he had been hired to do the murder."

"How can I help?"

"We're kind of going around in circles right now,

Chief McNeilly. The kid's story checks out—or at least, we found the money. Nothing much else to go on—the kid didn't give away anything about who hired him—except that Holt seemed to have a lot of enemies. We've worked up a list of likely suspects and are just digging as best we can to uncover something—anything—that would point to one of them. It hasn't come out in the papers yet that Holt's killer was hired, and we're trying to do as much as we can before it does."

"You mentioned Andrea Turnbull when you called me. Is she on your list?"

"Maybe. She was a big contributor to National Ballet and didn't get along with Holt at all, as near as I can figure out. Do you know of her?"

"Yes, I do," McNeilly answered. "It's pretty hard to have lived here over the years and not have heard of her. Her husband, Emery, was a pretty wealthy fellow. Made a lot of money in the farm-equipment business and, so they say, by playing the stock market. His wife didn't come from Syracuse originally, but boy, she sure made a splash once she arrived. She tried for years to start a dance company up here, but it was a disaster. She didn't have a good word to say about anybody, and she took off within weeks after her husband died."

"How did he die?"

"Car accident. Car went off the road and plunged down a hill. He was killed instantly."

"How long ago was this?"

"Let me see. Two or three years, I'd guess."

"You seem very informed about all this. Were the police involved with Mrs. Turnbull in any way?"

"Not really. We investigated the accident, as a matter of routine. The rest I just got from reading the papers. Mrs. Turnbull always managed to conduct her fights in the papers. And she was kind of a joke around here with her attempts to civilize us. This is a small town, Officer, and people know a lot of things."

"About the accident Mr. Turnbull had. Was there anything suspicious about it?"

"The coroner said it was accidental death," McNeilly said.

"Any doubt about that?"

McNeilly hesitated, then responded carefully. "Until you told me what you did just now, I never had any doubt that Emery Turnbull was killed accidentally. I was involved with the investigation myself, and I was satisfied."

"What do you mean about what I told you?"

"I think you should talk to Robert Lucas. He was Emery Turnbull's partner, and now runs the business. He bought out the estate. He disagreed with the coroner's findings at the time. I thought he was crazy as a bedbug. But now I think you should talk to him."

"Where do I find him?"

"Lucas Motors, out on the far end of Erie Boulevard. I'll call him."

McNeilly got the number from the directory resting on the table behind his desk and placed the call. Lucas was in his office, and would be happy to talk to Officer Bautista.

"When you going back?" McNeilly asked.

"I'm booked on a flight at seven-thirty."

"Well, Lucas will talk your ear off, but you should be able to make it."

"Is he the only one I should be speaking to?"

"I think so. There're plenty of people around that Mrs. Turnbull beat up on, but it sounds as if you already know what she was like."

"Yes, I believe I do."

"Okay, let me show you out and I can tell you how to get to the Lucas place."

"Thanks."

"You from New York originally?" McNeilly asked, as they went down the stairs toward the front door.

"Not quite. I was born in Puerto Rico. But I went to school in New York and have been there ever since."

"It's too big a place for me," McNeilly said. "I get lost every time I go there."

"Next time you come, give me a call. We'll show you around," Bautista said.

"Thanks, but I'm happy right here."

The two detectives parted in front of police headquarters, with McNeilly directing his visitor to his next destination.

Pleasant enough, Bautista thought, as he drove down Erie Boulevard. But what was he getting into now? What was this man Lucas going to tell him?

Bautista was soon driving in a grim, gray part of the city. Down-at-the-heels garages and supply houses lined the road. After going about two miles, he came to Lucas Motors, which, while larger than most of its neighbors, was in need of sprucing up. He parked his car and went into the showroom. A salesman descended on him, only to be disappointed when Bautista said he wasn't buying but wanted to see the owner. The salesman pointed at a glass-enclosed office in the back.

Sitting at a desk behind the glass was a beak-nosed, bald-headed man wearing a plaid flannel shirt.

"Mr. Lucas?"

"Yep. You the police fella?"

"Yes," Bautista replied, showing the man his badge.

"Long way from the Big Apple," Lucas said.

"Oh, not so far."

"Been up in these parts before?"

"No, I never have, sir."

"Well, you picked a good time. Winter up here is awful."

"I've heard that."

"You had lunch?"

"No, I haven't, sir."

"Want some?"

"Sure."

"Let's go. There's a place down the road a ways. Nothing fancy, but it fills you up."

"That's fine with me. You sure they'll be serving? It's almost three-thirty."

"Never known 'em to turn away a customer yet."

The restaurant Lucas had selected had plastic pretensions to grandeur, pretensions more cruelly exposed in the bright daylight. It was empty, except for three men sitting at the long bar that occupied one of the building's two main rooms.

Lucas, after amiable greetings to the bar patrons and the bartender, went into the dining room and asked the hearty, middle-aged waitress if he and Bautista could get lunch.

"Bobby, for you, anytime. Sit where you like," the woman said.

Without hesitation Lucas went to a table in the corner.

"This okay?" he asked.

"Sure," Bautista said.

"What about a drink?"

"I'm afraid not, thanks."

"I don't want one either. What would you like, a

steak?" Lucas asked. "Here, Elsie, let's see the menu."

"You recommend the steak?"

"It's good. Have it with some of their onion rings."

"Fine."

"Elsie, two steaks. Mine well done. How about you, young man?"

"Rare for me."

"Now let's go over and get some salad. They've got a good salad bar here."

Realizing that he had no choice, Bautista followed the man to a stainless steel counter in the other corner of the room. It was laden with all manner of greens, relishes, cottage cheese and vegetables, all looking slightly shopworn.

"Help yourself, young fella, it goes with the lunch."

Bautista took a modest quantity from the selection. His host completely loaded up a plate, with no attempt to keep the various items separated.

"That all you're going to have?" he asked.

"This is fine, thanks," Bautista said.

"You can always come back," Lucas explained. "This place is famous all around the area for its salad bar. All you can eat."

They returned to their table, where Lucas began eating with enthusiasm.

"How long you been a policeman?" he asked, between bites.

"Eight years, sir."

"How'd you ever pick that?"

"I don't know. I had a couple of buddies who went to the Police Academy. It seemed like a good life, so I took the exam."

"Ever been sorry?"

"No. It's not as glamorous most of the time as the stuff on TV, but it's okay."

"How about business—ever think of business?" Lucas asked.

"No, not really." Bautista replied with a laugh. "I never had the opportunity for that."

"Opportunity? You have to make your own opportunity, young man! Nobody gives away nothin' as near as I can figure."

Bautista refrained from mentioning his night law course; he somehow sensed that his luncheon companion might not regard law as a suitable vocation.

"That's all right," Lucas continued. "I know some damn fine policemen. That fellow McNeilly you were meeting with, he's okay. Not too smart, but okay."

Elsie brought the two steaks, each surrounded by gigantic onion rings. Lucas promptly doused his plate with ketchup and began eating with renewed enthusiasm.

"McNeilly said you wanted to talk to me about Andrea Turnbull," Lucas said.

"That's right. We're conducting an investigation of a crime that we think might involve her. I'd be grateful for anything you could tell me about her."

"What kind of investigation?"

Bautista hesitated, but saw no other course than to tell the truth. "Murder," he said.

"Hmn. And you think Andrea did it?"

"Well, not precisely—"

"She's too highfalutin ever to commit murder."

"We don't suspect her directly. But we think she might have had something to do with it."

"You mean putting somebody else up to it?"

"Yes, something like that."

"I'll be damned. Andrea up to her old tricks!"

"What do you mean?"

"Let me ask you something before I answer that. You're a policeman; you showed me your badge. Does that mean I can talk to you in confidence?"

"Yes, it does. Unless you say something that has to be used in a trial."

"Hmn. I hate legalities, hate lawyers, judges, the whole lot of 'em. Damn parasites on the society. But I doubt—though some damn lawyer probably might have another idea—that what I have to say could affect any trial. God knows it didn't affect the coroner's investigation of Emery's death."

"You think Mrs. Turnbull had something to do with her husband's death?"

"I do, but nobody else does. Let me go back and tell you the whole story. Emery Turnbull and I went to high school together. He was rich, I was poor. He went to college, I didn't. When he finished college, he came back here to Syracuse and his father set him up in the farm-machinery business. A couple of years later he got married, to this girl he'd met when he was in college. Andrea. They bought a big house down near the University, and pretty soon they had a kid."

"Would that be Mark?"

"That would be Mark. Anyhow, Emery worked real hard, but his new business didn't go so good. Emery was no salesman. And he was in a business where you have to be a salesman—convincing a farmer he's got to have a new tractor, or new baler or whatever you've got in stock. That's where I came in. I'd started working after high school as a salesman for a milking-machine company. Six years out of high school, I knew every farmer in Onondaga County, whereas Emery only knew people if they happened to wander into the shop. But Emery was smart. He knew his shortcomings, knew that he was shy around people, especially when he had to sell them something. So he came to me and asked me to be his partner. I didn't have any money, but Emery's father came through again. Made me a nice, soft loan so that I could eventually buy half the business.

"It all worked out just fine," Lucas went on. "I was the chief salesman, and Emery took care of the financial end of things, kept the books, all that stuff. We added a Chevrolet franchise, and we both were making a lot of money—Emery more than me because he played the stock market. But by local standards up here, we were both doing real good. Everything would have been great, except for Andrea."

"How do you mean?" Bautista asked.

"She had all these artsy-fartsy ideas. Wanted to start a ballet company. In Syracuse, for God's sake. But there was no stopping her, and Emery indulged his wife and gave her the money to do what she wanted. She actually got a company started. But then she began picking fights with everybody—the college, the newspapers, the banks. You name it. And the fights were all over the papers—everybody knew about them. That meant she had to use more and more of Emery's money to keep her damn ballet troupe going. And it also started hurting our business—she was stepping on too many toes.

"Emery couldn't control her at all and was getting pretty impatient. He didn't want to leave her and the boy, but he didn't want to read about his wife in the paper every night, either. Or keep putting his money down a rathole. He got physically sick, had an ulcer he got so worried. We were pretty close, but we never talked much about Andrea. But I had a pretty good idea he was about to give her an ultimatum—either give up the ballet bunch or he was going to leave. Then he had the accident."

"Go on," Bautista said.

"Everybody was shocked by Emery's death. I was real depressed about it, and it began to prey on my mind. The accident made no sense. Happened in broad daylight on a nice clear day. And up on Onondaga Hill, a road Emery knew like the back of his hand. He was a good, careful driver, too. I never saw him reckless in his whole life. I decided somebody had done something to his car. Somebody had fixed it good.

"Then I even decided who'd done it," Lucas went on.

"About six weeks before he died, Emery had fired a mechanic at the shop. Guy named Gaute, crazy French Canadian. He was a good mechanic, but he was bent. He was always pilfering from the shop. Finally, he started taking big stuff, so Emery and I set a trap for him, caught him red-handed, and fired him. Never turned him in or anything, just fired him. Gaute was about as angry a man as I've ever seen. He said he'd get even with Emery and get even with me. I figured he was just letting off steam—the worst thing you can do to a petty crook is find him out.

"But after Emery's death, I got to thinking. Gaute would never murder Emery on his own. He was a spineless little son-of-a-bitch. But if there was money involved, he just might. By the time I worked out my theory, Emery's car had long since gone to the compacter at the junkyard. I went and talked with McNeilly anyway. He said there was nothing he could do without more proof. I became obsessed. I went to Andrea and told her what I thought. She told me never to enter her house again, but in about a week's time she didn't have a house; she had left for New York."

"What about Gaute?" Bautista asked.

"I tracked him down too. He'd moved down near Utica—about thirty miles from here—about the time of Emery's death. I didn't know what I was going to accomplish, but I had to see him. I found him at the garage where he was working, called him outside and told him what I believed he had done. He started acting like a crazy man, and if he'd had a tire iron or something like that in his hand, he probably would've killed me on the spot. But, oddly, he backed off. Just said nothing and told me to leave."

"And that was the end of it?"

"Not quite. Two weeks later Gaute stuck a gun down his throat and killed himself."

"So you believe that Andrea Turnbull paid Gaute to doctor Emery Turnbull's car?"

"I do. But I have no proof. Except for the certainty that Emery did not die accidentally."

Both men were silent and drank from the coffee cups Elsie had refilled.

"Mr. Lucas, I appreciate your help," Bautista said. "As I told Chief McNeilly this morning, we've got precious few leads in the case I'm working on. Any strand of information is useful, and I think yours is."

"I've tried to forget the whole thing," Lucas said. "It didn't make my life any easier, since I had to buy out Emery's share of the business from a widow who was out for blood. Fortunately, we had a mutual buy-sell agreement, so she had to sell to me at a fair price. But it took a couple of years, and a damn lot of legal fees."

"I appreciate it. Can we split the check?"

"No, no. You're the visitor, Officer. Upstate hospitality, you know."

"Well, thanks. I may want to ask you some more

questions as our investigation progresses. Do you have a card?"

"Sure."

Once the check was paid, Lucas went back through the barroom and again greeted each of the patrons. Outside the restaurant, he directed Bautista back to the airport, shook hands and headed for his car.

Bautista was just too late to make the five-twenty plane, the last one before his scheduled departure at seven-thirty. He sighed. The prospect of two hours at the airport did not delight him. Although it had otherwise been a pretty good trip.

RETURN—AND A STREET BALLET

19

BEFORE GOING TO BED ON WEDNESDAY, REUBEN FROST had changed his plane reservation. He had been scheduled to fly out from Portland at six-fifty in the morning. He had once been able to keep such a schedule, flying to Portland, staying up half the night with Earle Ambler, and returning, with barely any sleep, to New York the next day. No longer, he decided. He should, of course, get back and report his findings about Gerald Hazard to Bautista. But then he remembered that Bautista had planned to go to Syracuse on Thursday. That decided him; he rebooked on the Northwest flight at eleven o'clock.

That morning, after an ample breakfast at the Benson Hotel (though the fresh orange juice to which he was accustomed was not available), he took a cab to the airport. This time the plane was full, and the aisle seat next to him was occupied by a young man he took to be a salesman. (At least that is what he guessed from peeking over at the sheaf of "call sheets" his companion was working on, atop an attaché case that served as a portable desk, complete with pencils in various colors, a pocket calculator and a stapler.)

Once again the stewardess in the first-class cabin pressed a drink on him. Neither he nor the hardworking salesman accepted her offer; Frost, after his large breakfast, declined any form of sustenance, knowing full well that the routine would later be repeated after the plane's intermediate stop in Minneapolis.

Instead, Frost decided to go to work himself. He took out a yellow legal pad and a supply of pencils from his carry-on suitcase and rested them on the meal tray in front of him. He turned the pad sideways and divided the page into four columns which he labeled "NAME," "MOTIVE," "SOURCE OF CASH" and "ACCESS TO WILSON." Then, on the theory that his seatmate might be a peeker too, he changed the word "motive" to "motivation"—surely a respectable and noncontroversial word in traveling salesmen's circles.

Frost entered the obvious names: Turnbull, Mattison, Maywood, Teresa Holt, Navikoff, Petersen—and Hazard. He was especially reluctant to include the last two, but felt that objectivity required it. Then he tried to describe the motive, or motivation, of each, the likelihood of each coming up with $24,000, and the possible ways each might have made contact with Jimmy Wilson. When he had finished, the chart looked like this:

NAME	MOTIVATION	SOURCE OF CASH	ACCESS TO WILSON
Turnbull	Hatred of H.; desire to run NatBallet— mentally unbalanced?	Inheritance	Son Mark?
Mattison	Public expos. of plagiarism	Book advance	?

Maywood	H. a threat to career; jealousy?	Perf. fees	?
Teresa Holt	Pent-up hatred	Money fr. Clif.	?
Navikoff	Fear of being cut out of will	Borrowed?	?
Petersen	Artistic advancement	Savings?	?
Hazard	" "	Perf. fees	?

Frost looked at his handiwork. The big gap was the link of each of the suspects to the actual killer. He could see only one link, and that was pure supposition based on his instant dislike of Mark Turnbull. But hadn't Bautista said that access to Wilson, or some other petty crook willing to commit murder, was easy? He remembered well Bautista's eloquent speech that the law-abiding and criminals coexisted almost side-by-side in New York. If Bautista was to be believed—and Frost saw no reason to doubt him—no one got crossed off the chart simply because Frost could not make a link to Wilson.

As for a motive, and access to the key $24,000, all seven of those listed had both. Frost shook his head in discouragement. The list, after his Portland excursion, was getting longer, not shorter. Ah, well, time for a nap.

The Northwest plane touched down at Minneapolis/St. Paul for forty-five minutes. Frost did not get off, but continued his nap. Once the 727 was back in the air, he felt revived and accepted a martini, followed by, once again, a steak dinner. His salesman seatmate had gotten off in Minneapolis and had not been replaced, so Frost was able to drink and eat undisturbed. Then he slept again until shortly before the plane landed at LaGuardia.

*   *   *

It was raining when Frost came out of the terminal in New York, approximately on time at eight-thirty. The line at the taxi stand was long, and there was not a single cab in sight, so he decided to take the Carey bus to Manhattan. He could get a taxi at Forty-second Street or the subway uptown to Sixty-eighth Street.

The weather had not improved when he got to Manhattan; nor had the taxi situation. So, overnight bag in hand, he took the Lexington Avenue local subway at Grand Central.

As he came up the stairs at Sixty-eighth Street, it was approaching ten o'olock and he headed on foot up Lexington Avenue to Seventieth Street. The rain had by now turned into a gray mist, more annoying than unpleasant. As he turned into Seventieth Street, he suddenly realized that the sidewalk, darkened with the foglike mist, was deserted except for three adolescent figures coming toward him.

Unlike many who walked about at night in New York, Frost was not frightened by the prospect of occupying the block solely with three teen-aged strangers. He had never had anything approaching trouble in his neighborhood and had never given his own safety there a second thought.

Then, without warning, the three boys were upon him. The smallest, who could not have been more than thirteen or fourteen, held a knife at his groin. The biggest stood over him. The third—was he an apprentice learning the technique or a lookout?—alternately watched the confrontation and the street beyond.

"Gimme your wallet, man!" the big one said.

Frost hesitated.

"Quick, man, quick! We ain't got all night!"

"Better give it to him," the little one with the knife said. "If you don't, I'll cut you good."

Frost looked incredulously at the whelp with the knife, barely out of knee-pants and blinking out of Coke-bottle glasses.

Thinking fast, Frost reached in his pocket and pulled out a crumpled mass of bills. He did not carry his money in his wallet, but loose in his pocket. He held the bills aloft, asking "Isn't this what you want?" and the big one grabbed them.

"What's in *there*?" the big one demanded, pointing to Frost's overnight bag.

"Dirty underwear," Frost answered.

"Yeah, well, we'll take that too, Gramps," the big one said. He grabbed the bag, and Frost did not resist. Instantly the three marauders were running toward the corner and disappeared around it.

Frost's instincts were to give chase, but then he realized how foolish that would be—a seventy-five-year-old man taking on three athletic kids. No, it was not time to play either Rambo or Rocky. He did shout "Thief!" twice, but his clarion fell on an empty street.

Satisfied that there was nothing more he could do, he walked on to his house and let himself in. He was not particularly frightened—the whole encounter seemed to have taken seconds—but he did feel relief—oddly, not so much that his life had been spared, but that his wallet had. Endless complications with the credit-card companies would not follow.

And he secretly had to admire the finesse of it all. He had been robbed, a felony had been committed, in a brief street ballet that could have been choreographed —one, two, three and done—such was its speed and efficiency.

As he thought of the word "choreograph," a vision

of Clifton Holt being stabbed in the Zacklin alley flashed into his mind and the horror set in. He had lost perhaps $200, but Holt had lost his life. Both in attacks by punks. But Holt's killer had been hired. The street creatures he had just encountered surely had not been. That was right, wasn't it? he asked himself. There was just enough doubt as to the answer to that question that Frost was sweating massively as he achieved the sanctuary of his own house.

20

"HELLO, DEAR!" CYNTHIA CALLED OUT TO HER HUS-
band as he came up the stairs to the living room.
"Welcome back!" She got up from the sofa, came
over to Reuben and kissed him.

"Reuben, you're out of breath," she said. "And
where's your suitcase?"

"To answer your questions in order: I'm slightly out
of breath because I've just been robbed by three young
men on the street. And second, I don't have my suitcase because the same young men took it."

"Good grief, Reuben! Are you all right?"

"Yes, I'm fine. No damage done. They got two
hundred dollars and some dirty clothes," Frost said.

"What about your wallet?"

"No, I saved that. I waved around the loose bills
from my pocket and that—plus the overnight bag—
satisfied them."

"Did they have a gun?"

"No, just a half-blind little pipsqueak with a knife
pointed at my groin. Which was practically eye level
for him."

"Look, sit down," Cynthia said. "Let me get you a
drink."

"Excellent idea. Scotch and soda."

"Now, tell me exactly what happened," Cynthia said, once she had fixed drinks. Reuben recounted the episode for his wife.

"Reuben, I don't want to alarm you, but let me ask one thing," Cynthia said when he had finished. "Are you sure these were just juvenile delinquents at play—not more Jimmy Wilsons?"

"Oh, God, Cynthia, I thought of that. But it can't be so. They had plenty of time to kill me if that's what they had in mind."

"Or maybe they just wanted to scare you?"

"I hadn't thought of that."

"I was only asking," Cynthia said. "We're paranoid, and it's going to get worse if Clifton's murder isn't solved soon. I know, I was paranoid last night."

"Why do you say that? What happened?" Reuben asked.

Cynthia told him about the figure in the shadows when she had come in.

"You couldn't identify him?" Reuben asked. "It wasn't nice Mark Turnbull, was it?"

"It could have been. But I couldn't really tell," Cynthia replied.

"Have we heard from Bautista, by the way?" Frost asked.

"Oh, heavens, I forgot. He called from Newark Airport just before you arrived. He's on his way here now. He claims he's got news."

"Interesting. It may surprise you, but so have I," Reuben said.

"News from Portland?" Cynthia asked.

"Yes, news from Portland."

"Like what?"

"Earle Ambler sends his love."

"Oh, I know that," Cynthia said. "But you said you had *news,* which I took to mean news about the murder."

"Well, if you'd be still long enough to listen, I do," Frost said. He told his wife about Ambler's description of Gerald Hazard's odd behavior the night Holt was killed.

"How awful. Poor Gerald, making an ass of himself like that."

"Ass of himself, indeed," Reuben said. "For my money he made himself a suspect in Clifton's murder."

"Gerald?"

"Yes, Gerald. He apparently was so exuberant nothing could contain him when he learned about Holt's death."

"But surely if he'd hired the killer, he would have concealed his emotions?" Cynthia asked.

"That's true if he were in New York, with everyone watching him. I'm not sure it's true at all if you're two thousand, three thousand miles away."

"Perhaps. God knows Gerald felt frustrated and held back by Clifton, but I'm not sure it's a reason to kill him."

"Look, Cynthia, none of the motives of anybody we suspect should be a 'reason to kill him.' But for someone, the motive was strong enough to push that person over the edge. And it could be Gerald just as well as anyone else."

"I suppose so. I know Gerald feels under great pressure, with those two boys to educate. I remember he asked me once, 'Cynthia, do you think I'll be strong enough, or last long enough, to dance for those boys' tuition at Harvard or Yale?' Gerald probably has more family obligations than almost anyone in the

Company; that's why he's always traveling around guesting to pick up a few extra dollars."

"And I guess there's no question, is there, that his guest fees would be higher if he were a principal dancer at NatBallet rather than a soloist?" Reuben asked.

"No, there is no question. He could get much higher fees, and better engagements, as a principal," Cynthia said.

"So he did have a motive for getting rid of the man who would not promote him?"

"But Reuben, it's so unlikely."

"No more so, I would have thought, than with some of the others we've talked about," Frost replied.

The front doorbell rang while the Frosts were arguing about Gerald Hazard. Reuben went to answer it and returned with Luis Bautista.

"Did you get mugged coming in here?" Cynthia asked, as the detective came into the living room.

"Mugged?" he asked, looking puzzled.

Reuben described his street encounter, and also the episode involving Cynthia the night before.

"Did you call the police, Reuben?" Bautista asked.

"Frankly, it never occurred to me. I assumed it would be hopeless," Frost said.

"Let me do it now. The perps are probably long gone, but you never can tell. What did these kids look like?"

"One was pretty tall, six feet I'd say. One was shorter, say five feet six, and one was tiny, not even five feet." Frost was rather proud of the precision of his description.

"Color?"

"All black."

"Light-skinned or dark-skinned?"

"I would say light, but it was a little hard to see."

"All of them?"

"Yes."

"What were they wearing?"

"I don't remember, exactly. Blue jeans, I think."

"Blue jeans, and knitted caps and sneakers, perhaps?"

"That's right. They all had these knitted caps. And white sneakers."

"Good. I'm glad they were wearing the standard mugger uniform," Bautista said. "I'd hate to think any of them was setting a new style trend."

"What do you mean, Luis?" Frost asked, chagrined. The detective was pulling his leg.

"Only that all muggers wear blue jeans, knitted caps to cover up their hairstyles and white sneakers for moving around fast. And unfortunately, most of them are black. Or sometimes Hispanic. Or once in a great while, plain old vanilla white."

"So you're saying I was right, it really would be hopeless to call the police."

"Probably. But I'm going to do it anyway," Bautista said.

"While you're on the phone, let me get you a drink," Frost said.

"Anything that doesn't have apple juice in it," Bautista said. "Bourbon and water would be fine."

When he reentered the room, Bautista told the Frosts that a patrol car would cruise around the neighborhood looking for Reuben's assailants—and his overnight bag.

"I doubt that you'll get your money back," Bautista said. "But you might get your dirty clothes."

"Luis, Reuben and I were talking before you got

here," Cynthia said. "Are we just being very foolish to think that what happened to us last night and tonight might be connected with Clifton Holt's death?"

"Offhand, I don't think it's very likely. But you can't ever tell. Maybe someone is trying to scare the two of you," Bautista said.

"As far as we know, Jimmy Wilson's little secret is not publicly known. Isn't that right?" Cynthia asked.

"That's right," Bautista said.

"And why would anybody pick on us, anyway?" Frost asked.

"Because we were with a police officer at the ballet the other night," Cynthia observed. "And most of our suspects knew it. Remember Arthur Mattison and Andrea Turnbull both found out that Luis was a policeman. Arne Petersen knew who he was too, and Veronica Maywood saw him backstage and may have recognized him from the hospital."

"We've *got* to solve this," Frost said. "We'll both be as jumpy as hens on a wire until the guilty party is found. And God help us all—and NatBallet—if the whole affair does become public."

"As I told you, Cynthia, I've got some news," Bautista said. "It may even bring us closer to solving the crime." The detective then recounted his day in Syracuse, and Robert Lucas' theory about Emery Turnbull's death.

"Lucas may be completely *loco* for all I know," Bautista concluded, "though he seemed sensible enough to me. But I think we've got to start investigating your Mrs. Turnbull very, very carefully."

"I agree with that," Frost said. "But I'm afraid I'm going to add to your work." He then told the detective about Gerald Hazard's reported behavior in Portland the night of the killing.

"Tell me about Hazard," Bautista asked. "Why would he want to have Holt killed?"

Cynthia explained Hazard's domestic situation and the pressures on him for money.

"Sounds like another candidate to me," Bautista said, writing in his notebook. "How many does that make now? Let's see: Mrs. Turnbull; the widow; the ballerina, Maywood; Navikoff, the producer; the newspaper guy, Mattison; that fellow Petersen. And now Hazard. That's seven in all."

"Lucky seven," Frost said.

"Yeah, some luck," Bautista replied.

"You know, on the plane this afternoon, I made a chart with all these lucky seven listed," Frost explained. He pulled the chart out of his coat pocket and let Bautista and his wife examine it. "Now," Frost went on, "even though I added to this list myself, I don't think we're going to get anywhere chasing after seven people when it's obvious that one stands out as the most likely suspect, either because she's absolutely cold-blooded or because she's crazy. I think, Luis, you should concentrate your attention on Andrea Turnbull. The others? What we've got is pretty vague. Take Teresa Holt, for example. I have down there that her motive was 'pent-up hatred.' That's mighty weak stuff. I think we've been a bit too imaginative for our own good and we shouldn't be distracted from proving that Andrea Turnbull paid the killer."

While Reuben was speaking, Cynthia carefully examined the chart he had made, putting on her reading glasses to do so. When he had finished, she looked up and spoke to the two men.

"I'm afraid, my dear, I disagree with you. Andrea may well be the most promising suspect. But I don't see how you can dismiss the others quite so easily," Cynthia said.

"But Cynthia, we have to set priorities, and after Luis' intelligence-gathering in Syracuse, top priority should be Andrea Turnbull," Reuben replied, somewhat impatiently.

"Very well," Cynthia went on. "But can I perhaps add to what you have here on the chart? While you two have been touring around the country, I've done a little spadework myself."

"By all means, let's hear about it," Reuben said.

"Let's start with Teresa Holt, Reuben. 'Pent-up hatred,' you say, and I agree that isn't very good. But I had drinks with her yesterday and it became quite clear that she knew Clifton was about to change his will—and to cut off her financial support as well. I know you had a different impression, Reuben, but she was very explicit with me.

"And another thing," Cynthia went on. "She told me—and I believe she had already told you, Reuben—that she had been in California for six weeks. Yet she said how wonderful Hailey Coles had been in *Summer Sonata*. It occurred to me that the girl has danced that ballet only recently. I checked the office this afternoon, and I was right. The only times she has ever danced the part were at two performances three weeks ago. Now, maybe Teresa was making it up about seeing Hailey in the part, maybe she was just parroting the reviews; but maybe she had seen her and was back in New York before Clifton was murdered. Now, all that should be pretty easy to find out, shouldn't it, Luis?" The detective nodded. "But I think it is something that should be checked before we scratch her name out.

"Who should we talk about next?" Cynthia demanded.

"Good God, Cynthia, do you have something to say about everyone?" Frost asked.

"Yes, I believe I do. Except Gerald Hazard. But I didn't know he was on your list until tonight."

"All right, what about Mattison?" Reuben challenged.

"There you've struck my weakest point," she answered. "I watched him at the screening of Vivian Brooks's movie last night. There we were waiting for the movie to start and we had to wait until he arrived. Can you imagine what that kind of power must be like, especially when it feeds a gigantic ego? I couldn't help but think how truly damaging to Mattison revelation of his plagiarism would be. It wouldn't just end a tiny little newspaper career; it would, in Mattison's mind, end his mighty reign over public opinion. Just an observation, I know, but I wouldn't forget about my dear friend Arthur."

"How was the movie, by the way?" Reuben asked.

"Absolutely terrible. But we can talk about that later."

"What about Arne?"

"That's more complicated than you think, Reuben. You have down here as a motive 'artistic advancement.' That's true enough as far as it goes. But Clifton Holt was doing everything he could to keep Arne from seeing Vivian Brooks. Don't ask me why, but he was. It's clear to me that Arne was absolutely tortured by Clifton, who made his trips to the coast to see Vivian as difficult to arrange as possible."

Bautista asked about Vivian Brooks, whose name he had not heard mentioned before. Cynthia explained the actress' bicoastal involvement with Petersen. When she had done so, her husband asked her whom she wanted to savage next.

"Reuben, I'm not trying to savage anyone," she

responded coolly. "I'm trying to solve a murder—and save the morale of a ballet company. And just possibly our physical well-being, too."

"I'm sorry, Cynthia. Please proceed," Reuben said.

"Shall I tell you about Veronica Maywood?" Cynthia asked. "She conducted Company class yesterday, and I had lunch with her afterward. I learned that she was desperate—desperate and depressed—about Holt's attitude toward her dancing. Despite the success of their artistic partnership, it seemed clear, or at least it seemed clear to her, that Holt was going to dump her. That Laura Russell was to be the new favorite."

"But we knew that already, Cynthia," Reuben said, again with some impatience.

"But what we didn't know," Cynthia continued, ignoring her husband's comment, "is that Veronica was made even more desperate by a failed love affair— with a dope addict who died of an overdose a couple of weeks before Clifton was killed."

"Overdose?" Bautista asked. "You mean of heroin, I assume?"

"That's what she said. She admitted that she was a cocaine user, though she said only in the 'off season.' And she claimed she didn't know that her rich, stock-broking boyfriend was an addict until shortly before they broke up."

"When was that?" Bautista asked.

"About six months ago, she told me."

Reuben picked up his chart. Under "Access to Wilson" another question mark potentially dropped away. Wasn't it possible that "through boyfriend" could be added after Maywood's name?

"What was this fellow's name?" Bautista asked.

"Oh, dear, I vowed I would remember it," Cynthia

said. "Ryan, Ryerson—no, Reyman. Bernard Reyman. Worked at Hughes & Company."

"And he died of an overdose?" Bautista asked.

"Apparently."

"When?"

"Three weeks ago," Cynthia answered.

Bautista was again taking notes.

"She also said everyone had covered the whole thing up," Cynthia added.

"We'll see about that," Bautista answered.

"All right, Cynthia, we're almost through the roster," her husband said. "What about Navikoff? What have you got new on him?"

"Not much, darling. Except that I was walking down Madison Avenue this afternoon when what, to my wond'ring eyes, should appear . . ."

"But?"

"But Jack Navikoff walking arm-in-arm—and I emphasize that, arm-in-arm—with Andrea Turnbull."

"Good Lord," Reuben said.

"He probably was just trying to hit her up for a loan," Cynthia continued. "But isn't it just possible that the two of them teamed up to have Clifton killed, each of them reinforcing the other as they talked themselves into their mad plot?"

"What did you do? Did you talk to them?" Reuben asked.

"I ducked into the Bermuda Shop—I'd never been in there in my life—and looked at bathing suits. I'm pretty sure they didn't see me."

"Is that all, Cynthia?" Bautista said. "You've given us quite a news broadcast here."

"I believe it is," Cynthia replied. "I hope you don't think I've been interfering."

"No," Bautista said. "I can't say that. But after

what you've told us, I don't think we can rip up Reuben's chart quite yet."

"Nor do I," Reuben conceded. "My dear, you must have had fifty-five drinks yesterday."

"Not quite, darling, though I felt about ready for the Betty Ford Clinic."

"I've got to go," Bautista said. "It's been a long, long day. Let me try to digest all this and I'll call you tomorrow."

"Fine. Let me see you out," Reuben said.

"Good night, Luis. And love to Francisca," Cynthia said.

She started up the stairs to the third floor and Reuben went down to the front door with Bautista.

"Are we making any progress?" Frost asked. "It certainly doesn't seem like it."

"Gridlock," Bautista said. "Everybody looks as guilty as everybody else. But don't worry, Reuben, even gridlock ends sometime. Let's just hope it's soon."

"Amen, amen."

"I'll call you tomorrow."

21

REUBEN WAS SCARCELY UP FRIDAY MORNING WHEN THE telephone rang, shortly after nine o'olock. It was William Burbank, the head of Hughes & Company. Although they were roughly the same age, Burbank was, unlike Frost, still very much in command of his firm, one of the few investment-banking houses left that had not gone public or been swallowed up by a giant conglomerate.

Hughes & Company, and Burbank personally, had been longtime clients of Chase & Ward. And Burbank had also been Frost's staunch ally in the maneuvers that had led to construction of the Zacklin Theatre.

The banker apologized for calling Frost so early at home. He said that he had called Frost's office, but that the secretary who answered did not know whether Frost would be in or not.

"Are you now fully retired?" Burbank asked. "I thought you still came in every day."

"No, I'm *not* fully retired," Frost shot back over the line. "I go into the office two or three times a week. But I do think at my age I've earned the right to do some other things." So there, Burbank, you aged work-aholic, Frost thought.

"You're still involved with NatBallet, aren't you?"

"Indeed I am," Reuben answered.

"Reuben, are you free this morning? Could you come down and see me? Something extremely delicate has come up that I'd like to talk with you about. But I'd prefer to do it in person, if that's possible."

"Of course. What time would be convenient?"

"I think the sooner the better," Burbank said.

Frost, who was not yet dressed, looked at his watch. "I could be there at ten-fifteen, ten-thirty."

"Fine, let's say ten-fifteen. Come to the thirty-eighth floor."

"I remember, Bill."

Frost was in the reception area outside Burbank's office at ten-fifteen precisely. If Burbank was anxious, so was he. Was his old friend about to seek advice concerning an insider trading scandal, or some other disaster threatening Hughes & Company? No, Frost guessed, it was much more likely that Burbank's "extremely delicate" matter involved Bernard Reyman. If so, Clifton Holt's murder might be a step nearer to solution.

"Reuben! Thanks for coming down here so fast," Burbank said, as he burst forth from his office and shook Frost's hand with enthusiasm. Frost, who was in perfectly good health, nonetheless envied the banker's obvious vigor. Ramrod-straight, he was wearing a finely tailored double-breasted pinstripe suit.

"You been away, Bill?" Frost asked. "You're looking very tan."

"Martinique. We're in a rut. Harriet and I've been going there every year for seventeen years."

"It looks like it agrees with you."

"It does," Burbank said, as he closed the door to his office. He got down to business at once, as Frost sat down in the chair in front of Burbank's desk. "I hope I didn't unduly alarm you this morning. But something's come up I think you ought to know about."

"Fire away," Frost said.

"I have to explain a little bit. About three weeks ago, one of our crackerjack salesmen, fellow named Reyman, was found dead in his apartment up in the Village. It turned out—and this is very confidential, Reuben, we managed to keep it quiet at the time— that Reyman died of a heroin overdose."

The banker spun out the story for Frost. How everyone had liked Reyman, and no one suspected him of being an addict. How he was found dead in his Village apartment, without any survivors. How a young staff lawyer, Jerry Hayes, had to look after the situation in the absence of family. How the police had been around the day before, asking about Reyman and checking out a list of names. How the police had not given out any information other than that the dead stockbroker's name had appeared in a dope peddler's address book and that they were investigating a homicide.

"Unfortunately, or maybe fortunately," Burbank continued, "Jerry Hayes, our staff lawyer, was out of the office at a meeting when the police came. So they went away and said they'd talk to Hayes sometime today. When he got back here late yesterday afternoon, I went over with him the names the police had asked about—I'd taken care to write them down. To my surprise, Hayes said there was a connection to one of them—your star ballerina, Veronica Maywood. He thought he remembered seeing an autographed picture of her in Reyman's apartment."

"Is that all?" Frost asked, with impatience.

"No, it isn't," Burbank said, reaching into a folder on his desk and handing Frost a single piece of paper. "There is this."

Frost examined the document. It was a demand promissory note, dated a month earlier, in the amount of $24,000. It was payable to Reyman—and signed by Veronica Maywood.

Frost could feel his heart racing beneath his shirt.

"I wanted to tell you about it, Reuben, because it's obvious there's some sort of scandal brewing here. I thought with a little warning you might be able to head off whatever it is."

"Bill, I appreciate your efforts. It's a scandal, all right, but there's no way to suppress it that I know of. But so be it. The important thing is to have it over and done with and behind us."

"And this promissory note does that?" Burbank asked.

"It certainly helps," Frost replied. "Is there a telephone I can use? I really should make a call about this right away."

"Use the one on the coffee table over there."

"But I don't want to disturb you."

"Hell, forget it. Take as long as you like, Reuben."

Frost moved over to the sofa at the side of the room and dialed Bautista's private number, then explained his new find when the detective answered.

"Reyman and Maywood, heh?" Bautista said. "I've already called the manager at the First Fiduciary branch we traced the twenty-four G's to and told him to check out Bernard Reyman in his forty-seven eighty-nine files. Is your friend still there?"

"Yes. I'm in his office."

"Ask him if he has a photograph of Reyman," Bautista requested. Frost lowered the receiver and asked Burbank the question.

"I'm sure we do. I know we do, come to think of it, because I saw his personnel file after he died. I'll double-check, though," Burbank said. He called his secretary on the office intercom as Frost resumed his telephone conversation.

"He's sure they have one," Frost told the detective.

"Good. I'll be down to get it right away. Where are you?"

"Thirty-eighth floor, Forty-six Wall Street. Hughes & Company. Mr. William Burbank."

"Oh, Reuben, one other thing. How can I get a picture of Veronica Maywood in street clothes? Nobody at the bank recognized her in her ballet picture. But they might in street clothes," Bautista said.

"Call Cynthia. She keeps the family photo album. And I know there are some shots of Veronica in there," Frost said. Pictures from some very happy occasions, he thought sadly.

"Oh, and Luis," Frost went on, "a couple of your colleagues are supposed to come down here today to talk to people about Reyman and Veronica. It seems like a waste of time to me until you check up at the bank."

"I agree. I'll call them off."

"Thanks." Frost put down the telephone.

"Is that the police you're talking to?" Burbank asked.

"Yes."

"And do I understand they're not going to talk to Hayes?" Burbank asked, making no effort to conceal that he had been listening to Frost's conversation.

"That's right. But another homicide detective, a

friend of mine named Luis Bautista, is coming down here now to collect that picture of Reyman," Frost explained.

"Fine. We have it."

"Good. Shall I wait outside, Bill? I don't want to take up more of your time."

"Heavens no, Reuben. I'm king of the roost here. I can do as much or as little as I want. And right now I want to talk to my old friend," Burbank said expansively. "Or rather, I wish my old friend would talk to me and tell me what the hell is going on."

"I would, Bill, but it's just too delicate. If things develop as I think they will, you'll hear about it soon enough."

"Will the circumstances of Reyman's death come out, you think?" Burbank asked anxiously.

"I suspect they will," Frost said.

"Damn. After all the trouble we took to keep this thing quiet. I should have known. Anything that involves dope is bound to be trouble. You have much of a dope problem over at your place?"

"I don't believe we have any," Frost said.

"You mean that, Reuben?"

"Yes, I do."

"You're naive. I suppose you think that dope's illegal so none of your bright young lawyers would ever touch it?"

"That's right," Frost said.

"You *really* are naive," Burbank said. "It's one of the biggest problems we have. Not heroin so much, thank God, but marijuana all over the place, and plenty of people with real problems with cocaine—and now this new stuff, crack. And I just don't believe we're any better or worse off than any other banking firm, or your law firm."

"I guess I've never thought about it," Frost said. "The subject has just never come up."

"Well, God bless you."

"If there is a problem, why do you think it's so widespread?" Frost asked.

"I've got a couple of theories," Burbank answered. "First, look at the money these kids make. Your young lawyers, our young MBAs. They've got disposable income to burn. Do they save it? No. Why should they? When every apartment they might buy costs a million bucks, there's no point in saving. The only way you can afford a million-dollar apartment is to claw your way up to a millionaire's income. Some of them will get that—they'll become partners in their firms, the big successes. And those that don't, they'll lower their sights and slink off somewhere else. But savings? Forget it. Buy coke instead!"

"You really believe that?" Frost asked.

"Talk to some of these kids sometime," Burbank replied. "It's very revealing."

"I guess it must be."

"Then there's my second theory, Reuben. We—you and me—just caught the end of Prohibition. But I remember what it was like, don't you? We worked hard, sure, but we were out every chance we got. Party as often as possible. Drink yourself silly. Even when you really didn't want to. Remember? Liquor was the forbidden fruit, the tempting apple everybody reached for. No great harm done—lots of fun. Except too many people became drunks. Ruined their health, caused hell for their families, lost their jobs. Remember, Reuben?"

"Yes, oh, yes."

"Well, somehow drugs have taken the place of bathtub gin. Cocaine is the new forbidden fruit, the new temptation. *Recreational* drugs, they call them. Fine. Great. Big party. Except once again there are the Reymans, who go too far and die, and the others who end up emotional and physical wrecks. Just like when we were growing up, except the forbidden fruit has changed. And I don't think for the better."

"Bill, you certainly have given me something to think about," Frost said. "You have to be right. There must be dope-takers at Chase & Ward. I'll pay more attention from now on."

"Is this thing you claim is going to be resolved got to do with drugs?" Burbank asked.

"In part," Frost said. "But I'm afraid it's not that simple."

Burbank's secretary came in and announced that Detective Bautista was waiting. The banker asked him to come in and told his secretary to get the picture of Reyman.

"You know each other, I gather?" Burbank asked.

"Oh, yes," Bautista said.

"We got to know each other when Graham Donovan died," Frost explained.

"Oh, I get it," Burbank said. "Well, I'm glad to make your acquaintance, Mr. Bautista. Your friend Mr. Frost has been very tight-lipped about what's going on. I assume I won't have any better luck getting information out of you?"

"I'm afraid that's so, sir," Bautista said. "But be patient. I hope everything will be cleared up very shortly."

"Well, I'm glad I could be of help."

"By the way, I want to take with me the promissory note Reuben—Mr. Frost—mentioned on the telephone. I'll give you a receipt for it," Bautista said.

The transaction was completed and Bautista and

Frost left the room. They stood together at the elevators, talking in low voices.

"Are you going home?" Bautista asked.

"I guess so. Either there or to the Gotham Club."

"Would you mind going home? I couldn't get Cynthia before, and I'd really like that picture of Maywood. I assume you can find it?"

"It's Cynthia's department, but I think I can."

"Good. I'll give you a ride. Once I get the picture, I'm going over to the bank myself and see what I can find out."

Bautista, after collecting the photograph of Veronica Maywood, went to the First Fiduciary branch at Second Avenue and Sixty-ninth Street and asked for the manager. A slight, middle-aged man with a prissy manner appeared, introduced himself as Lewis Frazier, and asked how he could help Bautista.

"I am Detective Bautista of the Police Department," he said, showing his badge. "I talked to you this morning, sir, about Bernard Reyman and any currency transaction involving Bernard Reyman."

"Oh, yes."

"Did you find anything?"

"Yes, as a matter of fact I did," Frazier said.

"A forty-seven eighty-nine?"

"Yes."

"May I see it?"

"Now, look here, Officer. Your people put us to a lot of trouble last week, giving us a whole list of names to check against our records, scaring our tellers half to death, and so on. I really don't think I'm going to do anything further about our records until I have a letter from the Commissioner."

"The Police Commissioner?" Bautista asked.

Frazier nodded.

"You've got to be kidding."

"I'm only going by the rules, Mr. Bautista. It's what the Federal regulations say. We can only show currency-transaction reports to a state or local agency when requested by the head of that agency."

"Mr. Frazier—may I call you Lew?—I appreciate your position. But please appreciate mine. We are involved with a murder investigation here, and one where time is important. I can spend the rest of today, and probably the weekend, trying to get you a letter from the Police Commissioner."

"I would like that very much."

"But I'm not going to do it, Lew. Lewis. Correct me if I'm wrong, Lewis, but I believe First Fiduciary just paid a fine of some three million dollars to the Treasury Department for failing to report cash transactions, for failing to file forty-seven eighty-nines. So don't talk to me about the rules. And second, if I have to delay my investigation until Monday because of some goddamn letter, I can assure you I won't come back alone Monday morning. There will be a squad of detectives here asking your depositors where they got the money they're putting in their accounts."

"But you couldn't do that! We'd have you thrown out!" Frazier said with great indignation.

"Fine. Then we'll ask them when they leave the bank. 'Excuse me, madam, I notice you just came out of the friendly Fiduciary Bank. I'm from the Police Department and I'd like to ask you a couple of questions. Did you make a deposit just now? You did? Let me ask you, and I apologize for the impertinence, but did your deposit have anything to do with a bordello operation? Or pornographic movies? Or drugs? . . .'"

"Okay, okay. Let me get the form. But all this is

highly irregular." Frazier went off in great dudgeon, but returned with the branch's copy of a form 4789, which he handed to Bautista. The detective read it carefully, noting with some excitement that it was dated the same day—March 2—as the promissory note from Maywood to Reyman. The form, signed by a teller named Lucy Menotti, indicated that $24,000 had been withdrawn by Reyman on that date, in bills of at least $100 denomination, the withdrawal being made from his money-market account.

"This is very interesting and very helpful, Lew," Bautista said. "Is Miss Menotti here?"

"Yes, she is. But this is our busy time of day. Couldn't you come back later?"

"No, I could not. And if she cooperates, I'll only be talking to her for about three minutes."

"I suppose I have no choice. Wait over there in my office," Frazier said, gesturing to a small cubicle in the corner. Within a minute, a diminutive and not terribly friendly-looking woman came in and introduced herself.

"Miss Menotti, this will only take a few moments, I'm sure. Is this your signature here on this form?" Bautista showed her the forty-seven eighty-nine concerning the Reyman transaction.

"Yes, it is."

"Do you remember the transaction? Do you remember Mr. Reyman?"

"I don't, really."

"Even though this transaction involved twenty-four thousand dollars in cash and you had to do up this report, you still don't remember it?" Bautista pressed.

"No, I'm afraid not."

"Even though it says here, right here on the form, that you verified Mr. Reyman's identity by looking at his driver's license?"

"That's right. We have lots of these transactions, you know. Twenty-four thousand dollars is probably a lot of money to you, but we have large transactions all the time, every day."

This was not going to be easy, Bautista thought. "May I say, Miss Menotti, this is a matter of great importance to us. We have reason to believe that the money Mr. Reyman withdrew back in March was used to hire a murderer. So every detail is important."

"I wish I could help you, Officer, but I don't recall this transaction at all."

"Perhaps this will refresh your recollection, Miss Menotti," Bautista said, producing the photograph of Reyman.

The woman studied the likeness carefully. "Oh, yes. It comes back to me a little. Yes, he was the man. Came in here in the morning, almost first thing, I remember, and wanted twenty-four thousand dollars in one-hundred-dollar bills. I had a deuce of a time getting that amount together, but I did. He was very patient."

"Do you remember anything else about the transaction? Was Reyman nervous?"

"No, he was patient, as I said. He had to wait, oh, probably five minutes while we got the money together. Then there was the business of checking his I.D., and all that."

"Was he pleasant? Was he laughing?"

"No, he wasn't laughing. He was just polite and patient."

"Was he alone?"

"I don't honestly remember," Miss Menotti said.

"Was he perhaps with this woman?" Bautista asked, showing the picture of Veronica Maywood.

"That rings a bell," the teller said. "Yes, he was

with a woman. She was right in line with him. Squeezed his hand once or twice. It comes back to me now. He actually had her take the money."

"And was it the woman in this picture?"

"It sure looks like her, but I can't be a hundred percent sure."

"Do you think you could recognize her if you saw her again?"

"I think probably."

"Then let me just make certain I've got everything straight, Miss Menotti. On the morning of March 2, Mr. Reyman, accompanied by a woman, who was more than likely the woman in the picture I showed you, withdrew twenty-four thousand dollars from his money-market account. The money was in hundred-dollar bills and he had to wait several minutes while you got it together. The woman was with him the whole time and occasionally squeezed his hand. When he got the money, he gave it to her. Is that all correct, Miss Menotti?"

"Yes, that sounds right."

"And you would be prepared to swear to all this in court, if necessary?"

"Yes, I believe I would."

"That's all, Miss Menotti," Bautista concluded. "Oh. Just one more thing. This woman didn't give Mr. Reyman a piece of paper at any time, did she? A sheet of paper with writing on it?"

"No, I didn't see anything like that."

"Very good. Thank you for your help, Miss Menotti."

Bautista felt there was no harm in asking about the promissory note. But he was not surprised, or disappointed, at the answer he got; after all, he had been quite lucky in what he had already discovered that morning and he shouldn't, he told himself, be greedy.

*   *   *

Luis Bautista used the branch manager's telephone to set up his next action and to call for assistance. Within two hours, the detective, armed with a search warrant and accompanied by two other policemen, went to Veronica Maywood's apartment on West Seventy-third Street.

The ballerina was not in, but the superintendent unlocked her door for them. Within another hour they found what they were looking for. Twelve thousand dollars in one-hundred-dollar bills, concealed in a box tucked under the springs of Veronica Maywood's bed.

22

REUBEN FROST WAS IN A STATE OF EXHILARATION AFTER receiving a call at home from Luis Bautista that Friday afternoon. The person who had hired Clifton Holt's murderer was unquestionably discovered, and discovered without frenzied disruption to NatBallet.

At Bautista's request, Frost tried discreetly to find out Maywood's whereabouts through the NatBallet office. He learned that she was out of town, making a guest appearance in Pittsburgh. But she was scheduled to return the next day and to dance with NatBallet Saturday evening. Ironically, the role she was to dance on Saturday was the lead in *Paganini Variations,* perhaps Holt's greatest ballet and the most important part the choreographer had ever created for Maywood.

He relayed his intelligence to Bautista, who cursed at the complication of Maywood's absence. Since the NatBallet office did not know when or on what flight she would return, Bautista decided that the best course would be to stake out her apartment building and arrest her when she arrived.

"I don't see any point in making a big stink in Pittsburgh," Bautista said. "We'll just have a welcom-

ing committee waiting for her when she gets to West
Seventy-third Street. Will you be home during the
day?"

"I'll be right here," Frost replied. But then he had
another idea and corrected his statement. "I'll be here
off and on. I may have some other appointments. But
one of us will certainly be around."

"I'll be in touch," Bautista said, ringing off.

Frost immediately called Andrea Turnbull. Except
for their brief conversation at the Holt memorial, he
had not talked to her since she had made her ridiculous proposal about her role in the Company earlier in
the week. There was no question that he would reject
it; the well-being of the Company—not to say of his
marriage—required it. The financial difficulty that the
withdrawal of Turnbull's support would create would
be severe, but he was sure that with some extra effort
new sources of funding could be found. And continuing on the terms she had dictated could only lead to
the diminution—if not the destruction—of the Company's reputation.

Now that the criminal-justice system would not be
solving the Turnbull problem for him, the sooner he
confronted the woman the better. Reaching her on the
line, he asked if she would be free for lunch the next
day or, failing that, would have some time to see him
in the afternoon. Turnbull declined lunch—to Frost's
relief—but said she would be happy to see him at his
convenience Saturday afternoon. Two-thirty was finally agreed upon as the time, Turnbull's apartment
the place.

Frost then called Arthur Mattison at the *Press*. Could
the critic meet him for drinks at their club Saturday
afternoon? Mattison readily agreed, but fought like a

terrier to find out the purpose of Frost's unusual invitation.

"I just have a couple of things I wanted to chat with you about, Arthur," Frost said, enigmatically. "I'll see you in the bar around five."

Andrea Turnbull was wearing one of her ill-fitting discount-store dresses, this time in a paisley print, when she let Frost into her Beekman Place apartment.

"I'm sorry I couldn't have lunch today, Reuben," she said. "I already had a commitment," she added, without further explanation. Given her raiment, Frost doubted this, but he let the matter pass.

"That's quite all right," Frost said. There was something different about the apartment, he thought as he sat down in the ill-kept living room. Then he realized what it was: no loud music and no stale reminders of marijuana.

"How is your son?" he asked.

"Oh, he's gone off to Florida with some friends. They're having a little holiday."

Florida seemed a long way from the University of Maine, but he kept still. Instead, he got down to his distasteful business.

"Andrea, I've given a lot of thought to what you said the other day about NatBallet," he began, telling a slight lie about the consideration given to her proposal. "I've also had a chance to discuss it with some other members of the Board," he added, telling another lie.

"Before I give you our answer, Andrea, perhaps I ought to review a little history," he continued. "Nat-Ballet was started over a decade ago, as you know, by a group of very dedicated people, including my wife, Cynthia, and Clifton Holt. They were determined to start a Company that would enable young artists to excel, to develop an eclectic repertoire of the best ballets wherever they could be found, and to provide Clifton with a base from which he could develop his own choreography. Financially it was not easy, since so many individuals with money and so many institutions were already committed to the other major companies with better-established records. But we did it—we begged and scraped and cajoled, and we got support.

"On the artistic side, we were very lucky. We brought along good dancers—first the famous American 'defectors,' and then more and more young ones just out of school. And we had the luxury of having Clifton's prodigious output, which has given the Company a unique body of work."

Turnbull, sitting opposite Frost, shifted uneasily in her chair. Frost ignored her signal and continued his explanation.

"We have always tried—and we've been pretty damn successful—to keep the financial side of things and the artistic side separate. Oh, sure, Clifton and Cynthia had to beg and grovel with the rest of us to attract donors, but never, ever have those donors had any control over what works are performed and who dances them. The result has been an artistic reputation that just keeps growing—to the point, I think, where NatBallet can hold its head up with the very best companies around today.

"I know I sound a little like I'm making a sales pitch, but I wanted to emphasize to you, Andrea, a basic principle that's been absolutely essential to the integrity of the Company.

"We have been deeply grateful for your part in making the Company what it is today. I don't want there to be any mistake about that. But I—we—do not see how, in good conscience, we can appoint you co–Artistic Director. I know you love the ballet and that you've had administrative experience running that group up in Syracuse. But we simply cannot—"

"Reuben, let me interrupt. It's obvious what you're going to tell me. You don't want me involved with NatBallet. You'll be happy to take my money, just as long as I keep my mouth shut. Clifton's death hasn't changed a thing. He wouldn't have anything to do with me—and now you won't either. That's fine. I now know where you stand. And you know where I stand. I have told you that quite clearly. So let's just say that NatBallet will not see another dime of my money. It's that simple." Andrea Turnbull's face had turned a mottled red. She was extremely angry and was having difficulty controlling herself. But having started to administer the *coup de grâce* to her lunatic ambition, Frost had to continue.

"Andrea, I'm sorry to disappoint you. And sorry about the way you feel. To my mind—though I can't speak as a rich philanthropist, because I'm simply not one—supporting NatBallet is one of the finest things that a rich, cultivated person can do. I know there are those who say charity should go to the hungry and the homeless. I'm all for that too. But if there isn't support for those things that make us civilized, that represent the best part of our natures and our culture, then what kind of a society would we have? Cynthia said the other night—I don't mean to quote my wife, but she was right—that NatBallet, and companies like it, are civilizing. And perhaps can reach at least some of the Jimmy Wilsons of tomorrow. And can expose not only New York but some of this country west of Manhattan to beauty and wonderful artistry. You are in a position to help make that possible, and it will be regrettable if you decline to do so."

"Oh, my dear Mr. Frost, *I* shall make it possible, all right," Turnbull said. "But I will do it where I'm appreciated. I love the ballet, and I'm very sure there are ballet companies that *will* appreciate me. Your New York arrogance is appalling, your notion that all good thinking about the arts must originate with people who do not provide the money. Well, you can have your purity. I will go to the New York City Ballet, or American Ballet Theatre, or one of those exciting smaller groups like Eliot Feld, and find a compatible artistic home. I'm only sorry I've wasted so much time and energy on your beloved Clifton Holt, and your wife, and all those other worthies at NatBallet, who now can't be bothered with my financial support. All you Wall Street lawyers, and culture vultures like your wife, can do anything you want. But you're not going to do it with my money."

"Andrea, I'm genuinely sorry you feel this way," Frost said quietly. "But in the circumstances, I think there is nothing more to be said—other than thanks for what you have done for us up until now." He got up and headed for the door. Turnbull followed him, but did not shake hands or do more than nod by way of a goodbye.

Frost was relieved to leave the oppressive apartment and its difficult occupant. He was relieved, too, that the relationship with Mrs. Turnbull was severed. He knew that he would probably have to sit through a long series of boring lunches and dinners, proselytizing for the Company with new sources of money. But it couldn't be worse than dealing with an irresponsible woman without a proper sense of the character and spirit of NatBallet. He was angry at her attitude, though none of what she said had surprised him. He had restrained his temper—even when the witch had called Cynthia a "culture vulture," whatever that might be— and had even refrained from mentioning Robert Lucas and the mysterious Gaute. What purpose would it have served? he told himself. Best to be rid of the woman, her son, her money and her past once and for all. Syracuse had been right; she was a shrike, even by the tolerant standards of New York City, where relentlessly demanding cultural organizations took support from any—or almost any—source.

Frost decided to walk to his drinks appointment at the Gotham. Walking along, he noticed a telephone-company ad at a bus stop urging him to make a call—to anyone. He responded and called home, but Cynthia had not yet heard from Bautista.

The Gotham Club was deserted when he arrived; late Saturday afternoon, unlike weekdays, was not a popular drinking hour there.

He ordered a Scotch and soda and waited, sitting by himself in the most secluded part of the room. Mattison soon arrived, slightly out of breath, and sat down opposite him.

"Reuben, I've been dying of curiosity all day," Mattison said. "I assume you have some wonderful scoop for me. Fernando Bujones is going to jump ship once and for all, leave ABT and join NatBallet? Or Violette Verdy is your new artistic director? What is it? I'm dying to know."

"Have a drink, Arthur, and I'll tell you, though it's not at all what you might think," Frost replied. He summoned the bartender, and Mattison ordered a gin and tonic.

"So what is it, Reuben?" Mattison persisted. "What is this late-Saturday-afternoon rendezvous about?"

"Arthur, you are not going to like what I say to you one bit. However, I deliberately asked you here because this is a civilizing spot; it is the best possible place to discuss the distasteful subject I have in mind."

"I haven't the faintest idea what you're talking about, Reuben," Mattison said, his voice betraying irritation and his hand, slightly shaking as he lifted his drink, betraying nervousness as well.

"Let me come straight to the point," Frost said. "As you may know, I am Clifton Holt's executor. In that capacity, I became aware of the letter he wrote to you last month."

"The bastard. He said right in it that he would not show it to anyone."

"He didn't. But a copy was found after he died."

"I can explain the whole thing," Mattison declared. "Holt was technically correct in what he said. The words he quoted were not originally mine, but Edwin Denby's. There's no denying that. But I absolutely stand behind the critical judgments they expressed—as applied to the performances where I used them. So no one was being hurt.

"It was silly of me to crib from Denby's old columns," the critic went on. "But as I say, no harm was done to anyone. And I only did it during a very short period when I was under great pressure—my column, my TV broadcasts, finishing my book. If I was going to cover the cultural front—as I try to do, and as my publisher wants me to do—I had to cut corners. And that's what I did, in a very small and wholly insignificant way."

"I'm not sure, Arthur, that your public—or even your publisher—would agree," Frost replied. "For their thirty-five cents, the readers of the *Press* may get clumsy and stupid prose, but I do think they at least expect that it's original."

"You're undoubtedly right, Reuben. And I certainly don't plan to take such a shortcut again, if that's what you're demanding."

"Arthur, I'm not demanding anything. The incident is closed as far as I'm concerned. I do not propose to tell anyone about Holt's letter. I'm not going public with it. I give you my word on that. I want to be very clear about that."

"I'm sure you're a man of your word, and I appreciate it," Mattison said quietly.

"I would, however, like to make one small suggestion to you, Arthur," Frost said.

"What is that?"

"That when you use the word 'elitist' in your commentaries, as you so often do, you make sure you know what you're talking about."

"What in God's name does that statement mean? What are you getting at?"

"I have in mind, my friend, those pieces you wrote on the grants program of the Brigham Foundation. I believe if you examined the Foundation more carefully, you would find that it is neither elitist nor snobbish, nor biased in favor of New York at all."

"Ahh, now I see. That's one of your wife's hobbyhorses, isn't it? So what you're telling me is that if I lay off the Brigham Foundation, you will keep quiet about Holt's letter."

"You haven't been listening, Arthur," Frost replied. "I gave my word that I would never reveal your letter—"

"—Not even to Cynthia?"

"No, I can't say that. But I think I can speak for her

too when I say that no one else will ever hear about it. I gave you my word on that, and I'll commit for Cynthia as well. As for the Foundation, I merely made the suggestion—the *suggestion*—that you look into what it does more carefully, find out how effective it is, before you dismiss it as a rich man's plaything. Once you've done that, you can write anything you damn please—I'm not trying to override the First Amendment. I know your publisher expects you to set off a populist rocket every so often, and you're entitled to do that, and so is he. But I suggest you look into the Brigham grants more carefully before aiming your rocket in their direction."

"Is the blackmail finished?" Mattison asked.

"Call it what you will, Arthur. As far as I am concerned, the discussion is closed. Would you like another drink?"

"I'm not sure. This isn't the pleasantest cocktail hour I've ever spent."

"Have another one anyway. I have another surprise for you."

"No, Reuben, actually, I think I'll be going," Mattison said. "But what is your second surprise? I don't quite see how you're going to top the first."

"The last edition of the *Press* is out for today, is it not?"

"Yes. Hours ago."

"And of course there is no Sunday edition."

"That's right."

"Too bad."

"Reuben! Will you get to the point?" Mattison demanded.

"That's too bad, because I think there's a story of some interest that is about to break."

"Well, what is it?"

"I can't tell you. It's in the hands of the police. But you might do some calling around later this evening."

"Me? I wouldn't have the faintest idea how to call the police! My mandate may be broad, but it doesn't include the jailhouse."

"Then you'd better get one of your police reporters on it. Ask him to call you when he gets the story, though. There might be a column in it."

"Reuben, I demand to know what you're talking about!"

"I'm a man of my word, Arthur. I told someone I wouldn't say anything about this police matter. So I haven't. And I won't. But keep your ear to the ground, Arthur."

Frost looked at his watch. "Actually, I should go too," Frost said. "May I say I've enjoyed this immensely?"

The two men stood up and went out together. As they parted, Mattison turned serious. "I hope you meant what you said about that damned letter, Reuben. And for my part, I think I'll have another look at the Brigham Foundation. Your comments have been most helpful."

"I did mean what I said about the letter. And I think some further looking at Brigham would be interesting."

"As will the report from the police station?"

"I think so. Goodbye, Arthur."

Frost felt both elation and anticipation as he walked home. He had not blackmailed Mattison, he told himself. He had merely relieved the man of what must have been a lingering doubt and worry—for which Mattison should have been grateful—and made a constructive suggestion about the man's criticism. All very innocent, yet he knew he would not tell Cynthia what he had done.

*   *   *

While Frost was going about his errands, Luis Bautista was sitting in the front passenger seat of an unmarked police car parked on West Seventy-third Street, between Broadway and Amsterdam Avenue. Within a few feet of the car was the canopy extending out from the front door of Veronica Maywood's apartment house.

Bautista was nervous. In his nine years on the police force he had arrested scores of murderers, of both sexes. Deranged psychotics holding innocents as hostages; desperate four-time losers barricaded behind tenement doors; monstrous young delinquents devoid of any trace of human emotion. He had seen all kinds, had arrested all kinds.

What Bautista had not done was arrest a celebrity. Granted, Veronica Maywood was not Elizabeth Taylor. But she was certainly well known—preeminently so in the ballet world—and, like most established New York celebrities, was probably tightly connected to those who ran at least one of the City's daily newspapers.

He had no doubt that Maywood was guilty of arranging Clifton Holt's murder. But he still was uneasy, wanting to make sure that she was arrested smoothly and quietly. A longtime colleague, Chris DuBois, was beside him in the driver's seat of the car. Down the block, two more detectives were posted in another vehicle, Dan Gallup and Betsy Crane.

A morning check with the airlines flying to New York from Pittsburgh showed Maywood with a reservation on a flight arriving at LaGuardia at three in the afternoon. The police stakeout had begun at one—just in case the ballerina had switched to an earlier flight. The doorman at Maywood's apartment house, normally a casual, laid-back young man impervious to third-party direction, had been sufficiently dazzled by

Bautista's shield—and those of his colleagues—that he had agreed to turn on the building's taxi call light to signal Maywood's arrival.

Bautista had cased the lobby of the building with care. The elevators were no longer manned, though it was clear that in more elegant days they had been. The tug-at-the-forelock operators of times gone by had been replaced by an electronic panel controlled by the doorman; no person could get by elevator to a higher floor unless the doorman activated a switch on this panel.

Bautista had never encountered this electronic compromise of the affluent before, but he understood its possibilities immediately: Veronica Maywood, as the owner of an apartment in the building, would arrive, get into the elevator, and be sent to her floor by the doorman. Except that if the doorman didn't activate the starting switch, she would be trapped in a closed, and stationary, box.

He instructed the doorman to entrap Maywood in just this way. The young man protested that he could not treat a tenant of the building like that, but Bautista convinced him otherwise.

"Buddy, the woman we're after may be your tenant, but we're here to arrest her for arranging a murder," Bautista told him. "We want as little trouble as possible, and no mess—no wild gunshots that hit innocent bystanders. Like you, for example. You follow?"

"Okay, okay," the doorman answered. "I'll turn on the taxi light and lock her in the elevator. What the hell, I just work here."

Once the ground rules were established, there was nothing to do but wait. It was at times like this that Bautista wished he smoked. Smoking was vile and unhealthful, but at least it was something to do.

Both Bautista and DuBois were staring at the signal light atop the canopy in front of them when a taxi drew up. Veronica Maywood, dance bag and overnight case in hand, got out and hurried quickly inside the building.

The four police were on the street before the prearranged light signal flashed. Once inside the entrance, the doorman indicated that their quarry was indeed in the elevator with the door closed. The quartet surrounded the door and called to the doorman to press the button that would open it.

As the door opened, Maywood leaned out to shout at the doorman. "Dammit, Tommy, will you press the button for six?" she demanded angrily. Then she saw the police arrayed in front of her.

"What the hell is this?" she asked, a frightened look in her eyes.

"I've seen you before," she said, turning to Bautista. "Aren't you Cynthia Frost's friend?"

"That's right, ma'am," Bautista answered.

"Well, what do you want from me?"

"We're here to arrest you, Miss Maywood," Bautista said.

"Arrest! May I ask what for?" the woman demanded, her voice defiant, but a look of fear still in her eyes.

"For arranging the murder of Clifton Holt," Bautista replied.

The mention of Holt's name, or the crime she was accused of, sent Maywood into a wild frenzy. She shouted obscenity after obscenity at her accusers and tried to break past them outside the elevator. Restrained by Gallup and Crane, she became even crazier, bending over and biting Gallup's hand so deeply that he collapsed on the floor, screaming in pain.

Any remaining politeness and deference disappeared

as Bautista and his two remaining colleagues realized what had happened to Gallup. They wrestled Maywood into submission and carted her, still screaming and cursing and dripping Gallup's blood from her chin like a vampire, to one of the waiting police cars. The one with the wire cage in the back for locking in violent prisoners.

When Reuben Frost got home, Cynthia was waiting for him.

"Where have you been? You missed Luis' call," she said.

"Nowhere, really. I got rid of Andrea Turnbull—I think once and for all—and then had a drink at the Gotham, which I needed after my session with her."

"Well, Luis called about a half-hour ago. Poor Veronica was arrested when she got home, a little before four."

"Did she go quietly?"

"She badly bit the hand of one of the policemen."

"Poor girl. I'm sure the whole thing was a crazy, drug-filled fantasy that unfortunately she made real."

"I know, I know. Combining cocaine with a ballerina's inherent selfishness was enough to undo her. But it's over, dear, with most of the players intact." She embraced her husband and held him tightly. "We're supposed to go to the ballet tonight, you know."

"Yes, I know. Has anyone told Arne he has to replace Veronica?"

THE SHOW GOES ON

23

REUBEN AND CYNTHIA FROST WATCHED THE EARLY NEWS on television and were relieved that, in the Saturday lull, there was no mention of Veronica Maywood's arrest. Reuben, in his earlier call to Arne Petersen, had told him the news, but had asked him not to tell anyone else. Frost had also asked him to assemble the Company and the orchestra members backstage at the Zacklin prior to the evening's performance so that he could tell the NatBallet personnel himself.

Frost also reached Teresa Holt, who, to his surprise, burst into tears when she was told the circumstances of her husband's murder. He then called Peter Howard, the Company's President, who, once he had recovered from the news, agreed to try to reach as many of the directors as possible to relay the startling message.

The Frosts arrived at the theatre a half-hour before the eight-o'clock curtain and sought out Petersen backstage. He embraced them both in the tight, clasping manner reserved for occasions of great emotion.

"I can't believe it, Reuben. Veronica could be a handful, but this . . ." His voice trailed off. "When did you know about it?"

Frost told him the story, tactfully omitting mention of Petersen's erstwhile status as a suspect.

"Arne, who will be dancing *Paganini* tonight?" Cynthia asked, when Reuben had finished his account to the dazed Acting Artistic Director.

"Hailey," Petersen replied. "Hailey Coles. She's never done it before, but she's been rehearsing it."

Frost was inwardly relieved, somehow, that Laura Russell would not be replacing Maywood. Besides, the chance to see a dancer as promising as Hailey Coles in her debut in a major role was exciting.

"I know it's not funny," Petersen said. "But we had an awful time with the slip for the program. You know, we usually say that due to an illness so-and-so is substituting for so-and-so. But what could we say tonight? 'Due to the arrest of Veronica Maywood, Hailey Coles will appear in tonight's performance of *Paganini Variations*'?"

"What did you say?" Cynthia asked.

"Just that Hailey would replace Veronica. No reason assigned."

Frost looked at his watch. The stage manager had given the call for the Company to assemble onstage, and the dancers began drifting in. Given the variety of the evening's program, almost all the dancers were performing. The members of the orchestra, in their tuxedos, and the stage crew, mostly in sweat shirts and jeans, joined the group.

At seven forty-five, Reuben, with Cynthia and Arne Petersen at his side, went to the center of the stage. The assemblage before them was obviously puzzled at this strange gathering. My God, Reuben thought, I hope they don't think we're going to disband the Company. He decided he had better speak right away.

"Ladies and gentlemen of the National Ballet," he

began. "I regret that I have some most distressing personal news for you. It's going to be particularly difficult for you because it comes so close to performance time. I'm sorry that this can't be helped, but the event I am about to describe did not occur until a few hours ago."

Reuben took a deep breath and went on. "As you all know, our Director, Clifton Holt, was murdered less than two weeks ago. Murdered by a young man who was thought to be acting entirely on his own. Unfortunately, that now appears not to have been the case. Late this afternoon the police arrested Veronica Maywood for having paid the murderer to kill Clifton. I am deeply saddened by this, as I know all of you will be. But I know also that tonight's performance will go on, and this Company will go on. What you—all of you—have created over the years is too resilient an organization to be brought low by this awful occurrence, horrible as it is. So to you all, I say God bless, and to all you dancers, break a leg tonight. Thank you."

Those standing before Frost reacted in a variety of ways—tears, mutual embraces, unbelieving stares. But the group soon broke up, with a performance about to begin. The orchestra members hurried down the stairs to the pit, and the dancers in Holt's *Mozart Concerto,* the first number on the program, began their warm-up exercises.

Those not involved in *Mozart Concerto* followed Reuben, Cynthia and Arne as they left the stage, eager to hear more details. The three of them quite unconsciously separated and began to talk to small groups that clustered around them. The Frosts both decided that they would miss the Mozart work; they were needed here to give what comfort they could.

They did not get to their seats until the lights were

dimming for the second number on the program, the Company's version of a suite of Bournonville dances. As he had so many times before, often rushing in from the office or a late business appointment, Reuben took comfort from the familiarity of being in his seat at the Zacklin. It was a setting that cleared the mind better than any other palliative he knew. Business problems, a dirty and delayed subway train or, tonight, the whole horror of Veronica Maywood's arrest, had a way of dissolving, or at least temporarily disappearing, when the lights dimmed, the conductor appeared, the music started and the curtain went up.

Watching the Bournonville, the average spectator would never have suspected that the dancers had so recently received catastrophic news. The buoyant cheerfulness of the peasant dances, the bright costumes and the dancers' unrelenting smiles gave nothing away. The Frosts were proud of them.

During the second intermission, they tried to be as inconspicuous as possible at the side of the mezzanine lobby. It was clear that the word had not traveled, as no one came up seeking further information. On the other hand, it was equally clear that the underground dance network had somehow found out that Hailey Coles was making her debut in *Paganini Variations*. The balletomanes who followed such things, the Company's equivalent of the most ardent rock groupies, were out in force.

Reuben had never figured out how this astonishing news network operated, nor how, some way, tickets were always available to these dedicated fans on short notice. But he was glad to see them there; their presence buttressed his hope that Hailey's debut would signal a rebirth for the Company and start it back on an upward course after the dreadful events of recent days.

The Company executed *Paganini Variations* as never before. The corps danced full out and with a sharp attack and a precision not, alas, always seen. Gerald Hazard danced the principal male role. Frost was struck by the irony as Hazard, so recently a suspected felon, danced the tenth variation, in which Rachmaninoff's frequent *leitmotif*, the *dies irae*, appears. The Hailey Coles did her solo variations with an authority that rivaled Veronica Maywood's. God, what good work the Company's school was doing! Reuben thought. Then more work for the corps was followed by the eighteenth variation, the unspeakably beautiful *andante cantabile* in which Rachmaninoff turns the basic theme of the piece on its head, where Hailey Coles, partnered by Gerald Hazard, achieved the magic that Clifton Holt had created for Veronica Maywood. Coles became a weightless, ethereal beauty in Gerald Hazard's disciplined arms; she danced with a softness that many, many ballerinas older and more experienced simply could not have achieved. Yet airless and weightless as she was, she projected both grace and authority.

The performance was stunning and, sadly or triumphantly as one viewed it, Veronica Maywood had been equaled, and perhaps even surpassed.

Then the ballet came to its end, with the corps dancing gloriously and then, finally, in tandem with Hailey and Gerald, reaching the abrupt, surprising and quiet end of the work.

As the curtain came down, in that brief interval before the audience responded, Reuben turned, with tears in his eyes, to Cynthia. She was in tears too, but they clasped hands, and looked at each other, as the tumultuous applause began.

EPILOGUE

THE FOLLOWING STORY APPEARED IN *TIME*, THE WEEKLY NEWSMAGAZINE, THE MONDAY AFTER VERONICA MAYWOOD'S ARREST:

DEATH DANCE

[All ballerinas] possess in common those elements necessary to make a ballerina; they are all tough, merciless, self-centered, narrow-minded, and without awareness of and interest in the needs of their male counterparts.

—Peter Martins, *Far from Denmark* (1982)

TWO WEEKS AGO, PETER MARTINS, CO-DIRECTOR OF THE prestigious New York City Ballet, and dance lovers throughout the world were shocked by the senseless stabbing of Clifton Holt, 52, artistic director of City Ballet's friendly rival, the National Ballet.

Holt, described almost universally as the finest world-class choreographer in the generations after George Balanchine and Jerome Robbins, was fatally stabbed in the stage-door alley outside National Ballet's headquarters theatre in New York on April 4. His assailant, James Wilson, a 22-year-old New York heroin addict and part-time drug peddler, was caught fleeing from the scene.

Wilson himself was fatally stabbed days later by a fellow prisoner at the Men's House of Detention on New York's Rikers Island, but only after he had bragged to his fellow inmates about Holt's murder, claiming he had been hired to do it for $24,000— $12,000 down, $12,000 after he carried it off. His jail-cell boast was given credibility by the presence of $12,000 in new bills in his walk-up apartment in New York's Hell's Kitchen.

Last week New York police traced the funds to a branch bank on Manhattan's East Side. Then, taking advantage of the federal forms required to be filed by banks for cash transfers over $10,000, Wilson's payoff was traced to Bernard Reyman, a high-rolling yuppie stock salesman—and dope addict—at the prestigious Wall Street firm of Hughes & Company.

Reyman, who died of a heroin overdose in early March, in turn was linked to Veronica Maywood, 32, the star ballerina of National Ballet, and investigation showed that he had apparently lent her the $24,000 the police say she paid to Wilson, Reyman's pusher, to murder Holt.

Maywood, involved romantically with Reyman for several months, had left him before Holt's murder, but nonetheless had allegedly persuaded him to lend her the $24,000 blood money. Reyman, deep into drugs and irrationally paranoid, had apparently made the ballerina execute a promissory note, which led the police to her last week.

At the time of her arrest, Maywood was one of the country's leading dancers. Born in an Ontario farm town in Canada, she studied ballet in Toronto before bursting onto the scene in New York. The sometime mistress of Clifton Holt, she had been the guiding star of the greatest ballets Holt choreographed for National Ballet from the time of its formation in 1970. Her collaboration with Holt, which dance cognoscenti compared to the legendary partnership between Suzanne Farrell and Balanchine, helped the fledgling National Ballet achieve its current international stature.

Sources close to the National Ballet indicate that not all had been well between Holt and Maywood in recent months. The breakup of their romance, although occurring much earlier, had not helped. Then Holt, by all accounts a genius but a difficult man to deal with, both personally and professionally, signaled in rehearsals for his major new ballet this season that Maywood—old at 32 in ballet terms—might no longer be the chosen female dancer on whom he would make his works.

The New York police completed their investigation late last week and arrested Maywood on Saturday when she returned to New York from a triumphant guest appearance with the Pennsylvania Ballet in Pittsburgh Friday night.

Maywood displayed the fiery temper for which she is famous when she was arrested at her New York apartment house, biting an arresting policeman on the hand so badly that he had to be hospitalized. She was clearly continuing to play Kate in John Cranko's *Taming of the Shrew*, which she had danced the night before in Pittsburgh. And, to the last, being tough, merciless, self-centered and narrow-minded to an extreme that even Peter Martins, who has seen them all, would not have imagined.

About the Author

HAUGHTON MURPHY is the pseudonym of a partner in a Wall Street law firm. He is at work on his third Reuben Frost mystery. He and his wife live in Manhattan.